fast money

A SHELBY NICHOLS ADVENTURE

Colleen Helme

Book Cover Art by Damonza.com Copyright © 2013 by Colleen Helme
Book Layout ©2013 BookDesignTemplates.com

Fast Money/ Colleen Helme. – 2nd ed.
ISBN 1466495154
ISBN-13: 978-1466495159

Dedication

To my sons
Jason and Clayton

ACKNOWLEDGMENTS

I would like to thank my family and friends for all the amazing support you have given me. To Erin, for your input and willingness to read as I write, even though it means re-reading through some of the changes. Thanks to Melissa and Clayton for your help with the web design and formatting. I couldn't do it without you! A big thanks to Kristin Monson for your willingness to proofread and edit this book within a short amount of time. You did a fantastic job! To Damon for the amazing cover art. To Tom, for your enthusiasm and support, especially when I needed it! And thanks to everyone who read CARROTS and wanted more – this one's for you!

Shelby Nichols Adventures

Carrots
Fast Money
Lie or Die
Secrets that Kill
Trapped by Revenge
Deep in Death
Crossing Danger
Devious Minds
Hidden Deception
Laced in Lies
Deadly Escape

Devil in a Black Suit ~ A Ramos Story

Contents

Chapter 1

I used to fantasize about how it would feel to be a millionaire, and what I would do with all that money. The only way I figured it would ever happen, was if I won the lottery, or the Publisher's Clearinghouse Sweepstakes. Which I'm not convinced is real. So the day it actually happened was a complete shock.

I was out shopping at the mall and, as usual, running a little low on funds. That cute pair of genuine leather boots was on sale and I didn't think I'd ever find another pair I liked better. At half off, I could hardly pass it up. That's when I remembered the account Uncle Joey had set up for me.

I'd used most of the money to buy a new car when a bank robber tried to kill me and totaled mine. Ramos, Uncle Joey's hit man, saved my life, but I ended up working for Uncle Joey. I had to tell him my secret that I could read minds so he wouldn't harm my family or me, and in the process, he opened a bank account in my name. Over the course of our association he put lots of money in there for me, and I dutifully spent it.

Now that Uncle Joey was out of my life, I had forgotten about the account... until I saw those boots. My husband, Chris, wouldn't mind too much that I bought such an expensive pair of shoes when I told him it wasn't his money I'd used. And the best part would be that I wouldn't feel so guilty about it.

With this happy thought, I rushed to the nearest ATM and put in my card. After entering my pin number I checked my balance.

That was when I nearly fainted. There was a five with a whole lot of zero's behind it – five million, two hundred forty-three dollars and seventy-eight cents to be exact. What the freak? I swallowed and took a deep breath, then glanced around, hoping no one had noticed how much money was in there and shove a gun in my ribs or something.

Call me paranoid, but the last few weeks had taught me to watch my back. Needing to turn the screen off, I punched withdraw and took out two hundred dollars. I got the money, logged off, and walked away like nothing was wrong.

I wandered over to the food court, and sat on a chair just as my legs gave way. There was only one way that money could get into my account, and that was through Uncle Joey. I thought I'd seen the last of him, but that must have been wishful thinking. How could I be so naïve?

I'd just have to call him and tell him to take his money out of my account or I would put it someplace where he'd never find it. On second thought, I'd better not. That would just get me killed. I'd have to be nice about it, and ask him what was going on, and hope I wouldn't have to do anything illegal or worse, to solve his money problems.

The last time we talked I worked pretty hard to convince him that my mind-reading abilities were gone, but I'm not sure he believed me. If he ever found out I still had them, my life would never be my own – ever.

Maybe an email would be the best way to handle it. Feeling better, I decided to go home and do just that. I passed the shoe store with the boots and slowed for one last look. I could probably still get them. I mean, I had two hundred dollars in my pocket so why not?

I'd always wanted a tan pair of cowboy-style boots, and these were fantastic. I tried them on and they fit perfectly. After paying for them, I left the shop with a smile on my face. I got halfway to the outside doors when a spot between my shoulder blades started to itch, like a warning that someone was following me. I slowed and glanced in the windows of the closest shop. Using my mind-reading ability, I opened my senses wide, hoping to catch a stray thought that would tell me if someone was thinking about me.

I heard nothing suspicious, but I'd learned to trust my instincts, and decided it wouldn't hurt to scan the mall. Trying to make it look like I'd forgotten something, I wandered back the way I'd come. Listening hard, I still didn't hear anyone thinking about me and why I had stopped. Hmm... I should probably go home. If someone were following me, I would know long before I got to my car.

The parking lot was crowded and my car wasn't too far. Still, I got out my keys and punched the unlock button. I didn't walk directly to the car, choosing to cross between the parking spaces so I could look back as I opened the car door.

It didn't look like anyone was following me. I swiveled into my seat and shut the door in record time, then locked it and let out a breath. So much for my instincts. Now I had to face the fact that I really was paranoid. All that money was starting to take a toll, and I hadn't even known about it for more than fifteen minutes. Even the thought of wearing my new boots couldn't lighten my mood.

I drove home in a daze, wondering what to do and if I should tell my husband. I knew Chris would not be happy about the money because of how it tied me to Uncle Joey. If I told him, he might question my honesty, and since I'd basically lied to him, he'd be right. He thought my mind-reading abilities were gone, and the stress of acting like I didn't know what he was thinking was one of the reasons I'd gone to the mall in the first place. It was hard, and I'd slipped up a few times. I knew he was a little suspicious, but trying to give me the benefit of the doubt. How would he feel knowing I'd lied to him?

To be honest, I was tired of keeping this secret. Maybe this was the excuse I needed to come clean and tell him my mind-reading abilities were back. It might make him mad, but he'd just have to deal with it. It's not like it was the end of the world or anything.

I pulled into the garage and hurried into my house. As I put my things away, I realized a big weight had been lifted from my shoulders. Telling Chris was the right thing to do, in fact, I was so ready to tell him, I wanted to call him right then and there. But I resisted, knowing it was always better to resolve big issues like this in person.

Three and a half weeks had passed since the shoot-out at Uncle Joey's office, and the bruising on my face from getting conked in the head had finally faded. I'd kept a low profile with two black eyes, but now I was ready to start a new life, and this might be just the way to do it.

I could come clean with Chris and that would open a whole new world of possibilities. I was sure Dimples, the police detective I'd worked with previously, would love my help solving crimes. They paid consultants all the time, or at least they did on TV and in books. I mean... look at Sherlock Holmes. I could probably solve cases a lot faster than him, and he was good.

Or I could have my own consulting agency. I could even help Chris with his clients. Wouldn't it be nice to know if people were guilty right off the bat? That could save a lot of time and money.

Helping people with their relationship issues might even be better. I could help them communicate with each other, and get them to admit their feelings. I could call myself a facilitator or something like that. Once word got around at how sympathetic and helpful I was, I'd have lots of clients. The possibilities were endless! Now all I had to do was tell Chris.

There was also the five million dollars hanging over my head. Why had Uncle Joey put all that money in my account? He must have needed a place to keep it safe that no one else could access. Maybe he'd caught up with Kate and Hodges, and this was the money they stole from him. That could be a possibility. I only wished he wouldn't have involved me. I thought about writing that email, but for some reason, I just couldn't bring myself to do it. It was probably something that could wait, at least until I talked to Chris.

I popped open a can of diet soda, and decided it wasn't too early to start dinner. Tonight I needed to have something nice for Chris and the kids to eat. They were always happier when food was on the table, and I needed Chris happy for what I was going to drop on him.

A twinge of guilt ran through me, and I knew I was walking a fine line. A few weeks ago, I had decided that a satisfying lie was better than the awful truth, and I still believed that to a point. I mean, so what if you tell someone you really like what they're wearing when you only sort-of like it. If you love them, you let little things like that go.

On the other hand, if you love someone enough, it's better to tell the truth when it's really important. They may hate you for it at first, but they would thank you later, because if it was the truth, they needed to know.

So telling Chris that my powers were gone had seemed like the best thing at first, but now, he would thank me for knowing it wasn't true. In the long run, it was better for him to know that I could read his mind, right?

My heart sank. Who was I trying to kid? He'd never thank me. Would it ruin our relationship? Would he decide he couldn't live with it? Maybe I shouldn't tell him after all. But how could that be better? I was keeping something from him that was important to me, and not talking about it was killing me. He was the only person in the whole world I could tell.

Breathing deeply, I pushed my doubts away and let my breath out. Telling him was the right thing, and I just had to have faith that we could work it out.

I found the hamburger and sausage in the freezer and started frying it up, deciding to make lasagna. I didn't make it very often because it was time consuming, but everyone in my family loved it. Plus I had all the ingredients, which didn't happen very often.

Fourteen-year old Joshua walked in from school and his eyes got big. "Is that lasagna?" he asked.

"Yup," I answered.

"All right!" He gave me a high-five. "When will it be ready?" He was starving. Feeling that raw need from his thoughts made me nervous... kind of how I imagined feeding a starving piranha.

"Here," I said, handing him the peanut butter and jam. "Make yourself a PB&J. Dinner won't be ready until about six-thirty, but that should tide you over."

"Thanks."

Savannah, who was two years younger than her brother, came through the door. She made a disgusted sound at Joshua stuffing his mouth, and went to her room, thinking something about a cute boy and wanting to call Ryan later. I sucked in my breath. Savannah and a cute boy? She was only twelve! I just about followed her into her room, but what could I say? Who's Ryan, and you're too young to have a boyfriend? That would go over well, besides, just because she was thinking about a boy didn't mean they were girlfriend/boyfriend.

I steadied myself against the counter and took a big swig of diet soda. On the positive side, at least I knew about Ryan. If I couldn't read minds, I wouldn't have a clue. That could be a big plus when I told Chris the truth. He was sure to appreciate my talent then.

I finished up the lasagna and put it in the oven, then made a salad and got the table set. At six-thirty, we were ready to eat. I was a firm believer in eating dinner together as a family and, since Chris hadn't called to say he would be late, we waited. The first few minutes were okay, but it slowly stretched to five, then ten. After enduring endless complaints from Josh and Savannah, most of them only in their thoughts, I relented, and we ate without Chris.

I kept hoping he would come in while we were eating, or at least call. Fifteen minutes later, we were through eating. After cleaning up, Joshua left for scouts and three of Savannah's friends came over to work on a group project for school. They disappeared into her room, but I knew they were mostly here to talk about boys.

At seven, Chris finally called. "Sorry I'm late, but I have a big case I couldn't leave. I'm on my way to the car, so I should be there in about twenty minutes."

"Okay, see you soon." I put a cheerful tone into my voice, so he wouldn't know I was mad, but inside it really bothered me. Especially after all the work I'd gone to in making lasagna. I don't know why I thought he would make it home in time for dinner. Most of the time he didn't, so I should be used to it by now. Still, I had to let it go. I couldn't let my anger get in the way of the truth I had to tell him.

I resisted the impulse to eavesdrop on Savannah and her friends, and turned on the TV, channel surfing until I found something that caught my attention. A few minutes later, the kitchen door opened and closed, signaling that Chris was home, but I didn't get up to greet him. I didn't necessarily care about the show I was watching, but I was feeling neglected so I stayed put. He could easily find me. Minutes passed without him doing that, so with a huff, I turned off the TV and got up to see what was going on.

I found him in the study, his rumpled hair standing on end, and a pencil in his mouth. His brows were drawn together in concentration so he didn't notice me for a minute. Finally, he glanced up. "Hey," he said, his voice low and husky, sending shivers up my arms. "I would have come down, but I didn't want to interrupt."

"That's okay. I wasn't really watching anything important, at least not as important as you."

He pursed his lips in a guilty pout. "I could have stayed at the office to finish this, but I thought I'd come home and finish here instead."

"What are you working on?"

"Just a case I have to argue before the judge tomorrow."

"What's it about?"

"It's not anything you'd be interested in." He was thinking that the messy divorce would just depress me, like it did him, and he didn't want to talk about it with me. He hated these kinds of divorce cases where no one could agree on anything, and it ended up going to trial. It was just stupid.

I took a step back. If I hadn't been able to hear his thoughts, I would have been offended. I would have thought he didn't think I was smart enough to understand his work, and it would have hurt me deeply. Now I knew he was try-ing to protect me.

I shook my head and sighed. I didn't need that kind of protection. What I needed was communication. I needed to be included in his world, and I wanted to include him in mine. This was the perfect opportunity to tell him. It was now or never.

My heart started to pound, but I stood a little taller and looked him straight in the eyes. "I don't need you to protect me, Chris. I know you see bad things. Some divorces are horrible, but don't you think that maybe if you talked about some of this stuff you wouldn't get depressed about it? Why do you think you have to shut me out?"

The pencil in his mouth fell, bouncing to the floor. He made no move to pick it up. His eyebrows arched into his forehead, and the color drained from his face. "You...you...how long...when??"

I couldn't answer. A guilty flush stained my cheeks and I lowered my eyes. Chris remained silent, his thoughts hushed by shock. I swallowed and licked my lips. Glancing up, I caught a flash of anger and rushed to defend myself. "Let me explain. I thought my powers were gone, and when I found out they weren't, you were so happy that I couldn't tell you the truth. Please try to look at it from my point of view before you get too angry with me. Think about it. You were so relieved. How could I disappoint you?"

His anger abated and I plunged ahead. "It just seemed like the right thing to do. And with all the trouble I'd gotten into with Uncle Joey and everyone, I thought it was better if it just went away. I really tried to ignore it. I promise. You have to believe what a terrible stress I've been under, keep-ing this a secret from everyone. But mostly from you. I can't do it anymore. I can't live like this. I need you to know and understand."

Chris was frozen. He didn't know how to feel or what to think. He was angry, disappointed, surprised, and mostly... relieved. It was the relief that shocked him. I took that as a good sign.

"Well... are you going to say something?" I asked.

"Why should I?"

That hurt, and my stomach clenched, but I guess I deserved it. "Okay. When you're ready to talk, I'll be in our room." I pulled the door shut before I heard his thoughts, and hurried to the bedroom. What had I done? Would he ever trust me again?

I took solace in the fact that he had felt relief from my confession. That had to mean he had been at least a little suspicious, and that maybe deep down he knew all along. When I thought about it, I realized that we were both protecting each other from unhappy things. That meant we loved each other, right? Even if we were stupid about how we showed it.

I waited for ten minutes thinking he'd come in. After twenty, and no sign of him, I climbed into bed and picked up the book I was reading. At nine-thirty I went to the kitchen for a glass of water. The door to his study was shut and I paused to listen. I was just about to knock when Savannah and her friends came downstairs. I followed them into the kitchen and broke out the cookies and milk, talking to them until her friends left. Joshua walked in as they were leaving, and Chris finally joined us. With him near, my heart did little happy thumps in my chest.

Watching him eat cookies and milk with Josh brought a sense of normalcy I'd been missing, so I did my best to block his thoughts. It worked because I was surprised when he got up and said goodnight to us, explaining that he still had a lot of work to do. He glanced my way with an apologetic smile and disappeared down the hall.

I went to bed hopeful that he'd soon join me, but after eleven I fell asleep. I tossed and turned all night and when I woke up the next morning, Chris was already gone. I realized he'd never come to bed and my heart broke a little. Why wouldn't he talk to me?

I stumbled into the kitchen and sighed with relief to find a note on the table. It wasn't much, but he said we would talk tonight, and he was sorry he hadn't come to bed. The case he was working on took most of the night, and he didn't want to disturb me, so he got a couple of hours sleep on the couch in his study.

He'd done this before, so I wasn't too worried, and he didn't seem unreasonably upset last night. Now that I didn't have to keep secrets, things were bound to get better. From now on, I decided I wouldn't tell any more lies. I'd stick to the truth as much as possible. I could tell him about the five million dollars in my account, and we could decide what to do about it.

Five million dollars. Just thinking about having that much money made my head spin. Too bad it wasn't really mine. What about the interest? Even if I only had the money for a short time, maybe I could keep the interest it was bound to make. I should probably put it in a higher yielding money market account while I still had the chance. How much interest could that much money make in a day? I had no idea, but probably a lot. I smiled. There was a bright side to this after all. One that even Chris couldn't disagree with.

Feeling relieved and less stressed, I made breakfast for my kids. They hurried to the kitchen, surprised and bewildered since I never made breakfast on a school day. Usually it was cereal or toast.

"What's going on?" Josh asked. "Did somebody die?"

"Don't be a smart-aleck," I said. "I can make breakfast for you if I want."

He shrugged like he didn't care, but I knew he was grateful, especially since he had a hollow stomach. Savannah didn't care about the food, only how she looked. I noticed the touch of eye shadow and lipstick with surprise. She'd never worn makeup before. Having this boy in her life must be serious. At least she wasn't wearing a lot of makeup, then I'd have to say something for sure. They ate quickly and, as usual, it was a rush to get them out the door in time for their rides.

After they left, I cleaned up and put the dishes away. The phone rang, and the caller ID said it was the police. For a second, my heart sped up. Was I in trouble? Had somebody died?

"Hello?"

"Hi Shelby, it's Detective Harris. How're you doing?"

Relief swept through me. It was Dimples. "Pretty good," I answered. "How about you?"

"I'm good, thanks. How's that bump on your forehead?"

"It's gone, and I don't have to wear my dark glasses anymore. So I guess I'm back to normal." I paused. "Well, almost normal." There, I hadn't lied. I could do this.

"That's great. The reason I'm calling is because I was wondering if you could come down to the station and help me out. You know... with your premonition thing? I haven't asked since all that went down with Joe Manetto... to give you some time to recover. But this case I have is important and I would like to get your input. I know it's short notice, but could you come down sometime today, maybe even this morning?"

"Sure, that will work. I'll get ready and come right in."

"Great! I'll see you soon."

We said goodbye and disconnected. This was perfect. Once I helped him, I could ask about being a paid consultant, just to see if it was a possibility. Things were falling into place and looking up. It was amazing how liberating doing the right thing could be.

I pulled into the police station an hour and a half later. Confidence radiated through me. I had a mission and a purpose, which didn't conflict with my 'ability' any more. This was the real me, not the scared, stay-at-home me, who was afraid to hear something she didn't want to.

Inside the station, I told them Dimples was expecting me, and they let me go back to his desk. He was on the phone, and motioned me to sit down. I didn't think I should listen to his thoughts, but that didn't fit with the new me. Now I realized my dilemma. To listen or not to listen, that was the question, plus this was a moral issue. I used to pride myself on not being nosey, but with my newfound powers, it was hard to stop. Like telling someone not to look at something was always a sure way to make them look.

Certainly I had more self-control than that. This was important if I was to manage around Chris and prove myself. I clamped down my senses just to see if I could do it. The whisper of voices receded and I opened my eyes.

"Shelby?"

I glanced at Dimples. His eyebrows were drawn together and he studied me with concern. He was thinking that maybe I wasn't ready to do this, and he'd pushed me too fast.

"I'm fine," I said, answering his unspoken question. I pursed my lips... so much for my resolve. Pulling myself together, I gave Dimples the smile he wanted. Reassured, he relaxed back in his chair. He thought I looked much better than the last time he'd seen me. The bruises were gone, and my forehead wasn't sticking out so much.

"Thanks for coming." He smiled back at me, and his dimples deepened into little tornados. "I hope it's not too much trouble."

This time, my grin was genuine. "Sure. Glad to help." Watching his dimples wobble always made me happy, and I realized I'd missed them.

"Good. Let me tell you about this case. There was a burglary from the Museum of Fine Arts. They just moved their entire inventory to a new building and that's when it happened. With so many people and volunteers helping, we can't even pinpoint the time it occurred, because the burglary happened during the move, and was only discovered once the museum reopened. I don't even know where to begin."

"Wow. That's big."

"Yeah, and I've got the Mayor on my back to get some results. You can see why I'm a little desperate."

He certainly was, and that desperation could get me a paying job as a consultant if I could prove my worth to the department, especially with the Mayor looking on. "What have you done so far?"

"Talked to the Museum curator and her assistant. Plus, I have a list of everyone who was there helping during the move."

I nodded. This was going to take some digging. "I will need to talk to the curator myself and all those who work at the museum. If I don't get any vibes from them, I'll have to talk to everyone on the list." Something occurred to me. "What was stolen?"

"Three paintings that were in the same crate. The curator, Jessica Palmer, said that although all of them were valuable, the Van Gogh was the museum's most valuable piece. They're all insured of course, but the members of the board are pretty upset." He glanced at the paperwork on his desk. "The total value is listed at around fifty million dollars."

"Whoa," I exclaimed. "That's huge."

"You're telling me."

I could feel the nervous energy radiating from Dimples. This was his case, and he needed all the help he could get. Even if asking me was a long shot, he was willing to take the chance.

My heart warmed. I understood his pain and the pressure he was under to solve the case. I wanted to prove that his trust wasn't misplaced, and that I could make a difference. "I'll do my best to help you. Where should we start?"

"Could you go to the museum with me?" he asked. "We could start there."

"Sure."

Chapter 2

The museum wasn't far from the police station, and we arrived just as it was opening. The curator wasn't in yet, so the receptionist had us wait while she tracked the curator down. The receptionist seemed nervous, but her thoughts were only about doing her job right and not getting into trouble. The curator, Jessica, intimidated her, and had a low tolerance for mistakes. Jessica liked things shipshape and running smoothly.

That was interesting. If Jessica was so conscientious, how had the robbers managed to take the museum's most prized possession? A few minutes later the curator walked in carrying a briefcase and wearing a navy skirt suit. Tall and thin, with long black hair and glasses, she was surprised to see us, but it didn't show on her face.

"Detective," she said politely. "How is the investigation coming?"

"We're working on it," Dimples said. "This is Shelby Nichols. Shelby, this is Jessica Palmer." We shook hands and Dimples continued. "Shelby is consulting on this case with me, and we'd like to ask you a few questions. Do you have a minute?"

"Of course," she smiled and ushered us into her office. The smile was all for show, underneath, she was rattled and worried. This had happened on her watch and was almost more than she could handle. She took her seat behind the desk and we sat in chairs across from her. "How can I help?" she asked.

Dimples glanced at me, not sure how to continue. I took the lead. "We'd like to go over the staff and volunteer list with you," I said. "Anything you can tell us about these people before we question them would be great."

"Like what?"

"Like... how long they've worked here, if you noticed any unusual behavior on the day of the move, that sort of thing."

"Okay," she answered, dubious that we'd find anything she hadn't already thought of.

We started at the top of the staff list and nothing popped out. Moving to the volunteer list was the same, until we came to the name of Greg Bowman. She didn't say it, but I got the distinct impression that there was something going on between them.

"Excuse me," I stopped her. "Is Greg Bowman one of the regular volunteers?"

"Not exactly," she said. Then she decided she might as well tell us the truth. "He's a personal friend. He came because I asked him if he could help with the move." She was thinking that she couldn't have made it through this ordeal without him.

"So, he's your boyfriend?" I blurted.

She was surprised at how quickly I figured it out. "Well, yes, but I trust him completely. I'm sure he's not involved."

"Oh, I didn't mean to imply that he was," I said. "Let's continue with the list."

We finished up and Jessica admitted that she couldn't see any of the people on the list involved in the theft.

"How long have you been the curator here?" I asked.

"I got the position about a year ago. Most everyone on the staff was here before me, but we've had a few newcomers. I still can't imagine it was any of them."

"But it has to be an inside job, right?" I asked

"It sure looks that way." She hated to admit that someone she knew could have done this.

We went over everything that happened on the day of the move. There were at least two people who attended the crates with double checklists. She supervised everything, and even watched the paintings that were stolen get loaded into the crate. That crate had a time stamp and a taped seal that went over it. The seal was unbroken when they opened the crate, but the paintings were gone. "I don't know how they did it," she exclaimed. "It's like a magic trick. It doesn't make sense."

Dimples stood. "We'd better get started with questioning the staff."

"Sure," she answered. "Most everyone should be here, and I'll have the phone numbers for all the volunteers ready with the list by the time you're done."

"Thanks."

Jessica set us up in a small office and we began our questioning with her assistant. He was polite, but not as forthcoming as I would like. It didn't take long to realize he had a grudge against Jessica because he had been passed over for the curator's position. He wouldn't mind if she failed, but he hated the fact that the paintings had been stolen. If he had been in charge, it never would have happened.

I scratched him off the list and we continued through the staff, ending with the security guards. It had taken about two hours, and I was starting to get a headache. "I'm not getting any vibes from these people," I told Dimples. "It must be one of the volunteers."

"All right," Dimples said. He tried to hide his discouragement with a smile. "Let's get the phone numbers and I'll set up another time we can meet with them."

The receptionist had the list ready for us. We were thanking her when a man came in wearing a big grin and strutting like he was on top of the world. He noticed us, and nodded dismissively before leaning on the receptionist's desk. "Is Jessica in her office?"

The receptionist smiled flirtatiously. "I think so. Do you want me to call?"

"No. I'd rather surprise her." He straightened and started toward her office, but there was something about him that caught my interest, and I couldn't let him get away.

"Excuse me, but you must be Greg Bowman?"

"That's right." He turned back toward me, and his eyes narrowed.

I held out my hand and smiled. "I'm Shelby Nichols." He clasped my hand firmly, and I continued. "And this is Detective Harris. We're working on the recent theft. Do you have a minute? We're going through the list to question all the staff and volunteers, and your name is on the list. It would save us a lot of time in tracking you down if we could just talk to you now."

"Um... sure, if it doesn't take too long. I was going to surprise Jessica and take her out to lunch."

"This will only take a minute and then we won't have to bother you again."

"All right. What do you want to know?"

"Just if you noticed anything out of the ordinary that day, and what your duties were. Let's go to the office we've been using and chat there. It's right through here." I led him back down the hallway, and nearly missed the correct office because I was listening so intently to his thoughts. He'd expected the questioning, but had hoped to put it off for at least another week. Maybe it was better this way. Now when he left in two weeks, no one would put it together.

My heart started to pound. This was the guy. "What kind of work do you do Greg?" I asked, motioning him to take a seat.

"Insurance, mostly disaster and homeowners. I'm an investigator. I look at the damage and then determine how much our company will pay based on the bids we get from the contractors."

"Oh, that sounds interesting."

"Yes. I'm not chained to a desk, so to speak. And I do a lot of traveling for the company." He was thinking that was a perfect cover for when he left, and even though he wasn't really an insurance investigator, he knew enough to know what he was talking about.

A chill went up my spine, but I kept an interested smile. He was the guy. Now all I had to do was prove it. "How long have you and Jessica been together?"

Greg narrowed his eyes again. "I fail to see what that has to do with your investigation." Why was I questioning his personal life? It wasn't any of my business, and he'd been more than cooperative already.

"Oh, you're right of course. I'm just a hopeless romantic," I smiled. "Didn't mean to pry, it just seems like you'd make a cute couple. Well, I guess that about does it for now." I stood. "If we think of anything else, can we give you a call? I know Jessica is frantic to find the thief."

"Yes. That would be fine. Glad to help." He stood, worried that he'd missed something, but couldn't figure out what. "Are you a detective with the police?"

"She's a consultant helping with the case," Dimples answered.

"So, you're a PI?" He couldn't let it go.

"No," I gave a small laugh. "Although I do have my own consulting agency." I heard Dimples think *you do?* at the same time as Greg. "Well, at least in my mind. I haven't formally opened for business, but I have helped the police a time or two, and I'm pretty good at what I do."

"Which is?" Greg asked. He wanted to know exactly what my place was in all this. Could I be an undercover agent with Interpol?

"I haven't decided which direction to focus on yet, but I guess what I do is more like a detective or private investigator. Wouldn't you agree with that, Detective Harris?"

I almost called him Dimples, but caught myself in time.

"Um... sure," he answered. He wasn't about to tell the guy I had premonitions, and that was why he'd called me. He stood, wanting to put an end to the questions. "That about sums it up Mr. Bowman. Thanks for your time. We'll let you know if we need anything else."

Greg smiled and shook our hands; unsatisfied with the answers we gave. He might have to step up his plans, just to be on the safe side. After all he'd gone through, he wasn't about to be thwarted now.

I almost squealed with delight at my discovery, shutting the door to our office as soon as Greg left. "He's the guy," I whispered, leaning against the door.

"He is?" Dimples eyebrows rose with surprise. "How can you tell?"

"I just know. Now all we have to do is prove it. I don't think Jessica is involved, but I think he's been using her. He's going to leave the country with the paintings soon, so we'll have to find them before he goes."

"How did you know all of that? You only just met him." Dimples was having a hard time believing how easy this was. I guess he'd forgotten the reason he brought me. He glanced at me and realized how he sounded. "Oh, of course... I forgot."

"We'll have to find a way to question him again. If we could make him sweat, and think we figured it out, it might be enough for me to get a reading on where he hid the paintings. Are there some kind of charges we could bring him in for?"

Dimples was beginning to think I was a little overzealous. "Um... maybe. But I don't want to scare him off if he's the guy."

"That could be a problem since he's planning to leave in two weeks."

Again, Dimples was faced with my 'uncanny' abilities, and he wondered just exactly how I did it. Could he really trust my instincts? To stem further questions from him, I opened the office door and noticed that Greg and Jessica were just walking out the main entrance and into the parking lot.

This was perfect. I motioned for Dimples to follow me and hurried over to the receptionist. "Wow," I said. "They sure make a handsome couple."

"Yes, they do." A tinge of jealousy escaped her tone and she glanced up to see if I'd caught it.

I smiled. "Have they been together long?"

"About three months I'd guess." She was thinking that he'd moved in with Jessica right after they met, which seemed pretty fast. She couldn't figure out what he saw in her. She was pretty, but she was one of the most uptight women she knew, and she didn't think that could be appealing to many men.

"Well, thank you for the list. You've been terrific." I glanced at both the staff list and the volunteer list, and didn't find what I needed. "Could I get Jessica's home address? I don't seem to have it here."

"Oh, sure." She found it on her computer and wrote it on a sticky note. I thanked her and hustled Dimples out the door.

"Where do you think a professional art thief would hide his paintings?" I asked.

"You think he's a professional?"

"Yes, I do." Something from Greg's thoughts popped into my brain. "I know! Let's check with Interpol and see if they have a most wanted list. It wouldn't hurt to see if anyone matching his description is there."

"Interpol?" Dimples wondered if I was letting this go to my head. "I've never worked with them before. I'm not sure I even know how to contact them."

"It shouldn't be that hard. You're a detective on the police force with some valuable stolen art. I'm sure they'd be interested."

"Okay." He was not overly enthused about where I was going with this.

We got into his car and I decided I'd pushed him enough for one day. "I'll leave it to you to decide what to do next, but I'm telling you... he's the guy."

"So in order for you to figure out where the paintings are, all you need is to be in the same room with him while he's being questioned?"

"Yes. That pretty much sums it up. I know that might be hard to arrange, and probably seems like a long shot to you, but I can do it. Think about it, and let me know what you want to do next."

He huffed out a breath, knowing he couldn't stake his entire investigation on my premonitions. He had to handle this the right way. "Are you sure you don't want to look at the other volunteers on the list?"

I considered it. Greg didn't seem like the type to have an accomplice, and his thoughts were pretty straightforward about his plans. He never thought 'we,' it was just 'I' or 'me,' so that had to mean he was acting alone. I waited until we pulled into the parking lot of the police station to speak. "I think he was acting alone, but I'll admit, I could be wrong."

Dimples shoulders relaxed. Just admitting that I could be wrong about something made him more comfortable with my premonitions. Go figure. "I'll talk to Interpol and see if I can figure out some reason to bring him in so we can question him," he said. "You're sure he's the guy?"

"Yes," I said firmly. "Let me know what you find out."

"Okay, thanks for your help."

"And Dimp... I mean Harris..." He glanced at me with a wry grin. "When we solve this case, will you check into maybe paying me for my services next time?"

His eyes widened. That was not what he expected me to say. Then it registered that I'd said 'when' not 'if and he smiled. "I think the mayor would be amenable to that, but we'll have to think of a better way to phrase what you do. I don't think he'd go for the 'premonitions' part."

I grinned. "You're probably right. I'll see what I can come up with."

I strolled to my car with a lighter step. I was happy and content to know I could make a difference. Telling them I had my own consulting agency made it seem more real, like I could really do it. It felt like the beginning of something important, and gave me hope that my ability wasn't such a bad thing after all. If it could be used for good, maybe it was all worth it.

I pulled into traffic and realized I would be driving right past Thrasher Development. Even though I didn't want to talk to Uncle Joey, there was no reason I couldn't see if his secretary, Jackie, knew where he was and when he'd be back. She might even know about the deposit. After all, she had set up my account in the first place. She must know something about his money and the business.

Before I could change my mind, I pulled into the parking garage and found a place close to the elevators. I put the car into park and turned it off, but hesitated to open the door. A shiver went down my spine and spread to my arms, raising goosebumps all over me. Cold fear seeped into my bones, and I found it hard to move. I knew this irrational fear was silly, but it was hard to shake it off. The last time I'd faced those elevator doors, Kate and Walter had tried to kill me.

I took a deep breath and pursed my lips. Walter was dead. Kate was gone, and Uncle Joey had followed her to Mexico. No one could hurt me now. There was nothing to fear. Filled with resolve, I got out of my car and marched to the elevators. I punched the button and stood with my head held high and my back straight. The elevator doors whooshed open, and I was proud that I only cringed a little. Inside the elevator, I hit the twenty-sixth floor, and allowed myself a small smile of victory.

I was still smiling when the doors opened, and I turned toward the suite of offices that belonged to Uncle Joey. "Thrasher Development" was painted in big letters above the wooden doors framed by green potted plants. That was new.

Curious to see what changes lay inside, I totally forgot my trepidation, and eagerly pulled the door open. Jackie's desk was in the same place as before, but the carpet and paint were new. Jackie straightened from a file she was working on, and a bright smile lit up her face.

"Shelby! What a pleasant surprise. How are you doing?" Jackie was genuinely happy to see me. She wasn't here the day all hell broke loose, but heard plenty about the huge bump on my forehead and my two black eyes. "You look great." She couldn't even tell I'd been clobbered in the head.

"Thanks Jackie. Yeah, I'm all back to normal, thank goodness. How are things going here?"

"Good," she said. "In fact they just finished the remodeling last Friday. Mr. Manetto's office looks great! Would you like to see it?" She was wondering what brought me here, especially since I'd nearly been killed, but figured I'd tell her when I was ready.

"Yes. I'd like that." She led me down the newly decorated hall to the double doors of Uncle Joey's office, and held the door open for me.

"Thanks," I said, and glanced around the room. "Wow this looks fantastic." It seemed almost sinful to step on the plush carpet. A deep mahogany desk and leather chair sat in front of the floor-to-ceiling windows overlooking the city. Matching bookcases and filing cabinets lined one wall, and at the near end was a fully functional wet bar. The other side held a conversation area with a small leather couch and leather chairs surrounding a coffee table. Earth tones and recessed lighting warmed the room. Beautiful paintings and potted plants gave it a professional feel. I wondered if Uncle Joey's safe was still behind the biggest painting.

While I admired the view, Jackie was thinking that she couldn't wait for Joe to get back. Besides missing him herself, Vic, Ricky and Marc were giving her grief, and it would be a relief to have Joe here to take charge. She didn't like feeling like their mother all the time.

"You should see the bathroom," Jackie said. She opened the door and flipped the light switch. Dark cabinets flanked by floor-to-ceiling marble covered the room. It was completed with a walkin shower that had several nozzles. An enclosed toilet was on the other side.

"Very nice," I said, awed by the sheer elegance. The money it took for this bathroom would probably buy me a new kitchen, appliances included.

"Mr. Manetto should like it." A burst of hopeful anticipation slid across her mind. Jackie was sure he'd like it since she was the one who'd picked it out for him. She enjoyed pleasing him in any way she could. She was excited for Joe to come back, mostly so he could show her just how much he appreciated everything she did for him.

To cover my shock at this revelation, I blurted the first thing that came to my mind. "Do you know when he'll be back? He told me he was going after Kate and Hodges, but that was a few weeks ago."

"No. He didn't say, but I'm hoping it won't be long." He'd told her about a big money transfer, so she knew he got the money back, but it hadn't turned up in any of the usual accounts and it worried her. When she'd asked him about it, he'd said the money was somewhere safe, but she didn't like not knowing where it was. She glanced at me with a gleam of speculation in her eyes. "Is there something I can help you with?"

"Um... no. I just thought I'd stop by and see how the remodeling was coming."

She smiled, knowing a lie when she heard one. "Did Mr. Manetto put some money in your account?" she asked in a teasing tone. "Is that why you're here?"

I didn't think she'd be so direct, so I wasn't prepared with a quick reply. "Why would he do that?"

She flicked her wrist in a quick wave. "It's just something he'd do. He doesn't trust too many people, but don't worry. I won't tell anyone." She was good, and she didn't seem too concerned that I had all that money. Now that I knew she was involved with Uncle Joey, I understood why he'd want to keep her around. She was loyal to him; so why didn't he give her the money instead of me? Didn't he know she was in love with him?

She ushered me out of the office and back down the hall. She was thinking that it was good to know where Uncle Joey had put the money. Now she didn't have to worry about it. She didn't think I'd take that money and run. It was enough money to live on comfortably, and was probably tempting. The only problem would be looking over my shoulder for Ramos or someone else Joe sent to kill me. She glanced at me and smiled, thinking it was something I already knew in my dealings with Uncle Joey, and it wouldn't be a problem.

"Well, thanks for showing me the office," I said. "And just for the record, Uncle Joey does put money in my account from time to time. I was hoping to talk to him about it, since I'm not working for him anymore. But I can wait until he gets back. And it's not that much money."

She smiled, sure that she knew where the missing money was. "I'll let him know you stopped by as soon as he gets back." She couldn't understand why I didn't call him if I wanted to talk to him so bad, but that was my business, not hers.

"That would be great. Thanks a bunch." I smiled and left, realizing I didn't know Jackie at all. I'd never had a reason to listen to her before, but she was pretty savvy when it came right down to it. Of course being Uncle Joey's love interest probably had something to do with it. She'd also thought about Vic, Ricky and Marc. I didn't know their names, but I had a pretty good idea they were Uncle Joey's men I'd been in all those meetings with, but to whom I'd never been introduced.

Now I knew three things for sure, Jackie was in charge of Uncle Joey's business while he was gone, she was in love with him, and she was pretty sure I had the money. But did that really make any difference? She was more than a trusted employee, right?

The drive home took me past the grocery store, and I decided I might as well stop there too, since there were some things I needed. I paid for my groceries and passed the ATM. It wouldn't hurt to check once more on the money in my account so I stopped. After entering my pin number, I held my breath, only exhaling when the amount came up. It was all there.

This time, I printed a receipt so I could show Chris. He'd need proof. It was the lawyer in him. I snatched the receipt and logged out as quickly as I could, casting a glance behind me to make sure no one noticed. Knowing I'd have to keep the receipt safe, I did the only thing I could think of and stuffed it in my bra. My grandma was like that. She kept all kinds of personal stuff in there, and I figured this was about as personal as it could get. Plus, it seemed like there was plenty of room. Hmm... time to go bra shopping.

Leaving the store, I noticed a big black SUV idling in the parking lot. The windows were darkly tinted, and I couldn't get a look at the occupants. Wasn't tinting your windows that dark against the law? My stomach did a nervous flip and I hurried to my car. Black SUV's seemed more like the kind of car a police detective or FBI person would drive, not someone connected to a crime boss like Uncle Joey. Still, it wouldn't hurt to be cautious.

Driving home, I kept a watch for the SUV in my rearview mirror. With no sign of it following me, my stomach finally unclenched, and I could breathe again. I pulled into the garage and closed the garage door behind me, just to make sure.

The door from my garage opened directly into my kitchen, making it easy to carry in my groceries. I put the food away, and spotted the leftover lasagna in the fridge. Yes! I did a happy dance. No cooking tonight! I briefly wondered if Chris would make it home in time for dinner, but since I'd already told him the truth, the pressure was off and I could relax.

I straightened up my living room and caught a glimpse through the window of a car inching slowly past my house. My legs went weak. It was the black SUV. Panic fluttered through my chest as it pulled to a stop, and I ducked out of view. From my vantage point, I waited to see who would come out, but it just sat there. After what seemed like an enormous amount of time, it continued up the street, and I could breathe more easily.

What was going on? I mentally slapped my head. I was such an idiot! Why didn't I get the license plate number when I was at the grocery store? I could have seen it then, but now it was too late.

I tried to think of who it might be, but only came up with who it wasn't. Not the police, and Uncle Joey wouldn't spy on me like that. Could it have something to do with the money? But that didn't make sense either. No one knew about the money, except Uncle Joey, and possibly Jackie, but I didn't think either of them would tell anyone.

The sound of a service truck going up the street caught my attention. My jaw dropped to find a FedEx van pulling to a stop directly in front of my house. The driver hurried to my front porch and rang the doorbell. Now what? He was holding a clipboard and an envelope. I opened the door and managed to sign the paper. He handed me the envelope with my name written in Uncle Joey's handwriting. Dread filled my stomach.

I thanked him and, after bolting the door, hurried into the kitchen and pulled the letter open. Inside was a single piece of paper. *Shelby*, it read, *I made a deposit into your account. Whatever you do, don't tell anyone, and don't try to contact me. It could be a matter of life and death. I hope to return soon, but if I don't come back in a few weeks, the money's yours.* He signed it, *Joe E Manetto.*

Oh great! What did he mean by all this secrecy? At least I hadn't tried to contact him, but what about my visit with Jackie? If this was such a secret, how come Jackie knew he'd made a deposit? If they were in a relationship, why didn't he tell her? The life and death part didn't seem very reassuring either. What had he gotten himself into? Why would he give me all this money if he didn't come back? Was this just another way to get me to work for him again? More likely, it was payment for the grief this money might cause me. He must be in some kind of trouble. And now, I was involved too.

This piece of paper was important, but I couldn't leave it lying around for anyone to see. I needed to put it where no one could find it. I went into my room and got out my journal. I'd had it for about eight years and it was only half full. Most of it was filled with little anecdotes about my kids when they were toddlers. Not so much recently, but that's what made it a perfect hiding place. I mean, seriously, who would want to read my journal? I stuck the letter in-between some pages and put the journal back on my shelf.

Things were getting complicated. When Uncle Joey said not to tell anyone, I had to take that seriously, especially since it was a matter of life and death. His or mine wasn't so clear. That didn't mean I wasn't going to tell Chris. He needed to know what we were dealing with, and hopefully it wouldn't freak him out. Telling him I'd stopped by Thrasher Development would probably make things worse, so it was better to leave that part out for now. I could tell him later if I needed to.

Through a blur of restless energy, I managed to get back on track with the day's schedule. I'd almost forgotten that

Josh had a soccer game after school, and it was my turn to pick up Savannah from dance class.

I sent a text message to Chris about the game, telling him to meet us there. It was almost over when he arrived, and his face was drawn with fatigue. I gave him a quick hug. "Hard day?"

"Yes." He was thinking that his client was a major pain in the... He jerked his thoughts to a stop and cut me with a razor-sharp glance, remembering last night's conversation. "I forgot..."

"Please... don't worry about it. I'm glad you made it to Josh's game. Look, they're ahead, that should take your mind off... you know." I was making a mess of it as usual. "Listen, I've got to pick Savannah up from dance class so I'll just meet you at home. Okay?"

"Sure," he gestured toward the game. "So, they're winning?"

"Yes. It's five to three." With his mind now focused on the game, I hugged him and left.

Savannah and I got home before the boys, so I warmed up the lasagna in the microwave while Savannah set the table. Both Chris and Josh were in a good mood when they came in the door, mostly due to Josh's team winning the game. The good feelings carried over through dinner, and I was relieved to feel like things were normal again.

Cleaning up after dinner, Chris started worrying what he was thinking about, and how he could manage around me. I tensed. How could I think things were back to normal with this looming over us? We needed to talk before he got worked up and made too much out of it. As soon as we had a free moment together, I pulled Chris into his study. "We need to talk. Might as well be now."

He pursed his lips and closed the door. "You're right. I don't know what I expected, but it wasn't this. I didn't expect you to lie to me. I understand why you did it, but this is hard for me to accept." He ran his fingers through his hair in agitation, and I knew enough not to say anything until he got it all out.

"I'm working hard at not being upset, but this whole thing is getting to me. I don't know how to act, or how to think. I was so relieved when you said it was gone! And now... you're saying it was never really gone... and you've been listening to my thoughts all this time? I feel... betrayed. And that makes me angry."

"When I told you it was gone, I really thought it was!" He needed to know that much. "You were blocking all your thoughts from me so well that I figured my powers were gone. I don't know how you did it, but you did. Don't you see? With both of us working on this, I'm sure we can find a solution."

He was trying hard not to let his anger get the best of him. "All right. So I can block you from my mind. How?"

"I'm not sure... but you did it before, so I know you can. Plus, I'm getting better at blocking thoughts too." He closed his eyes and rubbed the bridge of his nose.

"There's something else I need to talk to you about." I figured I might as well tell him about the money and get everything out in the open. My tone must have triggered his fight or flight response because his eyes widened, and he braced his feet as if in readiness for a physical assault.

"What?" His tone held acute displeasure, and my palms started to sweat.

"Today I checked the account balance from the bank account that Uncle Joey set up for me, and I found something you should know." His brows lifted, practically obliterating his forehead. This was not a good sign. "There's some extra money in there. Look... here's the receipt if you don't believe me." I found the receipt in my bra and held it toward him.

"You put it in your bra?"

"You actually said that out loud." I was surprised.

"I figured, why not?" Chris shrugged. "Since you can hear what I'm thinking, I might as well start blurting out what's going on in my head."

"Hey... that could work."

"Yeah, right. Until I think something that hurts your feelings, and you hear it and get mad at me."

"Chris... that's just silly! You hardly ever think or say anything to me that would hurt my feelings... enough that I couldn't get over it. I'm not that fragile... I promise."

He took a breath, considering it. "You're probably right. I do think you can be... a little exasperating at times, but for the most part... I think you're great."

I smiled and circled my arms around him. "See. This isn't so bad."

"So... you're just worried about some money Manetto put in your account?"

"I guess you could say that."

He smiled knowingly. "Because you're afraid I'll think you're still working for him? Right? But you're not. Right?"

"Of course I'm not." I said, starting to pull away.

"Hey, you're not supposed to get mad, remember?" He held me until I relaxed in his arms. "That's better. So when was the last time you talked to him?" I sighed, upset that he could ask such a thing. "Hey," he continued. "I'm just thinking out loud here. It's what I'm supposed to do, right?"

"I think you're enjoying this way too much," I said.

"Hmm... yup. I think maybe I am." His teasing smile was hard to resist. "And you're smiling back at me. This is good. I think I can live with this."

"Good, because there's more I need to tell you."

That made him pause. "Sure," he said, back to his kidding self. "Tell me. I can take it."

"Okay. Just remember you said that." I took the receipt from his fingers. "There's over five million dollars in my account." While that was sinking in, I continued. "And I got a letter from Uncle Joey telling me not to tell anyone. That it was a matter of life and death."

"Let me see that," he grabbed the receipt and studied it. "You're sure about this?"

"I just got the receipt from the ATM today. I didn't talk to the bank or anything because I thought it was best to keep this quiet."

"Where's the letter? I need to see it."

"I'll get it." I hurried into the bedroom for my journal and brought it back. He snatched it from my fingers and read, his brows drawing together.

"When did you get this?" He was hoping I hadn't been keeping this a secret for long.

"Today," I assured him. "The FedEx guy brought it and I had to sign for it."

"Hmm... I wonder if he caught up with Kate and Hodges, and this is the money they stole from him. But that doesn't explain why he put it in your account, or why it would be a matter of life and death. He clearly doesn't want anyone to know about it, probably because they would try and take it from you. So he must feel it's pretty safe where it is."

"What should we do about it?" I asked.

"I don't know." He was thinking it would be great if Manetto never came back and left us with all that money. He glanced at me sharply. "Did you hear that?"

"Uh-huh."

"You didn't tell Manetto your powers came back did you?"

"Of course not!" Hot indignation poured over me, then sputtered out with a wink. "But the last time I talked to him, he might have picked up something from me. I'm just not sure. That's why I didn't ever want to talk to him again. I was afraid he'd guess."

"That makes sense."

"So what should we do?"

"Let's just leave it alone for now. I'll check on the legal ramifications of getting a 'gift' like this tomorrow, and we can discuss what to do after that." He was thinking that he'd like to at least make some good interest on it while it was sitting there.

"I was thinking the same thing," I said. "About the interest."

"Oh." In all the excitement, he'd forgotten the mind-reading thing.

"There's something else." I might as well tell him more. "I'm working with Dimples on a case."

"You mean he knows about..."

"No! Remember before? When I told him I had premonitions? He called this morning and asked if I'd help him with a case. I figured it might be a good way to use my ability to get a paying job, like a consultant for the police or something."

Chris was thinking I was getting in over my head, and that somebody might figure it out.

"No one really thinks a person can read minds, so I don't think that's something I have to worry that people will figure out."

Chris blew air out of his cheeks. "I really don't like it when you do that. Could you at least wait until I say what I'm thinking like a normal person?"

"Oh... sure. Sorry."

"It's okay," he said, instantly contrite. "It's going to take some time to get used to this again for both of us. You're just springing a lot on me all at once."

"Yeah, well, that's kind of how it happens. But I'll work on that." Thank goodness I hadn't told him about my visit to Thrasher Development. "We can both work on blocking thoughts. You did it pretty well when I thought I'd lost my powers."

His eyes crinkled in a wince. "Yeah. But it wasn't something I liked doing. I guess I can work on it though."

I hated to think of him shutting me out again. "How about we see how I do at blocking first. If you're okay with that."

"All right," he nodded, his shoulders relaxing. "Tell me about the case."

I explained what had happened with the theft at the art museum and he was impressed at how quickly I'd figured out who the bad guy was. He admitted that I was in a great position to help a lot of people.

"So you think having my own consulting agency might be a good idea?"

"Yeah, if that's what you really want. I think we could come up with a small business plan and get a license, but let's wait until we figure out what to do with Uncle Joey and the money first." He knew how single-minded I could get. Plus, he didn't want me to get hurt. "Maybe you could just work for the police if they'll start paying you for your time, as long as it's not too much time." He was thinking that he hated to see me get involved with those kinds of people. Would witnessing a murder, even if it was only in someone's thoughts, change me?

"Oh, I hadn't thought of that." Oops, I did it again.

Chris just smiled, and pulled me to him. "If you're going to read my mind, maybe it's time I take advantage of it." His kiss seared my lips, and I had no trouble knowing exactly what he wanted at that moment. For some reason he didn't mind it a bit.

Chapter 3

The next morning dawned bright and clear. It was a beautiful spring day, and the tightness in my chest was gone. Talking to Chris had been the best thing I'd done in a long time.

Chris was in the shower and I wanted to join him, but I had to make sure the kids got off to school. I slipped on my bathrobe and got the cereal and milk on the table, then put in some toast and buttered it. Savannah wandered in wearing a tight button-up shirt with a short skirt and black tights along with some clunky boots. This was a new look. She was hoping I wouldn't freak out, but was ready to defy me if I did.

"Savannah!" I exclaimed. "You look adorable. Where did you get those clothes?"

"Oh," she tried to hide her surprise. "Um... Ash and Madi and I decided to share some of our clothes. You know... so we'd have more things to wear."

"That's generous of you. When I was your age none of my friends would have thought of doing that."

She mentally rolled her eyes, not in the least interested in hearing another 'when I was your age' story. I examined her skirt. If it was any shorter, I would have made her change, but it was within the acceptable range. Still, it wouldn't hurt to say something.

"That skirt is a little short, so I wouldn't bend over if I were you." That was more what she expected me to say. "Be sure to keep your knees together too." I was on a roll. "Is that makeup you're wearing?"

"Mom! I'm old enough, and I'm not wearing that much. Besides, all my friends are wearing it."

"Wearing what?" Chris asked, coming into the kitchen.

"Makeup," I answered, knowing Savannah was too embarrassed to admit it.

Chris did a double-take, studying Savannah in a new light. He was surprised to find his little girl changing before his eyes. "Umm... aren't you a little young for that?"

"No, Dad. Geeze, don't you even know how old I am?"

"Of course I do. You're about ten, right? Way too young for makeup." Chris was teasing, which was a good thing, since he couldn't remember if she was twelve or thirteen. This was one time I wished he could read my thoughts.

"Not funny," Savannah said, pouring cereal into her bowl.

Joshua came in and filled his bowl until it overflowed with cereal. Half of it spilled out when he poured in the milk. He took a big mouthful and noticed us staring. "What?" Milk and bits of cereal dribbled down his chin.

"Eww, that's disgusting" Savannah sneered, grateful to have the attention off of her.

Chris checked the clock and grabbed a piece of toast. "Got to run." He kissed me and picked up his briefcase. *We'll talk later*, he thought, and I smiled to let him know I heard.

Joshua and Savannah followed not long after, leaving the house in comfortable silence. After putting the dishes away, I put on my exercise clothes and headed for the gym. A complete workout with my friend Holly left me sweaty, but feeling good. My goal to keep the weight off I'd lost the last few weeks was working.

My euphoria vanished when I got home, replaced by a sick feeling in the pit of my stomach. A black SUV was parked across the street from my house. It was identical to the one I'd seen yesterday in the parking lot of the grocery store, and driving slowly up my street.

I swore under my breath and pulled into my garage, closing the door behind me. Safely inside, I watched to see what would happen. Sure enough, two men got out of the car and came toward my front door.

Both wore dark glasses and white shirts with black suits. Their hair was cut short and they looked official, like they were from the set of a CSI or FBI TV show. My heart pounded and, like a crazy person, I ducked into the hall where they couldn't see me.

What did these guys want with me? The doorbell rang and I peeked around the corner. My heart did little flip-flops, and my breath caught. Unfortunately, they knew I was home. I waited, hoping they would leave if I didn't answer right away.

The doorbell rang again, followed by a few hard knocks on the door. These guys weren't going anywhere. I might as well answer and get it over with. Besides, I had a secret weapon. I could read their minds. That gave me an advantage, right?

Walking to the door on trembling legs, I pasted an inquisitive smile on my face and pulled it open.

"Ms. Nichols?" one of them asked.

"Yes," I answered.

He took a wallet from his pocket and flipped it open, revealing a gold badge and an ID card. After I glanced at it, he snapped it shut and returned it to his pocket. "I'm Agent

Shaw and this is Agent Bristow. We'd like to speak to you for a moment."

"Um... wait a minute," I said. "Can I see that again?" I needed some time to process their thoughts and make sure they were legitimate before I let them into my house. Agent Shaw froze. He couldn't believe I was questioning his authority. No one had ever done this to him before.

"Oh... sure." He pulled his ID back out and handed it to me. I studied it closely, knowing if these were fake they'd be hoping I wouldn't figure it out.

"Yours too," I said, holding my hand toward Agent Bristow. He was thinking that either I was buying time, or I knew that the law gave me every right to check their IDs. I could call the agency before talking to them if I wanted. I could even tell them to get lost and they couldn't do a thing about it.

That meant they were for real. I took my time, trying to glean any more information off them before handing their badges back, but their minds were strangely quiet. "So... you're with the CIA?" I asked.

"That's what it says on the badge, ma'am." Agent Shaw's lips twisted to hold back a smirk. "We'd like to ask you a few questions, if that's all right?"

That smirk got my dander up. Just because he was a federal agent didn't mean he could talk down to me. "You know I could tell you to get lost and you'd have to leave. So you shouldn't be such a smart-aleck if you want my cooperation." Agent Shaw's mouth dropped open and his face flushed. Usually the only people who called him on the carpet like that were his partner and his mother. It rubbed him the wrong way to apologize, but if I filed a complaint...

"It wouldn't look good on your record if I filed a complaint," I finished his thought, and mentally kicked myself.

Why couldn't I keep my mouth shut? His initial shock left him speechless and Agent Bristow stepped in.

"There's no need for that. Agent Shaw meant no disrespect." He glanced at Shaw, sending a mental image of whacking him a good one. "We only need a moment of your time and then we'll be on our way."

Since I didn't want to arouse any suspicion about me, I opened the door and ushered them inside. "What's this about?"

They sat on my couch and Agent Bristow got right to the point. "Have you received any communication from Joseph Manetto recently?"

"Uh... not recently." The lie came automatically and I was a little ashamed, but when Uncle Joey said not to tell anyone with all that life and death stuff, I had to be careful until I knew more. "I used to work for him, but there was some trouble and I quit. Last I heard he was on his way to Mexico."

"Do you know why he went there?" Bristow already knew the answer. He was just fishing to see how well I knew Uncle Joey.

"Yes." It wouldn't help to lie about that since it was in the police report. "He went looking for his niece, Kate. Did something happen to him?" Dread tightened my stomach. Had he been kidnapped? Was that why it was a matter of life and death?

Bristow glanced at Shaw, gauging how much he should tell me. Joey 'The Knife' Manetto had shown up at the home of an arms dealer they were working with. Their operation was centered on their fight against the drug cartels, and they wanted to know why Manetto was involved.

The CIA was working with an arms dealer in Mexico? "Is this about the drug dealers in Mexico?" I blurted. "I can't imagine Uncle Joey getting involved in that. He must be in a lot of trouble if that's what you think."

"I never said anything about drugs," Bristow's voice was deceptively calm. And why had I called him Uncle Joey?

"Oh... I know that. I just assumed that since the CIA was involved that something big was happening. And Mexico is a hotbed for drugs and murders right now. It's in the paper. So I just put two and two together, but I'm probably wrong. I know sometimes my imagination gets the best of me. Too much TV I guess." Agent Shaw was thinking I talked too much for someone who didn't know what was going on.

This was not going well. "I have no idea what's going on with Unc...a...Joey. But if there's anything I can do to help..." What was wrong with me? I should tell them about the money, but something held me back. Probably that it would implicate me somehow, and I would get arrested. I mean... if I hadn't checked my account balance, I wouldn't know the money was there. So pretending I didn't know was okay. I would wait until I could tell Chris about them, and he would know how to handle this.

Bristow sighed and stood. "Thanks. Here's my card with my number. If he contacts you for any reason, will you please let me know?"

"Of course," I said.

Bristow gave me a tight-lipped smile and ushered Shaw to the door. There was something about me that bothered him, and he didn't trust me. Hopefully Shaw had been able to plant the bug in a safe place. He didn't understand how someone like me could be involved. I was a simple house-wife and, with no ties to Mexico, I did not fit the normal profile. But they had to check up on all their leads.

My eyes widened and Bristow glanced at me sharply. I covered it with a quick smile and gave a little wave. As soon as they were out I shut the door and leaned against it, my heart racing. I glanced out the window and watched them drive away. My shoulders slumped and I let out a big breath. This did not look good. And they'd planted a bug.

I had to get rid of it fast before it started working so they'd think it was broken or something. I sat on the couch where Shaw had been and ran my fingers under the edge. Nothing, but then again, I didn't know what a bug looked like in real life. It had to be somewhere close since this was the only place he'd been in the house.

The end table with the lamp was within easy reach. I checked the entire surface of the table and lamp but found nothing. Next, I checked the lampshade and everything in between. Still nothing. I ran my fingers under the table and my breath caught. On the inside curve was a small round object. I pulled it off and examined it closely. It was black with a little wire sticking out of it. This was it! Now what to do?

I ran into the bathroom, ready to flush it down the toilet, but hesitated. This little device was probably worth a pretty penny. Would I get in trouble if I destroyed it? Wait a minute. This was my house, and the fact that they could listen to my private conversations made me a little angry. Before I could change my mind, I threw it in, and flushed.

Bristow had only thought about one bug, so I was pretty sure it was the only one, but I went over every inch of where Shaw had been just to make sure. I found nothing else, but was mentally exhausted by the time I finished.

I decided to take a shower and go straight to Chris' office and tell him what had happened. With the CIA involved, this was getting too serious for me to handle by myself. If they could plant a bug, they could probably get away with just about anything, and that made me nervous.

An hour later, I walked into Chris' office. "Hi," I greeted his secretary.

"Hi Shelby. How are you?" She was wondering what I was doing there since Chris was in court.

"Dang, he's not here... is he?" I quickly added.

"No. He's in court for most of the day. You might be able to catch him, if you go over. If it's really important." She was thinking that he wouldn't like the disruption, especially since this case was pretty involved. But with my big eyes and pale face, I was looking desperate.

"I guess I could take a chance. Whose court is he in?"

She looked up the schedule. "Courtroom 400, Judge Benson."

"Okay, thanks." The courthouse was within walking distance, and I figured since I was already downtown, it wouldn't hurt to try, especially since I'd come all this way.

I made it through security and walked toward the elevators. Waves of violence and anger, along with determination to escape, hit me like a ton of bricks. A man with chains on his arms and legs, and dressed in an orange jumpsuit, entered from the back with an armed escort. He was thinking that if his partner didn't get him out of there, he'd be sorry. He wasn't going down alone. He'd tell them everything, including where the money was hidden.

I caught a quick flash of an open lid, like a casket in a dark room, and the word, 'underwear.' Then it was gone. What the heck did that mean? It didn't make any sense. Was the money hidden in someone's underwear? That couldn't be right.

Everyone within a short distance gave him and the escort plenty of room. The elevator opened and they disappeared inside, taking a mountain of rage with them. The anger and rage emanating from him was the single most awful thing I had ever experienced.

The woman beside me took a deep breath and glanced my way. "That was creepy," she said, hoping that guy rotted in hell. She turned her attention back to me, taking in my white face. "Honey, are you all right?"

"Who was that?"

She pursed her lips. "Keith Bishop, the bank robber who stole all that money and killed a hostage. Or I should say 'allegedly' killed her, since they haven't proven it. Hopefully the jury will today."

"He was seething with anger and determined to escape."

She glanced at me sharply. "Do you have ESP or something?"

I swallowed, realizing I'd spoken my thoughts out loud. "Something like that. Not that you needed ESP to feel the bad vibes he was giving off. You felt it too, right?"

"Yes, I suppose I did." She was thinking that she had a plan in place to keep him from escaping, but decided to put everyone on alert, just to make sure. She pulled a radio transmitter out of her pocket and talked into it. That was when I noticed her ID badge with SECURITY in capital letters.

A woman brushed past me, and I wouldn't have thought anything of it except she nearly lost her balance on her high heels. The string of expletives coming from her mind shocked me so much I couldn't take my eyes off her. She had huge ugly legs and walked with an awkward gait. Then it hit me what was wrong. The voice I heard was too low and deep for a woman. She was a he.

"Excuse me." I tapped the security woman's arm and pointed him out. "That woman is a man. I don't know if that means anything to you, but I just thought I'd mention it." She looked him over, and noting his hairy legs and the way he walked, knew I was right.

This was just the kind of thing the security agent was expecting, and she took off after him. "Miss, I need you to stop," she yelled. At that, the guy took off down the hall.

Several security officers converged on him at once, and with those high heels, he didn't stand a chance to outrun them.

His loud shouts of protest caught everyone's attention, and I decided I'd seen enough. I hurried over to the elevator's closing doors, and managed to get my arm inside before it shut all the way. The doors jerked back open, and I stepped in to find another occupant who frowned with displeasure that I had stopped his ride.

I averted my eyes as he let out a few expletives only I could hear. Good grief! Did everyone have to swear so much? He was hoping I hadn't gotten a good look at him, otherwise he'd have to whack me right there. He could probably do it if he had to. The hairs on the back of my neck stood up, and I managed to stick my arms into the door before it closed all the way.

I lunged out of the elevator and hurried back to the lobby, glancing over my shoulder. The man stuck his head out with narrowed eyes to watch me, but pulled back in when the doors started to close. Yikes! Did that guy have something to do with the bank robber? I inched back to the elevator and my heart dropped when it stopped on the fourth floor. That's where Chris was.

I had to go up there and make sure he was all right. When the elevator doors slid back open, I almost expected the man to still be there. Relieved it was empty, I stepped inside on pure adrenalin and pushed the button for the fourth floor. My legs were shaking as I got out and checked the hallway.

Several policemen were standing guard outside the courtroom doors, with no sign of the man from the elevator. What had happened to him? From the policemen's thoughts, I realized this was where the bank robber's trial was.

Oh no! Was Chris handling this case? My breath caught with shock. How come I didn't know about it? How had this happened? Above the courtroom doors was the number 401. I glanced at the other side of the hallway and realized there were two smaller courtrooms with the numbers 400 and 402 on that side. Now it made sense.

With relief, I backtracked to the courtroom with 400 on it, and pushed open the door. Slipping inside, I took a seat on the back row. Chris was talking to the judge about his client, and I realized this was the messy divorce case. I sighed, and the tension left my shoulders. At least Chris was safe. I glanced around the room to make sure the elevator guy wasn't there. So where was he? Was he planting a bomb somewhere so he could spring the bank robber?

I knew he was up to no good from the vibes he gave off, and I struggled to remember just exactly what thoughts and feelings I'd heard from him. The man dressed as a woman could have been a diversion for this guy to get in without anyone paying attention to him. That was probably why he was upset I got into the elevator with him. But he still had to get past security, so that didn't add up. Plus, there were security cameras all over the building, so why would he think he had to whack me for seeing him?

Maybe I was making too much out of it, but I couldn't shake the feeling that he was dangerous. So where was he now?

A loud crack jolted me from my thoughts and my heart nearly burst. The judge put down his gavel, adjourning court for one hour. My heart was still pounding when Chris spotted me. He finished talking to his client and excused himself.

"What's wrong?" he asked, his eyes narrowed with concern.

"I think a dangerous person is in the building," I said. "That sounds stupid, but from what I could pick up, I'm worried something bad is going to happen."

"Like what? What are you talking about?"

"I saw that man come in... the bank robber whose trial is across the hall? Keith Bishop? He was thinking about escaping and hoping his partner would get him out of here. Then someone else came in after that, and when I got into the elevator with this guy, he was thinking he'd have to whack me if I got a good look at his face. I got out of the elevator before the doors closed, but it stopped on this floor. So he must be here somewhere. Just before that, the security lady was thinking someone might help the bank robber escape."

Chris could hardly take it all in. He was thinking it sounded nuts, but since it was me, he had to believe it. "All right," he said. "It may not be anything, but we can alert the police in the hall. I just don't know how to do it without sounding..."

"Crazy?" I finished.

"Yeah." He smiled and shrugged.

"Hey Chris?" His client came toward us. "Were we going to go over my testimony during the break?" The guy was nervous because he wanted to get everything settled before his wife found out about all the extra money he'd taken from their savings account.

"Yes. Just give me a minute." Chris was torn. He needed to help his client, but this was more important.

The exwife walked past with her lawyer and smirked. She was thinking that it wouldn't matter how much he prepared since she had found the money he'd siphoned from their savings account and had the proof to show the judge. He wasn't going to get away with anything if she could help it. The jerk.

The door swished closed behind her, blocking her thoughts, and I was glad I was sitting down. Being in court with all these stray thoughts was giving me a headache.

"You've got that dazed look in your eyes. Are you okay?" Chris asked.

"Umm... sure, just a headache coming on..." Chris' client stood behind him and I didn't know if I should tell him what his wife was thinking or not. This was probably one time it was better to keep those thoughts to myself. "Maybe I should just go talk to the police in the hall about the man in the elevator and let them worry about it."

"Sounds like the best way to handle it to me," Chris agreed. "I'll come with you." He turned to his client. "I'll be right back."

The client huffed and reluctantly agreed, thinking he was going to keep track of the time Chris was gone and make sure it was deducted from his fee. I raised my brows at him, but turned away before he noticed. That clinched it for me. No way was I going to tell Chris about the money. I hoped his wife got to keep it.

We hustled out the doors and toward the policemen standing outside the courtroom. As we approached, I tried to figure out what I was going to tell them. How could I warn them about someone who hadn't said a word to me?

The officer glanced at me and I smiled. "Excuse me, but I was in the elevator with a man coming to this floor that seemed suspicious. He was hiding something in his jacket, and I just wanted to let you know to be extra watchful." I was improvising, but it was the only thing I could think of to make my story seem more plausible.

"Like what? Did you see anything?"

"No. But he turned his face away from me, like he didn't want me to see it, and it made me nervous. That's when I noticed his hand under his jacket, and I wondered what he was holding under there. I just wanted to let you know."

"Could you identify this man?"

He was actually taking me seriously. I'd only caught a glimpse of his face, but I was pretty sure I could spot him again. "I think so."

"And you're sure he got off on this floor?"

"Yes."

"Would you mind coming inside the courtroom to see if he's in there?"

I glanced at Chris who nodded his agreement. "Sure, if you think it would help." The policeman opened the door and I slipped inside with him. He ushered me to the side of the courtroom where I could look over most of the people. I focused on them individually, keeping my mind open for thoughts that would help me in my search.

Nothing popped out at me, and I pursed my lips in defeat. Then a trickle of awareness touched my senses. Glancing up, I noticed the elevator guy sitting just behind the bank robber. He was sitting forward and it looked like he was whispering something into the robber's ear while he leaned over to tie his shoe.

I concentrated on his thoughts and caught that he hoped Bishop went along with his plan because it was only a few more minutes before the alarm went off. That didn't give him much time to take care of the guy.

I nodded to the policeman and hurried out the door. In the hallway, I could hardly keep my composure. "The guy is sitting right behind the robber. He was whispering something to him." I blurted. "Is there some kind of an alarm in this building? Like a fire alarm? I think that's when he's going to make his move and break the guy out."

The policeman glanced at the other officer on duty. He was thinking that this was getting weird, and wondered how in hell I could figure all that out from just looking at the guy. Maybe it was me they should watch out for.

"I can read lips, and he was whispering something about an alarm, so I just put two and two together."

"Oh," the officer said, not really convinced, but going along in case I made any desperate moves.

I turned to Chris and explained. "He must have an accomplice who's going to pull the alarm. Are there any on this floor?"

"There should be," Chris said. "Down that way, I think." He motioned toward the end of the hall, but someone stood in the way and I couldn't see the little red box. The officers glanced at each other, then looked down the hall. The person standing there had his back to us. He was wearing a baseball cap with a jacket, jeans and sneakers, all in dark colors. I focused on his thoughts, but just then, an ear splitting bell sounded and I cringed, automatically hunching my shoulders, and covering my ears.

The officers jerked in surprise. The person standing in the hallway was running toward us with his head down and shoulders hunched. The side door where the prisoners were escorted in and out burst open with the elevator guy pulling the bank robber into the hall. Both officers took off toward the side door. The guy in the baseball cap veered into one of the officers, shoving him into the other, and kept on running.

With both officers down, the elevator guy and the bank robber hustled into the courtroom across the hall. The fallen officers got to their feet and rushed to the door, but it wouldn't open. One of them pulled out his gun to shoot open the lock, but stopped as people began to exit the large courtroom. Chris pulled me out of the way and we flattened ourselves against the wall. A shot rang out, and everyone scattered. Yelling came from inside the courtroom. The doors crashed open and Chris' client ran out, followed by another man whose thoughts were focused on getting away.

Was that the elevator guy? I stuck out my foot and tripped him. "That's him!" I shouted. Chris pounced on him and managed to pull his arm behind his back in a lock.

"Officer!" I shouted and waved my arms. "We caught him!" One of the officers in the hall hurried to my side. "This is the guy," I said. The officer cuffed the elevator guy, and turned him around. A look of confusion came over the officer, and I glanced at the guy, realizing that he looked different from just a few moments ago. Oh no! Had I made a mistake?

"What's going on?" the man complained. "I'm just trying to get out! Can't you hear the fire alarm? And what about the gunshot? What's wrong with you people?" Inside he was calculating how to get away. But he wasn't too worried.

"Oh, sorry sir," the officer replied. "We thought you were someone else."

"Wait!" I jumped in. "It is him. There must be a connecting door between the courtrooms."

"That's right," Chris broke in. "The judge has a chamber between both courtrooms. He could have used that."

Down the hall, several policemen broke through the door and the elevator guy began to sweat. "I don't know what she's talking about." He was glad he'd tossed his jacket in the other room.

"I'll bet he took his jacket off and it's in the other room," I said. "And that must have been a fake nose he had on before, but this is the same guy."

"What do you mean?" he asked. "What guy?"

"At least look inside and see if you can find the jacket he was wearing." I couldn't let him get away.

Another officer approached. "We found Bishop. He was in the judge's chambers. He's dead."

"Dead?" I asked.

"Yeah, and the place is empty. I guess the guy who did it got away."

"No, he's right here." I pointed at him. "He was wearing a disguise, but this is him." Both policemen glanced at the man again, then at me, doubt in their minds.

"Hey," the officer said to his partner. "See if you can find a jacket in there. She says he took off his jacket and left it in there." He turned to me. "If it's not there I think you'll have to admit you made a mistake."

"It's there," I said. I kept listening to the guy's thoughts, but he wasn't thinking about much except how furious he was with me.

The officer came back with a jacket. "Is this it?"

"Yes that's the one he was wearing," I said, relieved.

"That's not my jacket," the guy said. "You're making a mistake."

"Don't listen to him," I jumped in. "I was right about the jacket, wasn't I?" The officers looked at each other, unsure about what to do. If it was him and they let him go, there'd be hell to pay, but if it wasn't they'd be in real trouble. "At least take him in for questioning," I prodded. "You can't just let him go. What if I'm right and he just killed Keith Bish-op?"

"Okay," the officer said. "But you'll have to come and make a statement. It looks like you're the only person who thinks this is the same man." He wanted to make sure his bases were covered.

"I will," I agreed. "I have to talk to my husband for a mi-nute and I'll come right over."

The officer nodded and pulled the guy behind him. The guy shook his head and began to complain, but shot me a look of pure hatred over his shoulder. All at once, his eyes widened, realizing I was the lady from the elevator. What was going on? There was something weird here, and he was determined to find out what it was.

They rounded the corner and alarm tightened my chest. This guy was bad news, and now I was involved. He didn't seem like the kind of person to give up too easily. This was not good.

"Are you sure that was the same guy?" Chris asked. He had some doubt in his mind just like the officers.

"How can you doubt me?" I was surprised and hurt. "Of course it's him. Do you think I would say that about an innocent man?"

"Sorry," Chris quickly apologized, and pulled me closer. "What was he thinking?"

"He was thinking about getting away, and how furious he was at me."

"But why did he kill the bank robber?"

"I don't know," I sighed. "He wasn't thinking about that. When I go to the police station to make my statement, I'll see if Dimples will let me be there when they question him. That way I can probably find out."

"Okay," Chris sighed. He hated for me to get involved with men like that. "Let's walk back to my office, and I'll see if I can come with you to the police station."

Most of the people had cleared out, and we followed the stragglers down the hall to the stairs. Even though it was a false alarm, no one took the elevators. We made it to the bottom floor and out of the courthouse. Chris put his arm around me, and I leaned into him, surprised to find my legs a little shaky.

"I need to sit down," I said.

"I need to go to my office and make sure my client's taken care of before we head over to the police station. It won't take long, and you can sit down there."

"That's fine. I'm not looking forward to facing that guy again. I hope they can keep him long enough to gather more evidence. If he shot the bank robber, his gun must be somewhere."

"True, but how did he get it past security in the first place? Plus, even if they find the gun, tying it to him might be a problem."

"Wouldn't it have fingerprints on it or something?"

"Not if he was wearing gloves, but they might be on the bullets. Most guys don't think about that. Maybe he'll be one of those." Chris didn't think it was likely, but it didn't hurt to hope. "Hey," he said, stopping mid-stride. "That reminds me, what were you doing here in the first place?"

"Oh, yeah." I'd nearly forgotten, but it all came back in a rush. "I got a visit from the CIA this morning."

Chris' jaw dropped open. "What?"

"Yeah. Pretty crazy, huh? They even planted a bug in the house. But I found it and flushed it down the toilet."

"They planted a bug? And you flushed it?" Chris could hardly believe what he was hearing. "Why would they plant a bug? What's going on? What did they want?"

"They just wanted to know if I had talked to Uncle Joey recently." I heard Chris swear in his mind, but chose to ignore it, especially since I was thinking the same thing. "Apparently he showed up in the home of an arms dealer they're working with, so now they're suspicious of him."

"An arms dealer? They told you that?"

"Not in words." I pointed to my head.

"Oh yeah, right." He shook his head as if to clear it. "But what would the CIA be doing working with an arms dealer in Mexico?"

"My thoughts exactly! The only thing I could come up with is that they're trying to get weapons to the good guys to help get rid of the bad guys. You know... all those bad drug cartel guys that are killing all those innocent people? Isn't that what the CIA does?"

"I don't know." Chris was starting to get a dazed look in his eyes, and his mind was curiously blank, like it was just too much to take in.

"Anyway," I continued, hoping he would snap out of it. "They were checking up on me because I knew Uncle Joey. I was on their list, but they didn't really expect to find anything because I have no ties to Mexico, and I wasn't really a part of Uncle Joey's organization."

"Okay. So why did they plant the bug?"

"To see if I was lying, I guess." I shrugged my shoulders in an effort to make it seem like it wasn't a big deal. But Chris was starting to panic. He was thinking we were in deep shit. The CIA was not an agency you fooled around with.

We entered his building, only to be met by his client who was in a worse panic than Chris. "What the hell happened in there?" he asked, his brow covered in sweat.

Chris patiently explained that the prisoner in the other courtroom had tried to escape, and they would probably have to reschedule their court appearance. At this, the guy nearly had a meltdown. He was thinking that his wife was sure to find the money if they didn't hurry things up. Chris ushered him into his office and had the secretary call to find out what was going on at the courthouse for the rest of the day.

I told Chris I'd wait for him in the break room. I got a diet soda and, since I was starving, I also splurged on a candy bar from the vending machine. There's nothing like chocolate to compensate for bad things that happen, and I deserved the chocolate after all I'd been through.

Chapter 4

I finished the last bite of my candy bar and my cell phone rang. It wasn't a number I was familiar with, but I answered it anyway.

"Mrs. Nichols, this is Blaine Smith with Bank of America. You have an account with us, and we just noticed a large deposit. We were wondering if you would like to come in so we could talk about a portfolio of investments and money market opportunities. Your money can earn better interest with the right management. When could you stop by?"

"Um... how about tomorrow?" His request caught me off-guard, but I knew this was something I needed to take care of. "But I want my husband to be there, so it would have to be later. In fact, let me talk to him first and I'll call you back."

He repeated his name and number, and I thanked him and hung up, entering the information into my cell phone. I was starting to feel a little shell-shocked, like I had too much on my plate. The idea of leaving town to some remote island started to sound like a good idea. With all that money, I could actually do it. Chris could take some time off work, and the kids were almost out of school.

Before the idea carried me away, my cell phone rang again. I recognized Dimples' number. Was he calling about the fiasco at the courthouse?

"Hi Shelby," Dimples said when I answered. "Just curious, but have you been at the courthouse today? I just heard about a woman who fits your description who claims to have caught the man who killed Keith Bishop. By any chance would that happen to be you?"

"Oh, yeah," I stammered, realizing I had never given the police my name. "Yeah, it was me. I was there to talk to Chris."

"I knew it!" He shouted with enthusiasm. A rustling noise came through as he covered the phone with his hand and said, "It's her!" He came back on. "They said you promised to come down and give a statement."

"Yes, I'm coming. I'm just waiting for Chris. I'm a little worried about explaining my premonitions. The officers at the courthouse already think I'm a little weird."

"But if you're right, that means we caught the killer because of you. It could go a long way in getting you a paid consulting job with the police department." When I didn't answer right away he continued. "Hey," he said reassuringly. "I'll be there while you make your statement. I promise it will be easy. I won't let anyone give you any guff."

"Thanks. That will help." I let out a big sigh. "I'm at Chris' office, so it will only take me a few minutes to get there."

"Great!" He disconnected, and I frowned. I had to figure out how to make my statement sound like I was a normal person. That probably meant I had to lie again. It seemed I was doing that a lot lately.

Chris was still in his office with the door shut, but I could hear his client ranting about something. This was probably not a good time to interrupt so I decided to go by myself. It would be nice to have Chris with me, but since Dimples was being so accommodating, I figured I could handle it without him.

I headed to the secretary's office and told her that I had to go to the police station to make a statement. I also told her to tell Chris to join me as soon as he was through. I mentioned that they would want a statement from him as well, even though they hadn't told me that. But since he'd seen everything, it was probably true, and I really wanted him to come.

I got to the police station and, as soon as I walked in, everyone stopped and stared at me. Dimples caught sight of me and hurried over with a broad smile on his face, making his dimples huge. He escorted me to a back room like a proud parent.

As we passed through the office, I noticed a woman with bad hair and in handcuffs sitting beside another detective. Something about her was familiar. She turned her head and I realized she was the woman with the ugly legs who was really a man. He'd been caught, right before I got on the elevator. Was he the killer's accomplice? I listened intently and picked up that he was wondering if his day could get any worse.

With Bishop dead, he may never get a chance to find the money. Plus, the wig and heels were driving him crazy. How did women walk in these things? At least the police couldn't charge him with anything. Bishop's accomplice must have hired someone to kill him so he wouldn't have to worry that he'd talk. Now finding the money would be harder than ever.

He started thinking every swear word in the book, and I pulled away. This guy was after the stolen money. Had he hoped to talk to the bank robber? Maybe he had plans to get him out, but I'd spoiled them. Part of his plans must have included his disguise, but how he thought he could accomplish an escape with all the security was beyond me. Of course, someone else managed to kill Bishop, so what did I know?

We entered the back room and the two policemen from the courtroom stood. They were both relieved that I had showed up. It took the pressure off them to have me corroborate their story. Dimples introduced me to the police chief who also stood and studied me with great interest. After Dimples made the introductions, the police chief motioned for me to sit down and came right to the point.

"Detective Harris told us about your premonitions," the chief began. "Could you tell us what happened at the courthouse today?"

I remembered what I'd told the officers and kept it as close to that as I could, not really saying I had any premonitions about the man in the elevator. I wanted to keep it as simple as possible. "He was wearing a disguise when I first saw him in the elevator, but the jacket you found in the courtroom was the same. Did anyone find the fake nose in the jacket?"

"No," the police chief answered. "We have no proof that this guy was wearing a disguise. The only thing we have is your testimony. We have no gun, no disguise, nothing. If we don't get something more on him, we can't hold him for more than a day or two."

That was bad. "Who is he?"

He glanced at the driver's license in his hand. "His name is Trent Mercer. We ran him through all our databases and he has no priors. He's from New Jersey and says he's here on business. It all checks out."

The police chief let out a sigh. He was thinking that my story was a little farfetched, and so far, the guy had been cooperative. He had also insisted that he was innocent and was at the courthouse to look into a small claims judgment from seven years ago. There was no way the police could hold him only on my say-so. It seemed like I had accused the wrong guy.

"So he's told you that he's innocent and here on business, right?" I said. "And he was at the courthouse for some kind of claims judgment?" I hoped I wasn't giving too many details, but I had to say something that would give me some credibility.

His eyes widened, and he focused on me, wondering if there was some truth to my 'premonitions'.

"If you'd like to try, I might be able to pick up something from him," I offered.

"How would you do that?" he asked.

"I just need to be in the same room while he's being questioned. Sometimes I get premonitions that way, and even then, it doesn't always work." I had to leave room for doubt if I was going to get him to agree. "But it's up to you."

The chief glanced at Dimples, who nodded his head, indicating he thought it was a good idea. Of course I heard that in his thoughts, but it's amazing how much communication is done non-verbally. I'd have to remember that in case anyone ever guessed I could read minds, especially if I ever talked to Uncle Joey again.

"Okay," the chief agreed. "Let's set it up."

I waited in the interrogation room while they got Mercer out of his cell and brought him in. His step faltered when he saw me, but he kept his expression stone cold and took a seat across the table from me. His thoughts were a different matter. After swearing a blue streak, he wondered if I had been following him and that's how I'd ended up in the elevator. But if I was following him, it didn't make sense that I would make that mistake. So it must be something else. What had he done that had given him away?

He was meticulous in his planning, and nothing like this had ever happened to him. He'd never been caught before, and he was always careful to avoid personal contact and never leave a trail. Most of his clients never even knew what he looked like. Somehow this time it had all gone to hell. At least the bank robber was dead, and his 'helpers' had gotten away.

"Who hired you to kill him?" I blurted, then realized this was not part of the questioning process we'd agreed on. I focused my attention on his thoughts, rather than the surprise of the others in the room and caught a feeling of superiority from him. Mercer got hired because he did his job, and he did it right. If I hadn't interfered, he'd be celebrating with a lot of money by now.

"So... someone hired you to kill the bank robber because...?" I was flying by the seat of my pants, using his thoughts as a jumping point.

He'd talk he thought, but he said, "No one hired me to do anything!" He glanced around the room to catch the attention of everyone there. "You got the wrong guy. Are you charging me with something? Because if you're not, you have to let me go."

"Do you know where the money is?" I asked.

He huffed. That was the first stupid question I'd asked. He even had the audacity to roll his eyes, but still didn't say anything.

The others thought that was a dumb question too, so I decided to let them handle the rest of the questions. He didn't bother to think about anything they said, only focusing on me and thinking how some day he was going to kill me, and take great pleasure doing it for ruining his plans.

"How many people have you killed?" I asked.

"What?" He gasped. "Who is this crazy person? Why is she even here?"

The police chief widened his eyes at Dimples, who turned to the killer and asked why he was at the courthouse today. "I already told you," he answered. "I'm done answering your questions." He glanced at me. "Especially hers." Twenty-seven was the number he thought, and a shiver went down my spine. Some of them went through his mind, and I picked up a few images and a couple of names before he stopped.

I glanced at Dimples. "May I borrow your pen?" My voice was shaking, but this was something I didn't want to forget. Dimples handed me one and I wrote down the names on the palm of my hand since there wasn't any paper.

When I finished, I laid the pen down and kept my hand out of sight. "I'm done here." It came out whisper-thin, but Dimples could see how upset I was, and quickly ushered the killer from the room.

The police chief and the two officers waited until Dimples took his seat, and then waited some more to let me regain my composure. They knew something significant had happened.

I swallowed and began. "Do the names Derek Thompson, Abigail Johnson, or Calvin Reid mean anything to you?"

Dimples pursed his lips, then his eyes lit up with recognition. "Yes. Abigail Johnson. She was murdered about two years ago. We brought in her husband for questioning, but he had an airtight alibi. We never caught the killer."

"That's right," the police chief remembered as well. He studied me. "What's the connection?"

"I know this might be hard to believe, but that man killed all of them. I think he might be a hired killer. He probably killed the bank robber because he was going to implicate someone else, so that someone hired him." It was on the tip of my tongue to tell them he'd killed a lot more, but I decided to let it go for now. I didn't want to push my credibility.

They all sat there dumbfounded. Like I had two heads or something. "You're going to keep him locked up for a while, right?" I didn't want to die anytime soon. "You should at least check out his DNA and see if it matches any of the DNA you got at Abigail Johnson's crime scene. And check the courthouse again for the fake nose and the gun. They've got to be somewhere."

None of them moved. I glanced at Dimples and raised my eyebrows. It brought him back to his polite self. "Yes, of course we'll check." He was thinking he'd never been a witness to anything so freaky, but he had no cause to doubt me before, so he wouldn't start now. If the chief didn't feel the same way, he'd convince him that he had nothing to lose.

"Good. Thanks. I'd like to go now." I stood. "Using my premonitions like this takes a lot out of me." They could tell it had, so at least they believed me about something.

"Sure," the chief answered. "Thanks for coming in. Can we call you again?"

"Of course." I wanted to talk about getting paid, but didn't have the heart at the moment. It just didn't matter right then. All I really wanted was to never see that slime ball again. Or, at the least, see him put away for the rest of his life, and then hope he died in the electric chair. Not too charitable of me, but seriously, he deserved it.

I left the room with Dimples at my side. "Could you write down those names for me before you leave?" he asked.

"Sure, and thanks for checking into this. I know it's a leap of faith on your part, but I've never had such strong premonitions before. Plus, I think he's killed a lot more people than those three. He was so angry. He's never been caught, and I ruined all his plans. He would kill me if he ever got the chance, so you won't let him out will you?"

"Shelby, it's okay," Dimples handed me his pen and a pad of paper, then patted my arm. "We're not letting him out, and if he's killed these people, we'll get him on that too."

I relaxed my shoulders and let out a sigh, then quickly wrote down the names. I was looking forward to washing them off my hand. Too bad I couldn't wash them out of my mind as easily. "Okay, there you go."

"Sounds good." I tried to smile, but I don't think it worked since he was thinking I looked pale and scared. He smiled back and catching sight of those dimples lightened my mood. "Bye."

I couldn't wait to get home and maybe take a hot bath, or read a good book, anything to get my mind off that jerk.

I got home and realized Chris had never come to the police station. Maybe his secretary had forgotten to tell him. It was hard to believe that his client had needed all that time, but I decided not to complain, given all those billable hours.

It was later than I thought, so I had to scratch the bath and the book, going straight to fixing dinner. I tried to keep my mind off the killer, but it was hard not to see those dead faces every time I shut my eyes. Did I have post-traumatic stress syndrome or something like that? It was clear I needed some kind of help that would make me feel in control of my life and not so scared.

Maybe I should take a self-defense class and get a gun. Except that I hated guns. But at least a self-defense class might do the job. I got on the Internet and searched self-defense and found a close combat training program that looked pretty good. There were also things like stun guns, tasers, and pepper spray that I could carry in my purse.

Feeling better, I ordered the Stun Gun Flashlight that delivered one million volts of attack-stopping power. It was small, rechargeable and also worked as a flashlight. I ordered some pepper spray too. It came in a cute pink dispenser and I happily signed up for next day delivery. That done, I hurried back to the kitchen to finish dinner.

Chris came home and I gave him a big hug. "You won't believe what happened at the police station," I said. "I wish you could have been there. How come you didn't come?"

"My client is such a micro-manager. We had to go over everything before he felt prepared. If I didn't know better, I'd think he was hiding something from me."

"He is," I said, and Chris' eyes widened. "But I'm not sure I should tell you about it."

"Why not? If I don't have all the answers, the plaintiff and her lawyer could make mincemeat out of us."

"Do you get paid more if you win?" I asked.

"No, but I do have a reputation to maintain," he raised one eyebrow. "So spill it."

"Fine," I said. "Your client has been siphoning money off their savings account for years. He must have known the marriage wasn't going to last. But the other thing is... she knows about it and knows where it is. So at your next court hearing, she's going to reveal it all to the judge."

Chris just shook his head, thinking it had been a long day. "Okay, maybe that's something that's better for me not to know, and since he hasn't said anything to me, I'll try and forget what you said. The trial was changed to a week from Friday so I don't expect to see him before that." I followed Chris into his study where he put his laptop on his desk. "So tell me what happened at the police station."

"First of all, Dimples told them I had premonitions, so at least I didn't have to say anything about why I was suspicious of the guy in the elevator. His name is Trent Mercer and he's supposedly here on business. Since they couldn't get much information out of him, I kind of volunteered to sit in on the questioning."

Chris stilled, and fixed me with a penetrating stare, hoping I hadn't given too much away.

"Well... I ended up finding out quite a lot about him, so it was a good thing I was there." Chris took a deep breath for patience, and I quickly continued. "He was really mad that I'd spoiled all his plans. He never dreamed he would get caught. In fact, most of his clients have never seen his face. I ruined everything, so he was thinking how much pleasure he would take in killing me." I swallowed. "It made me kind of mad, so I asked him how many people he'd killed. That was when it got bad."

"What do you mean?" Chris asked.

"He's killed twenty-seven people. Twenty-seven! I even saw some of their dead faces in his mind. I was able to pick up three names. A couple came from newspaper clippings that he thought about. It was awful. I wrote them down without him seeing them, so he doesn't know I know, but I gave them to the police chief. Dimples actually recognized one of the names, so at least they believed me."

"That's nuts." Chris pulled me into his arms. "So you think this guy is a hired killer? This is bad. So why was he going after the bank robber?"

"Because they were afraid he'd talk. It must have been Bishop's partner or something because when I first saw Bishop at the courthouse, he was thinking that his partner better get him out of there or he was telling everything. The partner must have realized that, and instead of breaking him out, decided to kill him and keep all the money. Mercer would have gotten away with it if I hadn't intervened."

I shivered and Chris rubbed my arms. "Dimples promised me he'd keep him in jail for a while, and they'd see what they could do about linking him to one of the murders, but it still makes me nervous."

"Yeah," he agreed. He was thinking this was why he didn't want me to get involved with the police in the first place. On the other hand, I'd caught a really bad guy. Was it worth it?

"I don't know," I answered. "I don't want that kind of responsibility. I mean, yes I'm glad that guy is behind bars, but now I have to live with seeing his victim's faces in my mind, as well as worry that if he gets out, he's coming for me."

"If that's what he's thinking, I guess this is one case you're going to have to see through to the end. You might even have to listen to his thoughts again if the police need more help." He was sorry I'd gotten involved and that reminded him of my CIA visit that morning, which reminded me about the call I'd received from the bank.

"Oh, before I forget, the bank manager called about all the money in my account, wondering if I would like to come in and talk to them about investments and stuff. I told them I'd call them back and we'd both come in together."

Chris was starting to get stressed out. "I guess it's hard to keep five million dollars a secret." Now that was one more thing he had to worry about. He still wished I'd lost my powers, not that it would have stopped Uncle Joey from putting all that money in my account, but the rest of it... "I don't know what to do about the CIA. I guess nothing for now."

"I think you're right. Although they might be back since I flushed their bug."

He sighed, then caught a whiff of cooking food and perked right up. "What's for dinner?"

"Taco soup," I answered. "And it's almost ready."

"Sounds good. I'm going to change my clothes."

I hurried back to the kitchen and put the final ingredients in the pot. Joshua came in the door from soccer practice, and all his attention focused sharply on the food. As usual, he was starving, but I made him go wash up before he ate anything. Savannah was in her room talking on her phone, and a sense of accomplishment went through me to know that at least for tonight, we were safe, and could eat dinner together as a family.

Later, as we were getting ready for bed, Chris got out a pen and paper. He wanted to go over all the things we could do with the money and figure out how to handle the CIA. He propped himself up in bed with the pad of paper on his lap.

"I've been thinking about the money," he began. "And I think we should talk to the bank tomorrow and see how much interest we can make on it. We may not have the five million for long, but we can certainly take advantage of the situation."

"That's true," I replied, slipping into bed beside him. "Uncle Joey shouldn't expect us to fork over the five million plus interest, since he put it in my account in the first place. If for no other reason than the stress he's caused us, we should get to keep the interest."

Chris liked my reasoning skills. "Exactly. So tomorrow, why don't you call the bank manager and set up an appointment. I don't have any court appearances tomorrow, so as soon as you have a time, let me know and I'll meet you there."

"Sounds good."

"Now the other concern is the CIA. Did you pick up anything from them about the money?"

"No. They were only checking on Uncle Joey because of the arms dealer."

"Right." Chris wrote down CIA and under it put 'arms dealer' with a dash to Uncle Joey. "Why do you think he would get involved with an arms dealer in Mexico?"

"The only thing that I can think of is that he must need guns for some reason. It might have something to do with the money, but I don't think he would have put the money in my account unless he wanted it out of the equation."

"True," Chris agreed. "So the money needed to be hidden, and I think the proof of that comes from the letter you got where he told you not to tell anyone because it could be a matter of life or death."

"Maybe he was thinking that if anyone knew I had the money, they would try to take it from me." That was unsettling. "Like Kate?" I asked.

"Exactly so," Chris replied. "But I don't think we can rule anyone else out either. The other thing I don't understand is why he didn't just send it to one of his bank accounts here? Doesn't he trust anyone in his organization?"

"Probably not," I said. Did that mean he didn't completely trust Jackie? She seemed like a good person, plus she was in love with him. It didn't make sense. "He might have trusted Ramos with it, but Ramos went with him to Mexico." I thought they were probably in trouble, but it didn't bother me like it should. Did that mean I was getting callous? Or was it more along the lines of self-preservation?

"What should I do if the CIA agents come back?" I asked. "Since I flushed their bug, they might want to plant another one."

"I don't think they will, but if they do, we can figure it out then. I mean, you've done nothing wrong, so there's no reason for them to be suspicious."

"All right." I snuggled up next to him. "I'm so glad that we're working on this together."

He put the pen and paper on the bedside table and turned out the light. Slipping his arm around me, he held me close, hoping that we'd seen the last of Uncle Joey. Chris was encouraged that Uncle Joey had said we could keep the money if he never came back. That meant he might not, and that was fine with him.

I was a little hurt that Chris wasn't thinking about me, like I was about him, but then his thoughts changed direction, and my heart skipped a beat. I managed a squeak before his lips caught mine and I promptly forgot about everything else.

I woke with a start. Panic clawed in my throat, and sweat ran down my chest. I bolted upright, clutching the bedding and uttered a small scream. Chris woke and pulled me into his arms. "Hey, babe. It's all right. It was just a dream. You're okay now."

His words soothed me, and I melted into his warm embrace. The misty fog of my dream retreated, leaving me shaken and wide-awake, but glad it was only a dream. I calmed down and soon my breathing was even and the panic gone.

"What was that all about?" Chris asked.

"It was awful. The elevator guy... I mean Mercer was chasing me, and my legs wouldn't move, no matter how hard I tried to run away. Then he caught me and started to slit my throat with his knife. I tried to scream, but the knife was stabbing my throat and I couldn't breathe." I shuddered and Chris tightened his arms around me. "It was horrible!"

"It's okay now," Chris said. "It was just a dream. That guy must have scared you more than we realized."

"Yeah. I think seeing those faces in his mind really did a number on me." Talking about my dream brought it all back, and I fought to stay calm. "I didn't realize until now, that the faces I saw in his mind all had their throats slit. No wonder I dreamed about it."

Chris sighed. This was one more reason out of many he didn't want me to work with the police. That guy was an assassin and who knows what would happen if he ever got out? Seeing awful things like that was just part of it.

"You're right," I said. "I wish I hadn't seen that. Now I have to make sure that the guy is put away forever."

His irritation that I had read his mind again swept over me, then was gone. He couldn't be mad after that horrible dream, still...

"I sure do love you," I said. "Thanks for putting up with me."

He let out a laugh, I'd gotten the best of him that time, but he was okay with it. "I love you too. Now can you go back to sleep?"

"Yes." I hugged him again and turned over on my side to give him some space. He settled down and was soon breathing evenly. I hadn't exactly told the truth that I could go back to sleep. I was afraid to close my eyes, but at least the panic was gone. I decided to call Dimples in the morning and check up on the guy. Maybe they had found all the evidence they needed to put him away for good, and I wouldn't need to face him again. I kept those positive thoughts going through my mind and soon fell asleep.

Chapter 5

I woke up grumpy. Lack of a good sleep always does that to me, and last night was no exception. After that horrible dream, I decided that maybe consulting with the police was not for me. What else could I do? I could tell when someone was lying. That had to be good for something, right? In fact, that should be something any lawyer would want to know. But that still wouldn't keep me from knowing awful things.

How about a mediator or a counselor? I'd already thought about being a marriage counselor, but how about a family counselor? I'd know exactly what people really wanted and needed, and could communicate that with their family. That could work. I wondered if that was something I could do without a license. Probably not.

"Mom!" Savannah yelled. "Are you coming?" With a jolt, I remembered it was my turn to drive the carpool to school. I threw on a hoodie and hurried to the car. Savannah was embarrassed that I still had my pajamas on, but since I was already in a bad mood, I concentrated on shielding my mind. It worked for a while, but it was a relief when all the kids got out of the car and I could relax.

I got home to the ringing phone, and picked it up just before it went to voice mail. "Hello?" I said, catching my breath.

"Senora Nichols?"

"Yes." I answered, trying to think of why someone speaking Spanish would call me.

"This is Inspector Salazar from the Mexican Police Department. I was wondering if I could ask you a few questions?"

"Me? Why?" I asked.

He chuckled. "Ah... so blunt, you Americans. It is only a small matter, nothing to be concerned about."

Yeah, right. "Okay, sure."

"Gracias, you are very kind," he said. "I am hoping you can help me locate a certain individual. An American. Senor Joseph E. Manetto. I understand you worked for him. Have you received any recent letters or mail or phone calls from him? It would help us very much."

"Nope." The lie came easily. "I don't know anything about him, and I want to keep it that way. I hope you understand, but I'd rather not be involved." Then something occurred to me. "How did you get my name and number? I haven't worked for Uncle Joey... a... Mr. Manetto for a while."

"It is nothing," he said. "We are only following up on some leads. Sorry to bother you. Buenos Dias." The phone clicked and the dial tone buzzed in my ear. My heart sped up. What was that all about? How did they get my name and number? If I were a swearing person, I'd be swearing a blue streak right now. That's how bad it was.

I checked the Caller ID, hoping to get something official like "Mexican Police Department" but the number just said Out of Area. It had a zero-one-one area code, so that was probably legitimate. But that didn't mean it was really the

Mexican Police. It could have been anyone. So why call me? Did it have something to do with Kate? Was she trying to find out if I had the money?

I started to chew my fingernails and realized I was getting seriously stressed out. I had to call Chris. This was getting out of hand. "Hey," I began when he answered the phone. "Guess who I just got a call from?" I tried to sound like it wasn't a big deal.

He took a breath before speaking. I hadn't fooled him. "Who?"

"Someone calling himself Inspector Salazar, from the Mexican Police."

"What? That's crazy. What did he want?"

"He said he was trying to locate Uncle Joey, and wondered if I'd had any letters or calls from him recently. Sounds pretty fishy, huh."

"Yeah," he sighed, clearly distraught. "This just gets better and better. Have you talked to the bank yet? I think it's time the money disappeared from that account. If there was some way we could just send it back where it came from, that would be even better."

Now it was my turn to sigh. "I'll call them right away and let you know."

"Okay, thanks." We disconnected, and I slumped in my chair. He was right. That money was nothing but a headache. Why did Uncle Joey have to give it to me? This was getting to Chris too, and I felt bad.

I called the bank and set up an appointment for ten, called Chris back, and jumped into the shower. At least the bank people didn't seem sorry to have that much money in their bank. If only it were that easy for me.

I arrived at the bank and told them who I was. The worker immediately led me to a private office, and offered a choice of soft drinks, water, coffee or tea. The bank manager, Blaine Smith, stood to shake my hand with a friendly smile. After I was seated, he took a box from his desk and handed it to me, telling me it was a gift that they reserved for their best customers. I opened it to find a pair of earrings. They were small diamond studs about one quarter of a carat, and the manager assured me they were real diamonds.

Wow. I didn't know this side of the bank existed. Chris came in soon after that and was given a gift of a tie clip accented with diamonds. He wasn't surprised like me, but when he caught my eye he winked. He was thinking that with what the bank could use this money for, the gifts were hardly a pittance. A pittance? I almost laughed, but managed to only raise my eyebrows at him. He grinned and we settled down to looking at the portfolio Blaine had put together for us.

While he explained the portfolio, Blaine was thinking how thrilled he was to have all that money in his bank and was hoping we'd leave it there. Chris was thinking of moving it somewhere else, like an investment firm with higher-yielding money market accounts. Among other things, there were taxes to consider, and all the ways to get out of paying them.

Things got complicated, and I started to zone out, mostly because I was worried about the phone call from the Mexican Police, Who probably weren't who they said they were. There was also the CIA. What would they do if they found out we had all this money? Could we go to jail? Could they subpoena our records if they suspected anything? Would they think we'd stolen it, or worse, were working with Uncle Joey and his illegal operations? What if it was drug money? That would be bad.

This was all Uncle Joey's fault. What was going on with him? Ramos was with him, so he couldn't be in too much danger. So what was with his note? If I could find out what was going on, I'd know what to do with the money. I'd already tried talking to Jackie, but she didn't know any more than me.

The room fell silent, and I glanced up to find both Chris and Blaine looking at me expectantly. "I'm sorry, what did you say?"

Chris closed his eyes, thinking that since I'd missed the whole thing Blaine would have to explain it all over again, and he didn't have time for that. Then he had another idea and perked up. He thought, *Just say you like the portfolio, but want a little more time to check out some other options. In the meantime, you agree to transferring most of the money to our other accounts.*

I smiled and repeated Chris' words. After authorizing the money transfers, we were done. Blaine was thinking that we should decide soon because we could be making a lot more interest than we were by leaving it in our bank accounts. In a few years, it would be quite substantial.

As we walked to the parking lot, Chris was thinking about talking to the investment firm handling our retirement funds. It made sense to me. "Maybe we ought to transfer the interest we've made so far into our retirement account, and just keep doing that until we give the money back to Uncle Joey."

"That's a great idea," he said. "We can do an electronic transfer every day, and pretty soon that money can be giving us the best returns. I'll start on it when I get home tonight."

"Great," I agreed. He was lots happier now and less stressed, which made me happier too. I gave him a kiss and we said our goodbyes.

I spent the rest of the day cleaning the house, glad I didn't have to go anywhere else. I toyed with the idea of calling Dimples about Mercer, but shied away because of my terrible dream. I just didn't want to think about that right now.

The ringing doorbell sent my heart into overdrive. I ducked behind the curtains, thinking it might be the CIA, and peaked out the window. A deliveryman set a package down on my porch and ran back to his truck. What now? I opened the door and checked the return address before picking it up. It said The Security Store, and I realized it was my stun gun and pepper spray!

I eagerly opened the package and admired my new purchases. I had to charge the stun gun for eight hours before it was usable, so I plugged it in and read the instructions. With one million tooth-jarring volts of power and an intimidating arc-spark and crackling sound, I was impressed that it would do the job. Plus, it was a flashlight. The pepper-spray was extra insurance and seemed easy to use, so I put it in my purse where I could reach it quickly.

The rest of the day went smoothly, and night came with nothing out of the ordinary to mar my good mood. It was easy to pretend nothing was wrong when I didn't think about money, or Uncle Joey, or murderers, or the Mexican police. It was still there in the back of my mind, but maybe if I didn't pay too much attention, it would all just go away. Given enough time, things would resolve naturally. Plus, I had a cool stun gun that was all charged up and ready to go.

That probably wasn't the best way to handle it, but for now I was going to read a good book and put it out of my mind.

I woke the next morning, grateful to have slept through the night without dreams of anyone slitting my throat. It was Friday, my day to work out at the gym. There was nothing better than a good sweat to release the anxiety and stress of the last few days. I was feeling better from those happy endorphins, and ready to face reality.

My phone was chirping, telling me that I'd missed a call. It was from Dimples. He wanted me to come down to the station ASAP. That put a damper on my mood, but I tried to put a positive spin on it. Maybe they'd found the evidence they needed to send Mercer to death row, and I wouldn't have to worry about him anymore.

I got home and peeled out of my sweaty clothes and into the shower. I toweled dry, and hearing my phone ring, quickly slipped on my bathrobe. Thinking it was probably Dimples wondering where I was, I barely glanced at the caller ID before pushing the talk button. "Hello?"

"Hola. Senora Nichols?"

Hearing the woman's accent, I understood why I didn't recognize the area code. "Yes?" I answered curtly.

"Oh...Gracias a Dios!! I have finally reached you!!!" Her voice was high-pitched and frantic. "I am the housekeeper for Su Tío... your Uncle. Está en un apuro grande. He is trouble. Los narcos lo han raptado... they have kidnapped him. They wish un rescate... a ransom... or they will kill him muertos. Yo no sé qué hacer. Ah... El inspector de policía... un minuto por favor."

The phone was muffled as she passed it to someone else. "Senora Nichols. It is Inspector Salazar. I'm so sorry for you to hear such bad news. Your Uncle has been kidnapped and held hostage for ransom. We are doing everything we can to get him back, but I am not hopeful. These kidnappers wish for money, and say he will only be returned alive if their ransom is met."

"Are you sure?"

"Yes, I'm afraid so," he answered.

"What do you usually do in these circumstances?" I asked, concerned but wary. Something didn't seem quite right.

"If their demands are met they usually let the hostage go, but not always. I am sorry to tell you this."

"How much do they want?" If it were five million dollars, I'd know something was fishy.

"They have asked for one million American dollars. It is a lot, I know, but word got out that he was wealthy, and it put him in danger. We do not have that kind of money or resources, but we will do what we can to save him."

"You don't have much hope?" I asked.

"Not unless you can send the money, there is very little hope."

"But if I send you the money, you would see that he was rescued alive?"

"I would do all in my power to save him, yes." He spoke passionately. It almost made me sorry to disappoint him.

"Hmm..." I let him think I was considering it. "A million dollars is a lot of money. More money than I have. I don't know what to do. I'm not sure there is anything I can do."

"What about your Uncle's bank accounts? Surely you can get it from there?" My lack of emotion was getting through to him and he was starting to sound desperate.

"Nope."

"You can't? That is bad news. Your Uncle... he will probably be killed. They are usually beheaded. It is most painful and very tragic."

I swallowed, imagining Uncle Joey's head on a spike. Gross. "I'm sorry, but I can't help you. I'm late for an appointment, so I've got to go. Good luck."

"What??" His voice went up a notch. "You would let your Uncle die without doing a thing for him?"

"Looks that way," I said.

"If you don't help him, you will have to live with his death on your shoulders for the rest of your life. Are you willing to live with that?"

Now he was going too far. "Just a minute," I said angrily. "In the first place, Uncle Joey is not really my uncle. Second, I don't believe a word you've said. I know a scam when I see one. And third, I do not have access to Uncle Joey's money, and if I did, do you think I'd send it to you? That's just plain crazy. So I'm hanging up now. Please don't call me again!"

I ended the call on his muffled curse. Luckily, it was in Spanish, so I wasn't offended. My hands were a little shaky when I set down the phone. I hated to admit it, but I was rattled. A niggling doubt brushed my mind, but I pushed it away. Uncle Joey was fine. He had Ramos to take care of him.

But what if it were real? What if Ramos had failed or was dead himself, and Uncle Joey had truly been kidnapped? Of course I would feel bad. But deep down where it counted? Maybe not so much. What about keeping all that money? Hmm... I didn't think I would feel too bad about that either. Did that make me a bad person? I hoped not.

I got ready, but couldn't stop thinking about Uncle Joey. When I checked the clock, it was ten-thirty, later than I thought. I hoped Dimples had not given up on me, so I called to let him know I was on my way. He sounded relieved that I was coming, but his voice held a tinge of something else. Resignation? Despondency? Depression? Whatever it was, it wasn't the good news I was hoping for. Major bummer.

That meant I might have to face Mercer again. I shivered with dread, and it was hard to drag myself to the car. I sat behind the wheel with worries of Uncle Joey still on my mind, and realized the Inspector had succeeded in putting a major guilt trip on me. If I was going to get through the day, I needed to do something. Should I call Uncle Joey's phone? He'd told me not to. What about Ramos? Unfortunately, I didn't have his number.

There was nothing I could do except call Jackie, and I really didn't want to talk to her again. If she thought Uncle Joey was in trouble she'd probably want me to send the money, and I wasn't going to do that. If there weren't so many kidnappings going on in Mexico, I wouldn't have all this doubt.

I started the car with a sigh, and pushed the doubt away. For now, I had to believe it was a setup, and that the inspector and the housekeeper were just trying to scam me out of my money. It made sense looking at it that way. Besides, it was probably how Uncle Joey would handle it, so really, he'd be proud of me, right?

The drive to the police station was over before I knew it. All that thinking about Uncle Joey had kept me from being nervous about the reason for my visit. After parking my car, it hit me, and my stomach clenched. If they didn't have the evidence they needed to put the killer away, I would probably have to talk to him again. Yuk.

Getting out of the car was like going to the dentist. Something I had to do, but dreaded with a passion. The way I got through my dental appointments was thinking that I could do anything for an hour. That's hardly any time at all. Before I knew it this visit would be a thing of the past, and I could go on with my life. I might have to go back, but I had other things to concentrate on, and this was only a small part of my day.

That got me out of the car and into the police station. They were expecting me, and I was waved back to Dimples' desk. He stood, grateful to see me, his dimples doing that crazy dance when he smiled.

"Shelby, thanks for coming. I have good news." He was thinking it was always best to start positive, then the negative wouldn't seem so bad.

I smiled back, trying not to let my disappointment show. "Oh really? What's that?"

"The mayor has agreed to pay you a consulting fee. He was impressed with your... abilities the other day. When I filled him in on the progress we were making with the art theft, he felt it only right to compensate you for your time."

"Sweet." That was good news. "So does that mean I need to keep track of my hours?" I asked.

"Yes. He's hoping fifty dollars an hour is about right. What do you think? Will that work?"

"Um..." I stammered. I hadn't expected that much. "Yeah, that should be all right." I smiled.

"Good." Dimples smiled back, hoping that would help me deal with the bad news. "Why don't you sit down and I'll fill you in on what's going on."

I sat down with dread tightening my chest. "This is about Mercer, right? I hope you're not going to release him."

"Um... well, we don't have any choice."

"You can't release him! He's a killer!" I blurted.

"I know that's what you think," Dimples said. "But we couldn't find the gun or the fake nose you told us about, and we've run out of time. We've done everything we can to link him to Abigail Johnson's murder, but the crime scene was clean. The word in the department is, it was done by a professional hit-man." He glanced away from me. "He's got a lawyer and he'll be out in about an hour."

I was stunned. I had to do something quick. "Let me question him one more time. Maybe I'll pick up something that will help."

Dimples hesitated. He wasn't sure that was such a good idea. Besides, what kind of questions could I ask that would make any difference? On the other hand, what did he have to lose? "Okay, I'll have him brought out, but he probably won't say anything."

"That's okay," I said. I followed him to the interrogation room and took a seat.

"I'll be back." He left, but without much hope.

I thought I was prepared to face Mercer again, but his narrowed eyes and sardonic smile had me cringing inside. He shook his head in disdain before taking a seat. He was wondering why I was there, more curious than anything. Now that he was getting out, he wasn't as angry as he was before, which gave him the opportunity to study me more objectively.

I took a deep breath and let it out slowly to settle my nerves. "I know you killed Keith Bishop," I began. "I just don't know how you did it, or what you did with the fake nose and the gun."

"You're crazy," he said. But in his mind I caught a glimpse of an open window, and it came to me in a rush what he did with them.

"I get that a lot," I answered, wondering if I should ask him about the other murders. Probably not a good idea. I didn't want to give him a heads up that I knew any more about him. He was curious enough about me as it was. I glanced at Dimples. "I'm done. You can take him back."

Dimples hid his surprise with a quick nod and stood. Mercer couldn't understand what was going on, and it was driving him crazy. I just didn't make sense, and he didn't like that. He prided himself on reading people, and understanding their vulnerabilities. I didn't fit any mold he'd ever come across. At least he was getting out soon. He would be glad to put this fiasco behind him. Maybe he'd better lay low for a while. But he wouldn't forget me, and someday, he'd figure out what...

The door closed, and I missed the rest of that thought. Chills surged down my spine and I shivered. That guy needed to be stopped, and if what I gathered from his thoughts was right, I knew just how to do it.

I left the room and waited for Dimples at his desk. He came toward me with downcast eyes, and looking up, was confused by my smile. "We need to go to the courthouse," I said. "I think I know what he did with the gun and the fake nose."

Chapter 6

I pushed the button for the fourth floor and smiled at Dimples with encouragement. After explaining my 'premonition' about the window, Dimples was willing to check it out. We were on our way to the fourth floor, while two officers on the outside would head to the back of the courthouse. The plan was to see where the window opened on the fourth floor, and check the ground below it.

We entered the judge's chamber where the robber was shot, but there was only one window, and it was stuck shut with paint. "Guess it's not that one," Dimples said.

"Hmm... let's see," I said. "From here, he had to run through this door and into the next courtroom." We followed the path into the courtroom and I realized this was where Chris' client had been. Maybe he had seen Mercer standing by the window. My heart sped up to think we might have an eyewitness!

Dimples went to the window. "It looks like it's been opened recently." Excitement rippled through his mind. He took a cloth out of his pocket and gingerly opened the window. The screen was torn in the bottom corner, and he glanced at me with a grin. This was it! I hurried to his side and we both looked over the windowsill.

A dumpster stood directly below the window. The lid was open and it was full of garbage. Had Mercer somehow managed to drop the gun and fake nose inside? Dimples radioed the officers below, and told them to start searching the area around the dumpster.

I could barely contain my excitement. "This might be the break we need!"

"Yes," Dimples agreed. "We might have to go through all that garbage, but at least it hasn't been emptied."

"I know! How lucky can we be?" We hurried to the elevators and soon joined the officers outside. Sporting rubber gloves, they went through all the garbage around the dumpster. That turned up nothing, and it was clear the items must have fallen inside. No one wanted to get inside the dumpster, but Dimples surprised everyone by taking off his jacket, handing it to me, and doing just that.

With fresh rubber gloves on his hands, he was thinking this was the time to show some leadership. He was a detective after all, and it was part of his job. He glanced my way. "Want to join me?"

"Uh... kind of busy here," I held up his jacket.

He smiled and turned to the others. One of the officers offered to climb in and soon the dumpster was being emptied bit by bit. Dimples reminded them what we were looking for, and I studied each item as it was placed on the ground. Some of it smelled pretty bad, so I didn't get too close.

At this rate it was going to take most of the day, but I couldn't leave without finding the gun or the nose. It was the only thing that would keep that freaky guy away from me. About halfway to the bottom, Dimples shouted. He held up a squished rubbery thing that looked a little like play-

doh. Everyone watched him reshape the blob, until it slightly resembled a nose. Was that it?

"I need an evidence bag here." Dimples held out his
hand. An officer quickly responded, and Dimples placed the
blob inside. "Don't lose that."

I hurried to the officer's side to take a closer look. Relief
and excitement pulsed through me. It was definitely a fake
nose. A few moments later the officer yelled and held up
the gun, doubling my elation. He deposited it into another
bag and Dimples gratefully jumped out of the dumpster.

Not a moment too soon. The roar of the garbage truck
filled the alley, and it rounded the corner, coming straight
toward us. Everyone stopped in wonder. I caught the pre-
dominant thought that we had barely saved the day.

Dimples peeled off his gloves and threw them in the
dumpster with a shake of his head. "Talk about perfect tim-
ing," he said with a grin. His dimples twirled in his cheeks
and I grinned back.

Happy and excited, I laughed and clapped my hands. "We
did it! Now we can keep Mercer in jail!"

Dimples smile faded and he checked his watch. "I'm
afraid it's too late. He's probably out by now." My smile dis-
solved and my stomach clenched with panic.

Realizing my distress, he quickly continued. "But that's
okay. We can get him back. We just need to analyze these at
the lab. I'm sure we'll find evidence that will link him to the
nose and gun. From there, we can build the case and arrest
him."

That was not what I wanted to hear. He was out? What if
he disappeared? How would we track him down? Worst of
all, he was sure to come after me. What was I going to do?
He hated my guts.

"Shelby?" Dimples rubbed my arm. "Don't worry, we'll
get him."

I nodded and smiled agreeably, but inwardly I wasn't so sure. He was a hired assassin, and really good at his job. If he wanted to kill me, he could do it easily. "You know," I said, a little desperate, "Chris' client was still in the court-room when Mercer came in. Maybe he saw him drop the gun out the window without realizing what it was. He could be another witness.

"Wow, that's great," Dimples answered. "That would real-ly help a lot. Can you get me his name and number?"

"Sure," I said. "I'll go over to Chris' office right now and call you from there."

"Sounds good," he said. "And Shelby... good work today. Make sure you keep track of your hours, because you de-serve to be paid for this."

"Sure," I smiled, but my heart wasn't in it. Right now, I didn't really care about the money. "Oh... um... before you go back to the office, you might want to change your clothes. You stink." He laughed, and this time my smile was real. "See ya."

Although I could walk to Chris' office, I had driven my car from the police station to the courthouse. It was kind of a hassle to drive from one parking lot to another, but I didn't want to leave the car there. I entered the parking lot, and caught sight of a man sitting in his parked car. I couldn't make out his features, but I was pretty sure he was watching me.

My skin prickled, and I hesitated. Was he going to follow me? Was he the hired assassin, just out of jail and waiting to kill me? Was there a bomb in my car set to explode when I started it? Was it someone from the CIA watching me be-cause I'd flushed the bug? What about the Mexicans and Uncle Joey? Could it be someone wanting to kidnap me, and force me to give them all the money I'd received from

Uncle Joey before they cut off my head and threw the rest of me to the dogs?

Before I could decide what to do, the car's engine caught, and the man drove toward me. Thinking he might try to run me down, I jumped back and ran toward the building. I kept my eye on him to see where he went, and inadvertently ran into a side-view mirror on a car. I bounced from that car like a pool ball into the car parked beside it.

That hurt. Wincing, I straightened, and there was the car with the driver looking out his window, his eyes drawn together in concern. "Are you all right?" he asked.

"Yeah," I answered, and recognizing him, my eyes got big. It was number three from Uncle Joey's organization. I never did find out his name, but Jackie had thought about some names. If only I could think what they were. "You're..."

"Ricky," he supplied. "And you're Mr. Manetto's assistant, Shelby."

"Former assistant," I corrected him. "I got canned after the shooting in his office."

"Yeah right," he wasn't buying it. The way he heard it, I had something on 'The Knife' and used it to quit. Kind of like blackmail, only in reverse of the way Manetto used it. He was impressed. Which was why he was here.

"Are you spying on me?" I asked.

"Word out on the street is you might be in trouble," he explained. "So I just thought I'd watch your car until you came back. Make sure no one messed with it."

"Why didn't you say something?" I didn't want to mention that he'd scared me half to death since it was a good deed, but still.

He ducked his head. "You weren't supposed to see me." He glanced up apologetically. Now that his cover was blown, he might as well tell me the truth. He didn't think

'The Knife' would mind. "Before he left, Mr. Manetto told us to keep an eye on you if you were ever in danger. You know… you're like part of the family now, and he takes care of his own."

Would I ever be rid of Uncle Joey? The call from Mexico came to mind, and I flushed with guilt. Maybe he was already dead. It didn't look like Ricky knew anything about it, so that was good. Hopefully that meant I was right, and the call was a scam. If nothing else, having someone watch out for me was small compensation for everything else Uncle Joey had put me through. "Well, you're right about me being in trouble. So I appreciate the help."

"No problem," he said. "You going home now?"

"No. Going over to Chris' office first, then home."

"Okay, I'll try to stay out of your way, but be careful." He paused and rubbed his chin. "You might want to get a gun."

That reminded me of my stun flashlight and pepper spray. Like an idiot, I'd put them in my purse this morning and promptly forgot all about them. "I'll think about it," I said and smiled, feeling better. I wasn't so helpless after all. I checked my purse. Yup, there they were.

"See you." I hurried to my car, wondering if things could get any more complicated. Probably. The car started right up, and I drove to Chris' office. I kept checking my rearview mirror for Ricky's car, but didn't see it anywhere. If he was following, he was doing a good job.

Instead of parking in the garage, I found a place on the street and nabbed it, thinking that from now on, parking on the street might be a good idea. Right now, I hated parking garages, and a few quarters were definitely worth my peace of mind.

Chris' secretary was surprised to see me again so soon. She was thinking that with the amount of time I spent there, I might as well have my own office. Before I could ask, she told me that Chris had gone out to lunch. "Was he expecting you?" she asked.

I sighed. "No. But maybe you could help me."

She nodded politely, but inside she was rolling her eyes. "Sure. What do you need?"

"Chris' client from the other day? The divorce case?" She nodded and I continued. "I was just at the police department, and they think he might be a witness for the courtroom killing that happened there. I told them I'd find out his name so they could contact him."

Her smile faded. "Oh... I'd love to give it to you, but I'm afraid I can't. Client-attorney privilege and all that, and I don't want to get into trouble."

"Oh, right." I didn't think it was that big of a deal, and I was sure Chris would tell me. "Do you know where Chris went to lunch?"

"No, sorry."

"Okay, well, just tell him I stopped by and to call me when he gets back."

She nodded and I left, hoping she wouldn't forget this time. I got to the elevators and realized I should have just called him on his cell and saved me the hassle. What was I thinking?

I pushed the call button for his cell, but the call went right to voicemail. Rolling my eyes, I left a message to call me and punched the button for the elevator. The doors opened and I stepped in, pushing the button for the lobby. I watched the floors go by, hoping no one would stop the elevator and get in. For some reason, I felt a little jittery. When it slowed to a stop on the first floor, I panicked. Reaching into my purse, I grabbed my stun flashlight and held it ready to use.

A man stepped in and nodded politely, pushing the parking garage button. He was thinking that I looked a little scary with the cold stare I was leveling at him, and made sure he moved to the far side of the elevator. He kept his eyes down and hoped I didn't make any sudden moves.

When I got out in the lobby, his relief made me feel bad. At the same time, if I was intimidating to him, that could be a positive thing. I was a force to be reckoned with, not an easy mark, so watch out. Keeping a scowl on my face, I marched to my car, noticing that anyone who got close to me moved away. I heard a few random thoughts, like, *what's her problem?* And *wowza, keep out of her way.*

There was one mind that didn't fit, and I glanced down the street. Mercer stood a few feet away watching me, his eyes cold and calculating. Instead of cowering and running in fright, I faced him. His brows lifted in surprise. His stare usually worked on most people. Was he losing his touch?

I smiled as evilly as I could and walked toward him. "You got out," I said. "What are you doing here?" I knew he was here to watch me, but I had to play the game.

"No reason," he answered.

"You think I believe that? You're trying to scare me. Well it won't work, so you can just go back where you came from."

He raised his brows. Most people wouldn't dare talk to him that way.

"Most people probably wouldn't tell you what they think." I kept going, feeling invincible and on a roll. "But I'm not one of them. And before you think about killing me again because I ruined all your plans, just remember that I've got lots of friends that would hunt you down and make your life miserable... and then they'd kill you. Am I worth all that hassle and pain? Of course not. Besides, who would pay you for killing me? No one. See? So it would be in your best interests if you just forgot all about me."

Mercer was totally flummoxed. He was trying to understand how I knew he was a hired killer. Who would have
told me? Were the friends I was talking about the police?
Or was I bluffing him? I was right that no one would pay
him to kill me, but it would give him a lot of satisfaction to
end my life. Although that was probably not a good enough
reason to kill me, especially if the police had their suspicions. If I ended up dead, he would be the top suspect, and
his life could get really complicated.

I rolled my eyes. At least he was thinking twice about it
now. If it kept him from killing me, that was a bonus. "Well,
as much as I've enjoyed talking to you, I've really got to go."

"Wait a minute," he grabbed my wrist. "How do you
know all this about me? Who told you?"

"No one." I tried to jerk my arm away, but his grip tightened. "Oww. You're hurting me. Let me go." There would be
bruises on my arm later and my sense of invincibility disappeared, leaving me shaken.

He was upset that he seemed to be losing his touch. I
should be quaking in my shoes by now, and I wasn't. Then
it hit him that it was probably all a bluff. He relaxed his
hold, and dropped my wrist, realizing this was different,
more like a game. He'd never met anyone like me, and it
was refreshing. It was a challenge he'd never had before.
Maybe he'd hold off on killing me for a while. I had a lot of
spunk. That could be interesting.

Now I was starting to freak, and my bravado shriveled to
nothing. What was I doing, standing here talking to a killer?
"It would be better for you if you left me alone. I really do
know people."

He chuckled. "Yes, I'm sure you do." The mirth in his
eyes changed to concern as he glanced over my shoulder.

"Is this guy bothering you?" Ricky stood behind me, his
hand in his jacket, the gun evident in his pocket.

"He's just leaving. Isn't that right, Mr. Mercer?"

Mercer sighed. He glanced at Ricky, thinking that maybe I was telling the truth about knowing people. But on the other hand, that would just add to the fun. He wasn't afraid of someone threatening him with a gun. It put me on the same level as him, and evened out the playing field. I may have beaten him this time, but there was always tomorrow.

"See you around." He had enjoyed our little riposte, and looked forward to more. Smiling, he turned on his heel and quickly melted into the crowd.

"Thanks Ricky." My shoulders slumped. All I wanted to do was go home. I turned to face him and someone in the crowd brushed past my shoulder, making my purse fall down to my arm.

"Sorry," the man said, and kept walking. As I glanced at him, shock and recognition swept through me. The shock was because of the deep voice coming from a woman, and the recognition because it was the guy dressed like a woman from the courthouse. He had the same wig, but different clothes. Still, I'd remember those hairy legs anywhere. Couldn't he at least shave them? Then it hit me. He was following Mercer. Why was he doing that?

"Do you know who that is?" Ricky asked, catching my attention. He was thinking that Mercer was a hired assassin, and it was freaking him out.

"Yes, but don't worry," I assured him. "The police have evidence that will put him away for murder."

Ricky shook his head. "Don't be too sure. For guys like that, evidence has a way of disappearing." He was thinking it was time to call Mr. Manetto and let him know what was going on.

I glanced at him. He really didn't know about Uncle Joey. What if he found out Uncle Joey was dead or kidnapped, and I'd done nothing about it? Unless Uncle Joey really wasn't dead or kidnapped. It was all so confusing. "I'd better get home."

"You should be safe for tonight." He was thinking that guys like Mercer liked to toy with their kill, and draw it out for the enjoyment. I probably had a week or so. He glanced at me. "What did you do to him?"

I sighed, wishing I'd never gone to the courthouse that day. "He killed a guy and I sort of caught him." The bank robber probably deserved it, but what about all the others?

"You saw him?"

"No." I shouldn't have said that. "Nobody saw him, but I had a hunch it was him, so they put him in jail. He got released today because of lack of evidence, and he blames me for putting him there in the first place. That's why he's... you know... after me."

Ricky understood now. It was a matter of pride. Too bad I had interfered. Now Ricky would probably have to kill the guy, and that was usually Ramos' job. He'd better call 'The Knife' right away. This was getting too complicated for him.

"Well," I said. "Thanks again." I lifted my hand in a little wave and Ricky frowned.

"What's that in your hand?" He thought it looked like one of those stun guns that carried one million tooth-jarring volts of power.

"It's a flashlight stun gun," I admitted.

"Cool. Does it work?" He was thinking of getting one for his girlfriend.

"I don't know. I haven't tried it yet. I was going to use it on Mercer, but you got there first."

"Oh. Well, you should probably save it for when he tries to kill you, otherwise, you won't be able to take him by surprise next time."

"Yeah, that's true," I agreed. Why was talking about my impending death so easily?

"Okay, well, see you." He wasn't confident he could keep me alive, and was glad I had the stun gun. At least it would give me a fighting chance, as long as I knew how to use it.

"Bye," I said, and I hurried to my car, eager to get home. First, I needed to call Dimples and tell him the bad news. Maybe with the combination of the cops and Uncle Joey's men, I had a fighting chance against the assassin. He answered on the first ring.

"It's me again," I said. "Just thought you should know that Mercer was standing in front of Chris' office building when I came out. It looked like he was waiting for me. How soon can you guys pick him up?"

"Did he threaten you?" Dimples' voice was harsh. I'd never heard him sound that way before.

"Not in so many words," I said. "But it scared me just the same. I'm pretty sure he doesn't like me much, and would probably like to kill me if he got the chance."

The pause on the other end of the line made me glad I couldn't hear his thoughts, since I was pretty sure he was swearing. A lot.

"Okay," he said. "I'll have them rush the testing so we can get him back into custody. Hopefully by tomorrow."

"Do you think they'll find anything with the testing?"

"I think so. Even if the gun has no fingerprints, the fake nose was attached to his skin, so there should be something we can get from it. In the meantime, I'll have a cruiser drive by your house through the next couple of days and nights. That should discourage him from contacting you again."

"Sounds good," I said, relieved.

"Did you get the number of that client you told me about?" he asked.

"Uh, no." I had forgotten. "Chris is at lunch, and the secretary wouldn't give it to me. But I'll get it from him and call you back." Dimples said that was fine and we disconnected. I started the car, and pulled out onto the street, ready to get home where I felt safe. Since Ricky didn't think I had anything to worry about tonight, I was going to believe him.

I felt bad I'd missed Chris, and worried about how he'd take the fact that the killer was out of jail and I'd spoken to him. Maybe I should leave the speaking to him part out. It wasn't exactly lying, right? But I was definitely going to tell him he was out of jail. He would be happy we found the gun and fake nose, so it kind of balanced out. I figured it was best to tell him about Ricky, too. I mean... I was glad he was there, so Chris would be too. I hoped.

I let myself in the house, and relocked the door. The fact that it was locked when I got there didn't mean I could let down my guard. I knew how professionals broke in from Ramos, so I wasn't taking any chances. I held my stun gun in front of me and went through the house.

I checked every room and closet in the house before putting my stun gun back into my purse. My shoulders sagged with relief that I was safe. Taking my shoes off, I changed into jeans and a t-shirt, then checked the clock. Chris should be back from lunch by now. I called his cell again. I needed that guy's name and number, but after what I'd been through, I wanted to hear his voice even more. He answered this time. "Hey Hon, what's up?"

"We found the gun and fake nose!" I blurted, deciding to start with the good news. "They're at the lab for testing, but it should link Mercer to the murder."

"That's great. Now they can keep that guy behind bars where he belongs. Hey, can I call you back?" he asked. "I'm with a client right now."

"Um... first can you give me the name and number of your client who was at the courthouse? We think he might have seen Mercer throw the gun and fake nose out the window, and Dimples asked me to get it for him."

"Sure, just a minute," he said.

I heard some papers rustling, and he came back with the name and number. I thanked him and hung up, deciding to tell him the rest when he got home. Why ruin the rest of his day when there was nothing he could do about it?

I got busy with some chores and lost track of time, so I was surprised when the kids came home from school. It was Friday and, after dropping off his backpack, Josh left for a friend's house. Savannah came out of her room with a large bag containing her pajamas and a pillow.

Had I missed something? "Where are you going?" I asked.

"Don't you remember?" She realized that she had forgotten to tell me about her plans, and was hoping she could bluff her way out of it. "I'm pretty sure I told you about the sleepover at Madi's house. I'm sure I mentioned it a few days ago."

"I don't think so," I said.

"You probably just forgot. I know you've had a busy week helping the police and all."

She was good, but I wasn't going to let her get away with it. "No. I think I'd remember a sleepover." I couldn't understand why she didn't just come out and ask me. I usually gave my permission, so what was going on this time?

"Oh," she said, realizing I was on to her. "Well, can I go then?"

"It depends. What are you planning to do?" I asked.

"It's a sleepover, mom. Probably watch a movie and eat popcorn." She glanced down, avoiding my eyes, thinking it wasn't a total lie. The movie they wanted to see was at the megaplex, and if the boys met them there, that was just a happy coincidence. She really wanted to sit by Ryan like a real date. If I knew, I probably wouldn't let her go, and she wanted to go. Real bad.

"At Madi's house? You're not going to a movie theatre?" I asked, wanting to catch her. That part about sitting with Ryan like a real date kind of shook me up.

Her eyes widened, startled that I asked. Shrugging, she decided to go with it. "That's a good idea. Maybe we'll go to the movies instead. There's that action one I've been wanting to see."

"Yeah," I said. "Too bad it's rated PG-13, and you're only twelve." I was scrambling here, but how could I let her go, knowing she was going to be sitting by a boy in the dark? I knew what that led to. I wasn't about to let some hormonally challenged teenage boy paw my daughter.

"Mom," she moaned. "Why are you giving me such a hard time? It's just a movie."

Yeah, right! I didn't know what to say. It struck me that I was probably overreacting. "Okay," I thought quickly. "You can go, but you have to let me know what movie you're going to, and I'll pick you and your friends up after."

"After the movie?" She didn't like that idea. They already had it figured out. Madi's sister and her boyfriend were going to take them and bring them home. Having me come would be awful.

"Yes." I wasn't going to compromise. "Either that, or your dad and I will take you and your friends. I've been wanting to see that movie too. We could all go and watch it together."

Savannah sucked in her breath. That would be a fate worse than death. "Fine, you can pick us up."

"Great," I smiled. "Just let me know the details before you go."

She agreed, her face tight with defeat. It took some of the fun out of it, but at least she still got to go. If she didn't know better, she'd think I knew what she was up to. That was a creepy thought.

I offered to drive her to Madi's house, and that seemed to placate her a little bit. Now if only I could figure out how to get her to talk to me about boys and dating, I'd feel a lot better.

Chris got home, and I didn't know what to tell him first. He already knew about finding the gun and fake nose, so I filled him in on the details of that. From there, I told him about Mercer getting released from jail. To my surprise, he pretty much expected that. What he didn't expect was that I'd talked to him.

"You mean he was waiting for you, like he'd been following you?"

"I guess." I hadn't thought of it that way, but it was probably true.

"So, what did he say? Did he threaten you?"

"Not in words, but his thoughts were a different story." I explained what he was thinking, and how Ricky intervened.

"Ricky? Who's Ricky?" Now he was getting confused.

I told him he was from Uncle Joey's organization, and was watching out for me. Chris didn't take this news as well as I'd hoped. "Word on the street? Like someone's put out a contract on you?"

"No. I think it's more like Mercer letting people know he wants to kill me. Ricky said I didn't need to worry that he'd come after me for a while, and I agree. Mercer will want to scare me first. Make my life miserable. It's a matter of pride or something. Anyway, I think he'll be back in custody before he can follow through on his threats."

Chris glowered, his teeth clenching, and his brows drawn together, with his eyes tiny slits. By the time I got to Savannah, I decided not to tell him about her wanting to sit with the boy at the movie. I was afraid Chris would beat him up or something. So I just told him we needed to pick her up after the show.

"Oh, and Dimples said he'd send the police to cruise through the neighborhood every few hours until Mercer is back in custody. That's good, right?"

"Just great," he said. He was thinking he'd better apply for a concealed weapons permit, and buy a gun.

I sighed, sad that it had come to this, but silently agreeing. "Oh, I forgot. There's something I want to show you." I found my purse and pulled out my pepper spray and stun flashlight. I explained how it worked, and that I was ready to use it.

"Good," he said. "I wonder how long it keeps someone down. That might be good to know."

"Would you like me to try it on you?" I asked, a wicked smile on my face.

"Only if you go first," he said.

I reached out to touch him with it, and he grabbed my wrist. I playfully fought against him, and soon he had me pinned against his chest, the flashlight forgotten. I savored the feeling of his body against mine. As our lips met, he let go of my wrist and I circled my arms around him. A crackling, buzzing sound broke the spell, and I realized I had accidentally pushed the button on the stun gun. Lucky for me, it wasn't touching Chris. He jerked back, almost hitting his head against the wall.

"You'd better put that away," Chris said, his eyes wide. He was thinking that the sound alone gave him the creeps. No way did he ever want to know how it felt.

"It's got one million tooth-jarring volts of power, so I'm sure it would feel pretty icky." I put the stun gun back in my purse, and snuggled back into his arms. "Now where were we?"

Later that night, we got Savannah and her friends from the movie, and dropped them off at Madi's house. I picked up that Savannah had a great time snuggling with Ryan, but she wasn't ready to kiss him or anything. She liked having his arm around her though. It made her feel all shivery inside. I smiled, grateful she hadn't done more than that. The girls were probably going to stay up all night talking about it.

The rest of the weekend was uneventful, which suited me just fine. No phone calls from Mexico. No strange vehicles stopped in front of my house. No assassins loitering at my door. The only thing out of the ordinary was the police car that drove through the neighborhood, parking every now and then in front of my house. Even with the extra police presence, I couldn't help being nervous, and it started to bother Chris too.

On Saturday, he purchased a gun and took me to the firing range. We took the firearms safety class and I got pretty good at understanding how to load and fire a gun. It didn't make me want to use one, but I knew I could if I had to. But seriously, I'd rather stick with my stun flashlight.

Chapter 7

Monday morning came with the hope that the police had found something to put Mercer behind bars again. After getting the kids off to school, I called Dimples to check on the case. He was hopeful that by this afternoon or the next morning it would happen.

Not quite what I wanted to hear, but at least they were making progress. After my regular workout at the gym, I showered and got ready for the day. I finished fixing my hair when the doorbell rang. My pulse quickened. Now what? I ran down the list of who it might be, and none of them were people I wanted to open my door for.

Peeking out the window, a familiar black SUV was parked across the street. The CIA was back? What did they want? Had they come to replant a bug since I'd flushed the last one? A loud knocking followed the ringing of the doorbell. Somehow, they knew I was there. Maybe they'd seen me come home from the gym.

I pushed down my fluttering nerves and hurried to the door. Agent Bristow and Agent Shaw smiled politely. "Hi Mrs. Nichols," Agent Bristow said. "May we come in for a moment?" I hesitated and he continued. "We just have a couple of questions we'd like to ask, if that's okay."

"Sure," I said, pulling the door open. Agent Shaw was relieved he didn't have to show me his badge again. After last time, he'd decided to let Agent Bristow do most of the talking.

I ushered them into my living room where they took a seat on my couch. "How can I help you?" I asked.

"As you know, we've been monitoring Mr. Manetto's whereabouts in Mexico," Agent Bristow began. "And he's dropped off our radar, so to speak. A few days ago, we found out he was helping a woman, Ms. Carlotta Juarez. She works for the Mexican police, and we think she might be involved with the drug cartel there. We don't know what her role is, but we have some suspicions." He was thinking they didn't know if she was being blackmailed, or on the drug lord's payroll.

"I know you're probably wondering what this has to do with you, but we have information that they might try to contact you." He looked at me expectantly, wanting to know if they'd called me already.

"I did get a phone call from a police inspector last week," I said. Had the phone calls been real? If so, it was something I should probably tell the CIA. "His name was Salazar, and he told me Uncle Joey had been kidnapped and held for ransom. He called me twice. First, to ask if Uncle Joey had contacted me, and a second time, to ask me for money to pay a ransom."

"How much did they want?" Agent Shaw asked.

"One million dollars," I said. "I told him I didn't have that kind of money, and that I thought he was scamming me. I kind of hung up on him."

Agent Bristow's eyes got big and he wondered how I could be so cold hearted when Manetto was my uncle. At least I kept calling him that. Somehow the kidnappers were under the impression that he was my uncle as well, so it only made sense that they would contact me. They had to think I had access to Manetto's money. When he'd talked to Manetto's secretary, she'd seemed upset and surprised. It was obvious she didn't know anything about it. That left me their only lead.

Oh no! Jackie already figured I had the money, but she didn't know the kidnappers had called me. What would she do once she found out? Since I knew she had feelings for Uncle Joey, it was ten times worse. Maybe she'd tell Ricky to let the assassin kill me. This was bad.

"Mrs. Nichols," Bristow said, his lips drawn into a frown. "Did you just say you hung up on your uncle's kidnappers?"

"Just a minute," I said. This was getting out of hand and I was starting to panic. "In the first place, I am not related to Uncle Joey. That's just what I call him, but he is not my uncle! I only called him that to bug him, and it sort of got into a habit with me. But believe me, I am not related to him. Nor do I have access to his money. I only worked for him for a short time, but I quit. Okay? I don't work for him anymore. I don't want to have anything to do with him. I don't know why you people, and those Mexicans, keep bothering me. Who tells you these things? Who told you they would contact me?"

Agent Shaw glanced at Agent Bristow, a small smile on his lips. I was rattled. That was good. It meant they were getting closer to the truth. It also meant their anonymous informant was right, since I just told them I'd been contacted for the ransom money. Shaw wasn't fooled one bit with my little song and dance routine. He figured I knew what was going on, and would make it his mission to get me to crack so he could get to the bottom of this.

I closed my eyes and rubbed my forehead, wondering how in the world things had taken such a bad turn. I wondered if I should just tell them about the money and have done with it. But could that backfire? Could they arrest me for something? I was pretty sure I had done nothing wrong, but for some reason that did not reassure me.

"We can't tell you that," Bristow answered my question. "But since our source was right, you can understand why we had to ask. I believe you, by the way." At my confusion he continued, "That he's not your uncle."

"Oh, well that's good," I said. "Since it's true."

He nodded, thinking there was still something I wasn't telling them. Did I have access to Manetto's money somehow? It seemed the common thread in all this. Why wouldn't I tell them unless... I was being bribed?

Shaw pulled his hand away from the end table and wondered what had happened to the bug he'd planted. He was pretty sure that was the spot. Maybe it didn't stick and had fallen on the ground. He glanced under the table and I decided I'd had enough.

"Did you lose something Agent Shaw?"

He jerked his gaze back to my face and satisfaction ran through me to catch the guilt on his face. "No," he stammered. Then his eyes lit up with speculation, and my stomach dropped. Did I know? Had I removed it? If so, maybe there was a lot more to me than they thought.

Oh great! Just great! What was wrong with me? Why couldn't I keep my mouth shut? "Um... I've got to go. Is there anything else?"

"Yes," Bristow said. "This is serious. If you get any more calls from Mexico, we need to know immediately." His tone made me flinch a little. He noticed and tried to sound more agreeable. "We have some good men down there, and any info we can get to help them would be appreciated."

"Sure," I said. "If they call me back, I'll let you know." I didn't add that I didn't think they would, but they could tell from my tone that was what I thought. They both stood, and Bristow handed me another one of his cards.

"Be sure to do that," he said.

I took the card and led them to the door. They left and I flopped onto the couch. What was I supposed to do now? Maybe I should come clean with Jackie. If she could get in touch with Ramos, maybe she'd find out what was going on. I could just let her handle it, and then I'd be off the hook.

I picked up my cell phone and hesitated. This is what the CIA would be waiting for. I'd seen it a hundred times on TV. Right after the agents left, the guilty person always called his cohorts and told them what the agents wanted. The agents were always listening, and the poor guy got caught.

Well that wasn't going to happen to me. I checked out my window to make sure they had really left. They were gone, but that didn't mean they hadn't parked down the street out of view. Next, I felt under the end table, just to make sure Shaw hadn't planted another bug.

I couldn't feel anything, but I checked the whole area again just to make sure. Nothing. Did that mean it was okay to make my phone call? I had no idea. Maybe I should leave to call Jackie, just to be safe.

I grabbed my keys and got in my car. I could drive to the grocery store and see if anyone followed me. Then call from there when I was sure the coast was clear. I sat in the parking lot for ten minutes. Nothing seemed suspicious, so I picked up my cell phone and dialed Thrasher Development.

While it rang, I remembered Uncle Joey's warning not to tell anyone about the money and my heart sped up. Maybe this was a mistake.

"Thrasher Development, may I help you?" Jackie answered. I froze, my breath caught in my throat. "Hello?" she asked.

"Hi, Jackie... this is Shelby," I said. "Um... do you have a minute to talk?"

"Is this about Joe? Do you know what's going on?" Her voice sounded a little frantic.

"Not really," I stalled. "I was hoping you could tell me."

Silence on the other end made me wish I knew what she was thinking. "I was just leaving for lunch," she said, her tone in control and calculating. "Would you like to join me?"

"Sure, sounds great," I answered, not really sure at all. We decided to meet at a café that was famous for its sandwiches and espresso. I hung up and wondered if I'd done the right thing. Doubt and frustration coiled in my stomach, giving me heartburn. Hang Uncle Joey. I was tired of worrying. Sharing this with Jackie would take some of the pressure off of me. If something needed to be done, she could take care of it.

At eleven-thirty, it was a bit early for lunch, and easy to spot Jackie in a corner booth. She gave me a curt nod and I hurried over, realizing she was one of those people that I wanted to please, mostly because I had a feeling it wouldn't be good to be on her bad side. Which didn't bode well for me at all.

"Hi," I said, smiling. She returned my greeting and we made small talk until our food arrived.

"I had a visit from the CIA this morning," she said, jumping right in. "Is that why you're here? Did they visit you too?" Her thoughts were quiet, totally focused on what I had to say.

"Yes, but that's not why I'm here. I mean... it's not the only reason." I tried to figure out a way to sugarcoat the phone call from the inspector, but finally gave up, and told her about the kidnapping and demand for ransom. "I don't think it's for real," I explained. "I was sure it was a scam, at least until the CIA came around. That's when I decided to call you."

"What did the CIA tell you?" she asked.

"Just that Uncle Joey's dropped out of sight, and there was a woman, Carlotta something, whom he was helping." Jackie's eyes widened, and then a glint of cold steel came into them. "They thought she might be involved with the drug cartel..." Jackie blinked and the coldness was gone, re-placed with worried concern.

"How much money did they want?" she asked.

"One million dollars," I said. "I told the kidnappers I didn't have that kind of money and to get..." I stopped, real-izing that Jackie knew I did have the money but wasn't will-ing to pay the ransom.

She smiled at the fact that I had told them off. But how they knew to call me in the first place was a mystery. She was pretty sure I had the money, but how did they know? Unless I'd called Joey 'Uncle Joey,' and it was just a fluke. That would certainly explain it. "You handled it well. If any-one understands bribery, it's Joe Manetto. You were right to tell me. I'll call Ramos and see what I can find out. In the meantime, you should watch your back. Those kinds of people will stop at nothing for a few bucks."

"All right." I was surprised that she wasn't mad at me for not giving in to their demands. She didn't seem too worried either, and I was grateful to have her handle things. "Let me know how it goes."

All the way home, I was counting my lucky stars that she'd taken it so well, and I didn't have to worry about Un-cle Joey anymore. Hopefully it would all blow over, and I could focus on the more important job of keeping a vengeful assassin from killing me.

That night, Chris got home from work, unhappy about his day. A couple of things had gone undone, and it put him behind. He used to keep his frustration to himself and leave work at work, but now that he knew I could hear his thoughts, he wasn't sure what to do. Plus, he was worried about me and everything I was involved in. It was starting to get to him.

"Do you want to talk about it?" I asked. He exhaled, puffing his cheeks out to keep from saying something he'd regret. "Oops," I said. "I guess that means no."

"Shelby," he hesitated to get under control. "Yeah, it means no." At least he toned down what he was thinking. He could have let me have it about how I wasn't supposed to read his mind and answer his thoughts without him vocalizing them. And where the hell were my shields? So even though he was thinking he wanted to strangle me, he was really being nice about it. "I'm going to go for a run," he said instead.

He hurried from the room with a tight smile, and I got out of his way. Hmm, this might not be a good time to tell him about the visit from the CIA, or my lunch with Jackie where I spilled the beans. There was also the bad news that I hadn't heard anything from Dimples about Mercer.

Yup, this was one of those times I needed to put up my shields and try to act normal. Which was easier said than done, but what choice did I have? Savannah came home from Madi's house with Ryan on the brain. Lately, that was all she thought about and it was driving me crazy. Of course, the fact that I wasn't supposed to know about it was even worse. What do you say to your teenage daughter who has a crush and can't think straight?

That was one reason why I worked hard to keep my shields up around Josh. I didn't think I could handle the thoughts of a hormonally-challenged teenage boy. So far, it was working out, and I decided to do the same with Savannah. I would work on having an open relationship without being intrusive. Of course, that didn't mean I wouldn't put my foot down if I thought for one minute she needed it.

What about Chris? I realized I hadn't held up my end of the bargain. I listened to his thoughts when I shouldn't. He needed the same boundaries as my kids, and I hadn't given him that. He had every right to be upset with me.

After his run, he seemed more relaxed, which was a huge relief. He showered and was getting dressed when I walked in on him and softly closed the door. "Honey," I began. "I'm sorry that I listened when I shouldn't. I promise to work harder on that."

He paused. His boxers were on, but nothing else. He reached for his t-shirt, and I wandered over to him, taking the opportunity to touch his bare skin. He exhaled, letting me run my fingers over his chest. "Am I forgiven?" I asked.

"You are such a manipulator," he said, his voice low. But he didn't pull away, and I put my arms around him, circling my fingernails lightly over his back the way he liked it. He moaned and caught my lips in a kiss. We came up for air, and I smiled sweetly.

"Um... are you hungry?" I asked. "Because dinner's ready."

"Yes, definitely," he replied, not thinking about food.

"Great." I pulled away. "We'll save that for later." My eyes widened, wondering if he'd be mad again, but he just smiled. I didn't want to ruin the moment by telling him my shields were up, so I pulled away.

He was having none of that, and jerked me back in his arms. "Where do you think you're going?" I squeaked in alarm and his smile deepened. "Is dinner going to burn if we're not there right away?"

"Not this dinner. It's in the crock-pot."

"Good. Then since you're groveling for my forgiveness, I know just how you can earn it."

I laughed, more than willing to do what I must. "There's only one thing wrong with your plans," I said between kisses. "Josh is starving."

"He can wait a few more minutes," Chris answered.

It was a little longer than that before we sat down at the dinner table, but all in all, the evening was going much better than it started. I did my best to keep my shields up, and Chris could tell how hard I was trying.

"I'm sorry I was such a grouch when I got home," Chris said later. "I guess I just needed some time to unwind."

"I know what you mean," I agreed. "It's been nice to relax and not worry about everything."

"Yeah," he answered. He took a breath and with reluctance added, "Did you hear anything about Mercer? Have they got him back in custody?"

"I talked to Dimples this morning. He said it should happen today or tomorrow. So he might be in custody by now. I'll call him in the morning."

"Good. I'll feel a lot better about things once he's back in jail."

"Me too," I agreed. "Do you want to watch something on TV?" I asked, knowing how worried he was, and that he didn't want to talk about it anymore.

His face cleared, and the tightness around his eyes relaxed. "Sounds great."

The next morning after Chris left for work, worry hit me like a ton of bricks. I hadn't told him about my conversation with Jackie or the CIA, mostly because he was already worried about Mercer, and I didn't want to make it worse. The thing that churned my stomach was wondering if Mercer was still out there gunning for me. If he were smart, he'd leave town and forget all about me.

I called Dimples for an update, but he wasn't available, so I left a message to call me ASAP. It had been a few days since I'd last seen Mercer, and if what Ricky said was true, my reprieve was probably over. I checked my stun flashlight and made sure it was fully charged.

The gun Chris and I bought over the weekend was safely put away, and I couldn't bring myself to load it. I didn't feel comfortable with a loaded gun in the house, even with the safety on. Of course, I would probably change my mind if I didn't get good news from Dimples. Soon.

After locking all the doors and windows, I put my nervous energy to work and started the laundry. Then I decided to clean the kitchen cabinets. I kept my eye on the street for anything that looked suspicious, and found that I spent more time watching the street than I did cleaning. Finally, I just gave up.

I picked up the phone to call Dimples again, and noticed a white industrial-type van parking across the street and up one house. My pulse leapt and my mouth went dry. There was no writing on the side to identify it as belonging to a business, and the windows were tinted so I couldn't see if anyone was sitting inside. The hairs on my arm stood up, and a chill went down my back. I knew I was in danger.

My hands shook, but before I could push any numbers, the phone rang, and I fumbled it in my fingers. The phone number on the caller ID wasn't familiar, and I debated whether I should answer. I glanced out my window to find that the passenger door of the van had opened, but I couldn't see anyone. Maybe whoever was on the phone could help me.

"Hello?" I said.

"Shelby! You're all right." I recognized the voice, even though it was a little high-pitched for him.

"Ramos? Is that really you?"

"Listen," he said forcefully. "You've got to get out of there."

"What?"

"I don't have time to explain, but I've been following some people and I think they're coming after you."

"Are they in a white van with no windows?" I asked.

"Uh... I don't know. Why?"

"Because there's a van parked up the street from my house, and I have a bad feeling about it."

"Okay... listen... just get in your car and leave. If they follow you, you'll know you're in trouble. Take your cell phone and call me. Got it?"

"Yeah," I answered.

"Good. Go!" The line went dead and I started to shake.

I slipped on my shoes and grabbed my purse. Pulling the back door open, I came face to face with a man whose fist was raised to knock. I screamed and slammed the door in his face. With my chest heaving, it dawned on me who it was, and I cringed. What had I just done?

I pulled it open again, this time with a smile plastered on my face. "Agent Bristow. What a surprise. Sorry about that, you startled me."

"Do you always slam the door in people's faces?"

"I was just leaving, and I didn't expect anyone to be standing there," I explained. "Usually people come to the front door, not the back door." I noticed the side door to the garage was standing open. "So... what are you doing here?" I thought it was a fair question. "Hey, is that your van up the street?"

I checked to see if it was still there so I wouldn't look like a total moron. It was. He didn't answer, so I turned back to him and he had a puzzled look on his face. Then he started to slide forward and I reached out to steady him. His weight took me by surprise and I couldn't hold him up. The momentum carried us both to the floor, and I gasped.

"Bristow! What are you doing?" His eyes rolled back in his head, and I struggled to push him off me. My fingers touched something sticking out of his back. Dread that it was a knife turned to relief to find a dart-like thing in his shoulder. At the same time, fear twisted around my heart. My door was standing wide open!

I yelped and wiggled out from under him, trying to get to my feet and shut the door. In complete panic, I lurched to slam the door, but his feet were in the way. I bent down to move them, and something whizzed over my head. A dart hit the stove and bounced across the floor. I ducked behind the door and pushed against it, smashing Bristow's feet between the door and the doorframe.

Bristow groaned, and I worried that I was breaking a bone or something. I let go of the door and shoved against him with my legs. The force rolled him out of the way and I pushed against the door, only to find it blocked from the outside by a person's foot.

I let out a yelp and, still pushing on the door, looked for something to hit the foot with. Not far from me, the dart was lying on the floor. Keeping my feet firmly planted against the door, I scooted back on my butt and straightened my legs. Stretching, I managed to grasp it. I brought the dart down with all my strength, plunging it through the person's shoe. The man yelped and jerked his foot away, allowing me to finally get the door closed. I jumped up and locked the dead bolt, then ducked down to catch my breath.

I heard some movement coming from outside my door, but it was muffled. Did that mean the man was waiting for me to make a move? Or was he now lying in a drugged sleep in my garage? Where was Agent Shaw? Was he the one I just darted? I crawled over Bristow to peer through the window.

The van was gone. I scanned the street, but couldn't see it anywhere. Was it over? Had they left? Maybe the presence of the CIA had scared them off. Ramos told me to leave and call him. He could tell me what was going on. For now, that was probably my best option. Bristow stirred. He'd be awake soon, and I wondered if I should involve him or leave. Which was safer? The CIA or Ramos? Hoping I wasn't making a huge mistake, I decided to go with Ramos.

I grabbed my purse, but this time I opened the door a crack and peeked out. I couldn't see anyone in the garage, although the side door Bristow had come in was still wide open. I took a deep breath and pulled the door wider. I strained to hear movement, but all was quiet. I pushed the remote to unlock the car and made a run for it.

I got to the car door and pulled it open, ready to jump inside. Arms wrapped around me in a tight grip and I screamed. A hand clamped over my mouth, and I struggled for all I was worth, almost missing the sting of a prick against my neck.

My legs went weak, and I couldn't move. The man holding me began to drag me out the garage door. I kept blinking my eyes to keep the darkness away, but it was getting hard. The man hauled me into the back of the van that was sitting in my driveway, and lowered me onto the floor next to another still form. He closed the doors, shutting out the light, and I couldn't fight the darkness any more. The last thing I heard was the engine starting and someone speaking in Spanish.

Chapter 8

I opened my eyes to find myself lying on a piece of carpet in the back of a van. It had stopped moving, and I sensed that I was alone. I tried to sit up, but found my hands bound with rope. At least my legs were untied, and nothing covered my mouth.

Loud, angry voices came from outside. My captors were arguing about something, probably what to do with me. I listened carefully, but couldn't make out a single word they said. Then it hit me. It was all in Spanish. My heart skipped a beat, knowing that these men were probably from the drug cartel or Inspector Salazar. Maybe they were working together, or one and the same. Did they still think I could give them the million dollars? Was there anything I could tell them that would keep them from killing me?

The only thing that kept me from sinking into despair was the fact that Ramos had been watching out for me and could be somewhere close. If not, then at least Agent Bristow had been in my home when they came for me. He would know I'd been kidnapped, and could possibly be looking for me right now. Since they'd only darted him and not killed him, I had hope they wouldn't kill me either.

I held my breath at the sound of footsteps on gravel. They were coming to get me. The doors swung open, and the light coming in blinded me. I jerked my bound hands to cover my eyes, and a man spoke.

"Ah, you are awake. Good. You will talk, and we will let you go. Si?"

"What do you want?" It was still too bright to lower my arms. Maybe that was a good thing. If I couldn't see what he looked like, maybe he would let me go. I listened to his thoughts. This might be my only chance to know what he wanted. The words were there, but I couldn't understand them. Then I realized it was Spanish. If he was talking in English, why wasn't he thinking in English? This was terrible!

"We came because of your Uncle Joey. He told us all about you, and told us that you had our money. All we want is our money back, and you can go free."

He sounded sincere, but since I couldn't understand his Spanish thoughts, I wasn't sure I could believe him. I groaned, laying my head back against the floor. What should I do?

"Senora? I need an answer. If you want to leave this van alive you will do what I say."

"Okay, okay. I can see about getting the money. But it's not going to be easy. I put it in a mutual fund, so it's not like I can just go to the bank and make a withdrawal. And there's something else you need to know. Joey Manetto is not my uncle. So quit calling him that. I don't even like the guy. He's made my life a living hell, and I want nothing to do with him. Got it?" That last part came out in kind of a shriek. My captor jerked back as if astonished by my outburst.

"You don't care if he lives or dies?" he asked.

"No," I yelled. "This whole thing is all his fault. He sent me this money, and you know what? I didn't want it. I'm supposed to keep it safe for him, and not tell anyone. Now why should I do that? I didn't want his money. I wish he'd never sent it to me."

"Then why did you put it in a mutual fund?"

I thought that was a pretty good question. And it calmed me down.

"Because the interest rates were better. I figured he'd want his money back someday, and that was fine with me. But I was hoping to keep all the interest it had earned. I figured it was the least he could do for dumping it on me in the first place."

"Ah," he nodded his head. "Yes, that makes sense now. So, you will get the money for us?"

"Of course." I was trying to sound reasonable. "Knowing Uncle Joey, I'm sure it was your money in the first place, and I don't blame you for wanting it back. But it puts me in a bind. I mean, when he finds out, he's not going to be happy with me."

He let out his breath, and rubbed his forehead. I could tell he was getting a little exasperated with me. "You want us to kill him for you? Is that it?"

Shocked, I inhaled and choked on my spit. I couldn't seem to catch my breath and my eyes watered, sending tears gliding down my cheeks. I swallowed, taking small breaths until it was easier, and then began to cough my head off. The gunmen were saying something in Spanish, and one of them started pounding me on my back. The other one shoved a bottle of water in my hands.

I gratefully took a drink and then coughed some more. Finally, I could breathe again, and I wiped my mouth and nose on my sleeve, still catching my breath. Under control, I took another swig of water. "Thanks," I said, my voice sounding like gravel. "Sorry about that. Do either of you have a tissue?" I sniffed, but my nose was running along with my eyes, and I couldn't keep from coughing.

One of them uttered what sounded like a swear word and opened the van's jockey box. Luckily a box of tissues was inside, and he handed me the whole box. "Thanks," I muttered. After blowing my nose, wiping my eyes, and clearing my throat a few times, I felt almost normal.

I glanced at my captor and noticed the big frown on his face. Had I given Ramos enough time to find me? I'd better answer his question. "Um... no, don't kill him for me. I mean, it might solve some of my problems, but I can't ask you to do that. Thanks anyway, though."

"So, how do we get to the money? We need it today."

"Sure. I can talk to my bank and see if they can pull all the funds together, and write a cashier's check. You want one million dollars, right?"

His lips curved upward in a smile. He glanced at his companion and started to laugh. They were both chuckling as if sharing a funny joke. After a moment, their focus turned on me, and their laughter abruptly stopped. The one who had done most of the talking leaned closer, and looked me straight in the eyes. "That was a joke, right?" His eyes narrowed into little slits.

I pulled back and swallowed. "Um... just how much did you want?"

My question did nothing to alleviate the tightness around his eyes. "Five million dollars." He said each word with a pause between them for emphasis.

"Oh, okay," I said. "I just wasn't sure, you know, because Inspector Salazar told me it was one million."

If it were possible, his eyes narrowed even more. "Inspector Salazar talked to you? When?"

He pulled back and I breathed a sigh of relief. "Let's see, it was a few days ago. Thursday or Friday, I think." I honestly couldn't remember.

He glanced at the other guy and they moved away from the van, speaking heatedly in Spanish. I was grateful for the reprieve and started undoing the knots around my wrists with my teeth. The bad guys seemed pretty flustered, which led me to believe that maybe Inspector Salazar was a rival. Who knew, maybe he was on his way to kidnap me too? My stomach clenched. Could that be who Ramos was watching, and he really wasn't onto these guys at all?

No. I couldn't let myself start thinking like that. Instead, I concentrated on untying the knots. I drew my legs up and maneuvered back against the same side of the van as the doors, noticing my purse for the first time. It was lying sideways and most of the contents had spilled out. My heart raced. There was my stun flashlight! I grabbed it, holding it firmly in my lap out of sight. With time to spare, I also found my wallet, and shoved in into the waistband of my jeans where it wouldn't fall out.

Just then, the arguing outside stopped. Footsteps approached, and I held my breath, then checked to make sure my finger was on the right button. One of the men walked around to the driver's side, and the other one stuck his head in to find me. I knew he was going to close the doors, so I lunged for his throat and pushed the button.

He gave a strangled gasp and slumped to the ground. I scooted out of the van, landing off-balance and skidding on the gravel. Righting myself, I started running. The other guy let out a string of Spanish and jumped out the driver's door after me, but I had a head start.

I took in my surroundings, realizing I was in a gravel parking lot filled with all kinds of junk. There was only one road leading in or out next to a small broken-down building. I focused on that, and tried not to think about the foot-steps getting closer behind me.

Just then, a car careened around the corner of the build-ing, sliding into the parking lot, and spinning in a half turn on the gravel. It came to a halt between my kidnapper and me. The man inside opened his door and started shooting at the kidnapper.

"Get in!" Ramos yelled.

I fumbled with the door handle, not willing to let go of my stun flashlight. The other guy raced back to his van, es-caping the barrage of bullets, and jumped in. Ramos ducked back in the car, and pushed open my door. He roughly jerked me inside the car and stepped on the gas. Half lying on the seat, I pulled my feet in, just as the door slammed shut.

Out of breath and panting, I closed my eyes, relieved that I was safe. I felt the car skid around the corner and merge into traffic. When the car straightened, I pushed myself into a sitting position.

"You okay?" Ramos asked.

"Yeah," I said, breathless. "You got there just in time."

He shook his head. "I would have been there sooner, but some goon in an SUV cut me off." He glanced at me sharp-ly. "Wouldn't have anything to do with you, would it?" I smiled shakily, and he continued. "He pulled into your driveway."

"Oh," I said. "It's the CIA."

He stilled for a fraction of a second, then shook his head again. Checking the rearview mirror, he said, "Hold on."

Dropping my flashlight, I grabbed the handle above the door. Ramos deftly turned the corner and took a quick right down another street. In a bold move, he accelerated across two lanes of traffic and pulled into a parking garage. Taking the ramp that led upward, we were soon at the top of the structure. He pulled into a parking place a safe distance away from all other cars, and killed the engine.

He glanced at my hands still clutching the handle. Chagrined, I let go. "Here, let me help you with that." Pulling out a pocketknife, he cut through the coils of rope.

"Thanks," I said, rubbing my wrists and sending him a grateful smile. He dipped his head, and I turned away to look out the window, not wanting him to see my eyes get misty. I tamped down my emotions and cleared my throat. "I sure hope you can tell me what's going on."

He was thinking that I was in one helluva mess, and it was all Manetto's fault. Not that Manetto had planned it that way. Manetto had a soft spot for me. When it looked like he might not get back alive, he thought putting the money in my account would not only hide it, but also give me something nice to remember him by. As it turned out, it was a big mistake. Now how was he supposed to explain all that to me?

"Why don't you start with the money?" I prompted, quickly adding, "You do know about that, right?"

He glanced at me with narrowed eyes. I was doing that weird thing again, almost like I was reading his mind. He shook it off. That was nuts. "The money is what we call 'collateral damage control.' Mr. Manetto thought he could hide it in your account, and no one would know he had it. But that's getting ahead of the story. First of all, as you know, we went to Mexico after Kate and Hodges."

"Right," I said with enthusiasm. "Did you find them?"

He huffed. "No. They weren't there. I don't know why we thought they would be, especially since they knew we knew where they were going to disappear. Kate was smarter than that, and probably the one to change their plans."

"Oh." I was confused. "Then where did the money come from?"

"It's kind of a long story," he answered.

"I'm not going anywhere."

Ramos decided he might as well tell me everything. It wouldn't make sense otherwise. "A long time ago, Mr. Manetto had a relationship with a woman."

"Carlotta?" I jumped in.

"Who told you about her?" he asked.

"Um..." I knew he wouldn't like it, but he had to know. "The CIA."

He swore a blue streak, but only in his mind. I cleared my throat and he got back under control. "So," he said. "That's what they were doing at your house. You'd better tell me the rest."

"They stopped by not too long after I got the money, asking if I'd heard anything from Uncle Joey. Of course, I didn't tell them about the money. They thought Uncle Joey was working with an arms dealer in Mexico and wondered what he was up to."

The name Cisco came to Ramos' mind. "How did they know about that?" He was basically asking himself, but I answered anyway.

"They're working with the same arms dealer."

"What for?" he asked

"They're trying to help the good guys take out the bad guys?" I shrugged. "I guess that's what the CIA does."

"Go on," he said, dismissing my reasoning.

"They came by the other day asking me if I'd heard about Uncle Joey's disappearance and if I knew anything. They said he was involved with a woman, Carlotta, and that she worked for the police, but they also wondered if she was working for a drug cartel. Maybe because she was being bribed or something? They said they had reason to believe that someone might contact me."

Ramos glanced at me sharply. "Did someone contact you?"

"Yes," I admitted. "Police Inspector Salazar. First he asked me if I'd talked with Uncle Joey recently. I told him no, and the next day he called to tell me that Uncle Joey had been kidnapped, and was being held for ransom. Then he wanted to know if I'd pay the million-dollar ransom. I guess he thought he was my uncle. Probably my fault," I conceded.

"Anyways, I told him..." I hesitated, then decided Ramos would understand and continued. "That he wasn't my uncle, and I wasn't going to pay. Then I sort of hung up on him." I raised my brows and widened my eyes, giving Ramos my best innocent look. "It sounded like a big scam to me."

Ramos' lips twitched, holding back a smile. He knew it was hard to pull the wool over my eyes. That was what he liked about me. I seemed to ferret out the truth, no matter what it was. "So, you told this to the CIA?"

"Yeah," I admitted.

"What else?"

"Well... when the CIA said Uncle Joey had really disappeared, I got a little worried. So I went to lunch with Jackie to talk it over. She said she'd call you and find out what was going on. Did she?"

"Nope," he said. He narrowed his eyes. "Did you happen to mention Carlotta's name to her?"

"Yeah." I remembered how hurt she'd seemed. "I don't think she was very happy about it."

"Shit," he said. Realizing he'd said it out loud, he quickly added, "Sorry." I shrugged, and he continued. "No wonder she didn't call me. I wonder what she's up to."

"So, who's Carlotta?" This woman seemed to be the key to everything.

Ramos frowned. "She's Manetto's old flame, from a long time ago. She left him, and I don't think he ever got over her. Since we were down there on a wild goose chase, Manetto thought we should make the most of it, and stop by for old time's sake.

"Anyway, she was pretty happy to see him, but mostly because she was in trouble. You see, she never approved of Manetto's occupation, but now that it looked like it could actually help her, she was happy to use him."

"How?" I asked.

"She was being bribed by the drug cartel." At my wide eyes, he nodded. "Yup, the CIA got that much right. Since she works for the police, she had a lot of inside information that would help the cartel escape capture. She needed a way out and figured Manetto would help her."

"Why? Just for old time's sake?"

"Not exactly. They were holding her son hostage," he paused, locking his gaze with mine. "As it turns out – the kid's Manetto's son too."

"Holy hell!" I covered my mouth with surprise, but Ramos just laughed.

"That pretty much sums it up," he agreed.

"What about Uncle Joey? Is he all right?"

"He's fine. He hired mercenaries and we went with them to get his son back, then for good measure he took their money. He's pretty ruthless when he wants to be, and the fact that they had his son wasn't something he could forgive. The leader and most of that particular cartel are dead, but not all.

"That's where these guys who found you come in. They got to you because Manetto lost his phone in the confusion. Passwords, things like that, were all on there. By the time we blocked the phone, they had already hacked his accounts and found your phone number and address along with the info about the money transfer made to you. I'm really sorry," he said.

"As soon as we figured it out, he sent me back to protect you. I got lucky and picked up their trail, but not before they got to you. I'm really sorry," he repeated.

"Hey, it's all right. I'm okay. I got away." He was still beating himself up, so I changed the subject. "So... now what do we do?"

"You don't need to do anything," he said. "It's my job to take them out. After that, you'll be fine." Meaning they'd be dead and wouldn't be bothering me anymore.

"Oh." I guess that would take care of it all right. "What about the CIA? Won't they be looking for them too?"

"Yes," he said. "But I have a solution."

I clamped down tightly on my shields before I got a glimpse of what Ramos had planned. I really didn't want to know. "Is Uncle Joey coming back?" Who knew? Since he took out most of the drug cartel, maybe he'd stay and run things.

"Yes, but it's complicated. Now that he has a son, he wants to bring him into the business, but Carlotta is... opposed. She's not sure she's ready to leave Mexico, but it's unsafe there, so Manetto is trying to work it out so they can come here. If they can't come here, he's got to figure out a safe place for them elsewhere. So whatever happens, it's going to take some time."

"So he might not be coming back here?" I asked, a little hopefully.

"No, he'll come back. I just don't know if it will be with Carlotta and his son."

"How old is his son anyway?" Uncle Joey seemed too old to have a child.

"He's seventeen," Ramos said.

"Oh. That should make things easier."

"Yes," Ramos agreed. "The problem is Carlotta. I think Manetto still loves her." He glanced at me, realizing he'd said more than he wanted. "We'd better get you home."

"How are we going to do that? The CIA knows I was kidnapped. What am I going to tell them?"

"You got away," he shrugged. "Have you got your phone?"

"Yes, it's in my pocket."

"Then all you have to do is call your husband, and tell him what happened. Just leave out the part about me. He's probably at your house with the CIA right now. Tell them all you can remember about the men and what they wanted."

"But how will I explain how I got here?"

"I'll drop you off a little closer to the junkyard. They will find evidence of a shootout. Tell them that another car came in and the two groups of gunmen got into a fight. That's when you made your escape." I crinkled my forehead in disbelief. He smiled and continued. "You were right about Inspector Salazar. He's after you for the money, too."

"Good grief. Does everyone want a fast buck around here?"

Ramos shrugged. "This will put the CIA on the right trail. When they find all of them dead, they will figure it was a shootout and they all killed each other. It's perfect!"

"But Inspector Salazar isn't really here..."

Ramos smiled, and I realized my shields were still up and I'd missed that. "He's here, and I know where. It won't be too hard to bring these rivals together, and my work will be done, and you will be safe."

He made it sound like he was doing it all for me. I wasn't sure I liked that. "What about the money?"

He frowned. "You'd better put it someplace where you can make a little interest on it, because Manetto's going to want it back."

I sighed, shaking my head. "Already done."

"Good. Let's go"

As we drove closer to the junkyard, I went over my story with him. Satisfied, he dropped me off in the parking lot of a discount store around the corner. "I'll be watching," he said, and drove away. I pulled out my phone and called Chris. He answered on the first ring.

"Shelby? Where are you? Are you all right?" His voice was frantic, and I was sorry to put him through that.

"Yes, I'm fine. I got away." He was at home with the CIA, just like Ramos thought. I told him where I was and he told me to stay put while they came to get me. While I was waiting, I scanned the parking lot for any sign of Ramos, but he had disappeared. I also couldn't help looking for a white van, but after searching for a moment, I decided it would be safer to wait inside.

The black SUV pulled into the parking lot, but I waited until Bristow, Shaw and Chris got out. As soon as Chris stepped out of the van, I ran out the door and into his waiting arms. I realized then how frightened I'd been, and what a close call it was. He held onto me tightly, and didn't let me go, even holding me against his side on the drive home.

We entered the house, and I noticed the kitchen rugs were messed up, and Bristow was walking with a limp. There were also several more agents there, including some with FBI on their jackets. Bristow introduced me to the FBI agent in charge and explained that since it was a kidnapping, his agency was involved as well.

We sat in the living room, and I was grateful to have Chris' arm around me for this part. Bristow rubbed his ankle, and a guilty flush rose to my cheeks.

"What happened to your foot?" Chris asked, making small talk to ease the tension.

"I don't know," Bristow drew his brows together. "I got darted in the back, and it kind of hurts there, but my ankle feels like someone stepped on it or something." He focused his attention on me. "I'd sure like to know what happened after I blacked out."

I took a deep breath and began my story. "You slumped, and it kind of took me by surprise. I tried to catch you, and with your weight, we ended up on the floor. You were on top of me." Chris stiffened beside me, and Bristow flushed a bright red. That was probably too much information. "When I felt the dart in your back, I knew something bad was happening and I was in trouble. The door was still open, and I had to roll you off me to shut it. When I shoved the door closed, your foot was in the way."

As the truth dawned on Bristow, I grimaced. "Sorry about that." The rest of my story went pretty much how Ramos and I practiced it. I ended it by telling them about the shoot-out at the junkyard. "I don't know what's going on, but when they started shooting at each other, I was able to get away." Bristow and Shaw glanced at each other, impressed that I held it together well enough to escape. They were thinking it made sense, but something was missing.

"Do you think they were both part of the same drug cartel that kidnapped Uncle Joey?" I asked, trying to help them figure it out. "If they were, why were they shooting at each other?"

Bristow was wondering the same thing. He narrowed his eyes and glanced at me. "Tell me again about the phone call."

I told them about Inspector Salazar, and that he'd called me twice. "It wasn't until the second time that he called Manetto my uncle. He must have thought I could get the money because of that. But the guys who kidnapped me were different."

Shaw perked up. "How?" he asked.

"They said the money was theirs," I answered. "And they wanted me to get it for them because Uncle Joey stole it."

"So it's like two different groups fighting over the same money," Chris said. "And they both came after you without knowing about each other?"

"It looks that way," I said. I didn't want Chris to say too much, so I squeezed his leg kind of hard. I heard his inward yelp and sent him an apologetic smile. He was thinking I didn't have to do that, since he knew not to tell them about the money. Geeze. He wasn't a moron. Oops. Now I was in trouble with Chris.

"Do you think they'll come after me again?" I asked Bristow.

"I don't know," he answered. "Only if they think you still have the money, I suppose." He thought that was the only reason they came for me in the first place. He glanced at me again, trying to assess if I was lying or telling the truth. Both groups thought I had the money. Now why would they think that?

"I never should have called Mr. Manetto Uncle Joey. That must be why they came after me." My stomach clenched and tears came to my eyes. The pressure from the CIA, and all I'd gone through, was catching up with me. "I'm so sick of this mess. I wish I'd never taken that stupid job." This time I wasn't acting. I turned my face into Chris' chest, letting the tears soak his shirt. The realization that I'd almost been killed sent shudders through my body.

Chris held me tight, soothing me with his words that everything would be all right. I calmed down, and the tears stopped. Shaw offered me a tissue, which I gratefully accepted. Back in control, I apologized. "Sorry about that."

"It's okay," Bristow answered. "We've got agents looking for the van. If we find anything, we'll let you know."

"Do you think they'll come back?" I asked.

"We'll keep your house under surveillance for a few days," the FBI agent spoke for the first time. "But I don't think they'll try here again. I think after this, they'll go after Mr. Manetto's people." He was thinking that he wouldn't be surprised to have a few dead bodies show up. With all of them probably from Mexico.

Bristow wanted to get his hands on Uncle Joey. Word had reached him that one of the main drug lords had been killed, along with most of his organization. If Uncle Joey had done that, he wanted to know why, and then he wanted to thank him. He didn't think the people who had come here would survive for long. This might be one of those times when he didn't dig too deep. Let them kill each other off, and save him the worry of losing his own people. He felt sorry for me though.

"I think he's right." Bristow nodded toward the FBI agent. "We'll let them take care of this, but please call me if you get any more phone calls. Especially from Mr. Manetto. I'd like to ask him a few questions myself." He handed me his card and left with the others.

Chris closed the door behind them, and I sank deeper into the couch, finally relaxing. Chris sat beside me, equally drained by the day's events. "So, is that what really happened?" he asked.

"Not exactly," I said. "Ramos is the one who pulled into the junkyard and saved me. He'd been following those guys and knew they were after me."

"How did he know that?"

I told Chris the whole story about Uncle Joey, his son, and Carlotta. "It was losing his phone that got me involved.

They found out about the money transfer and everything. That's why they came after me."

"So how does the story with the two groups come in?" Chris asked.

"That part is true. One group is the guys who kidnapped me wanting their money back. The other group belongs to Inspector Salazar who's after me for the ransom money."

"He's here too?" Chris asked. He was thinking it was getting ridiculous.

"I guess so, at least according to Ramos he is. Ramos has been watching both of them. That's why he came up with the story about the shoot-out. He's hoping to make it happen for real, or at least make it look like that's what happened once he finds them."

"So," Chris said. "He's planning on taking them all out?"

"Yes."

Chris nodded, like it was something he'd expected, but was thinking how he'd like to go with him and make sure they were all dead.

Then he'd like to find Uncle Joey and put a few dozen bullet holes in him too. This whole thing was his fault, and when Manetto got back, he was going to tell him to leave me the hell alone. And if he ever did something like this again, it would be the last thing he ever did. His lips turned into a grim line as he envisioned doing all this, and it made me a little nervous.

It was time to calm the raging beast, but all his violent thoughts reminded me about Mercer, and I wondered if Dimples had him behind bars. I didn't want to bring it up with Chris in this mood, but I thought it was something that would be good to know.

I checked the home phone to see if there were any messages. Nothing. I knew there weren't any calls on my cell phone, so I guessed Dimples hadn't called. Did that mean Mercer was still out there? Not good.

"What are you doing?" Chris asked, coming out of his vengeance trance, and noticing the phone in my hand.

"Just wondering if Dimples had called. He's supposed to have Mercer in custody by now."

Chris shook his head, and his shoulders slumped. He wondered how this day could get any worse. In the excitement, he'd forgotten all about Mercer. Maybe he'd better get his gun loaded and carry it in the waistband of his pants at the small of his back like the guys on TV. He should have bought that shoulder holster he'd been looking at after all. Even with the FBI watching the house, that wouldn't stop a trained assassin. "Honey, you'd better get your stun gun recharged."

"Good idea," I said. "But before you load the gun, let me call Dimples and find out what's going on."

He glanced at me narrowly, scrunching his eyes together. Didn't I believe in following my own rules about not reading his mind? What was up with that?

I ignored him and made the call. Another detective picked up the phone, telling me that Dimples was unavailable. If I didn't know better, I'd think he was avoiding me. "That's okay," I said. "This is Shelby Nichols. Maybe you can help me. I just need to know if Mercer is in custody."

"Um... I think that's where Harris is right now. Out to apprehend the guy."

"Will you tell him to call me as soon as possible?" I asked.

"Sure," he answered. I thanked him and hung up. Turning toward Chris, I explained what he told me.

"So the bottom line is... he's not in custody yet," Chris said. With nervous energy, Chris jumped up and went into the bedroom for the gun.

"Are you sure that's necessary?" I asked, trailing behind.

Chris sent me a tight-lipped grimace and nodded. I shook my head and followed him, needing to put my stun flashlight in to recharge. "I still think you should wait. It's only three in the afternoon. He could be behind bars before the day is over."

He stopped and I bumped into him from behind. Turning, he grabbed me by the arms and gave me a little shake. "Do you realize you could have been killed today? And that was from some people we didn't even know about. We know about Mercer, and I'm not taking any chances."

His eyes were hard and his grip intense. It didn't take a mind reader to know he had reached his limit. "Okay," I said. It was on the tip of my tongue to apologize for this mess, but I held back, knowing that wasn't what he wanted to hear. His grip relaxed and he pulled me into his arms and held me tightly, like an apology for being so rough.

In our bedroom, he methodically loaded the gun, making sure the safety was on, and put it in the waistband of his pants. "Do you have Ramos' number?"

"What?" That hit me out of the blue, and I realized he was shielding his thoughts from me. "Wait just a minute, you are not going to get involved with Ramos. Defending me is one thing, but going after those guys is not... you can't!"

He shook his head before I finished. "It's not what you think. I don't want to get involved in that. I just want Ramos to let me know when those guys are out of the picture, so I don't have to worry about them."

"You already don't have to worry about them," I said. "Ramos will take care of it. That's what he came here to do."

I caught a flicker of annoyance from Chris, and I realized that wasn't the real reason he wanted to call Ramos. He wanted help to get rid of Mercer, and figured Ramos was the man for the job.

"Chris," I said. "You're freaking me out. Let Dimples do his job. They'll get Mercer."

"Yes, but can they put him away for long?" he asked. "He might go to prison, he might not. Even if he does, he'll get out someday. Then where will you be? He'll come after you. He won't rest until you're dead."

"Okay. I'll talk to Ramos about him and see what he says." With that, I left to get dinner started.

Trying to act normal around a couple of teenagers and an angry husband frazzled my nerves. I could only smile and sound positive for so long. Especially when I was the only one trying. The good thing about it was that my children, being the self-absorbed teenagers that they were, mostly ignored me. It kind of hurt that they didn't notice the strain I was under, but on the other hand, it was good that they were oblivious.

Chris didn't want to tell them about any of this, and I concurred. We would tell them if they needed to know, and only then.

At eight-thirty p.m. the phone rang. My heart sped up, hoping it was good news. "Hello?" I said.

"Shelby," Dimples answered. "Sorry it took me so long to get back to you. It's been a long day."

"Is Mercer in custody?" I needed to know. Now.

"That's what I'm calling to tell you." He paused. "It's bad news. We tried to pick him up, but he's gone, and we don't know where he is."

I had a feeling that would happen, but hearing it was ten times worse. "What do you mean? He can't be gone. He wants to kill me. Do you know how that feels?"

"I'm sorry, Shelby. I can keep the patrol cars in your neighborhood for a little longer. Until we catch him." He took a deep breath. "If you had actually witnessed him kill-ing someone, we could put you in the witness protection program, but all we have are your premonitions, and they don't qualify for that sort of thing."

"Yeah, I get it." I couldn't help the sarcasm in my voice.

"We're not going to stop looking. We've got several leads, and we'll follow them until we track him down." His voice got louder, like he was trying to convince me of his sincerity.

"It's okay," I answered. "Right now the FBI is watching the house because of an incident that happened earlier."

"What? What are you talking about?"

I decided to tell him a shortened version of my day. When I finished, there was silence on the other end. "Dim-ples? Are you there?"

"I don't know how you do it, Shelby." He sounded stunned. "Why didn't you tell me about the CIA and the phone calls? I might have been able to help you."

"Honestly, I didn't think about it. I never thought this would happen – that's for sure."

"So now, besides an assassin for hire, you've got a crook-ed inspector and a Mexican drug cartel after you as well?" His voice got higher with each word. I was sure if I could hear his thoughts, there would be plenty of swearing going on.

"Um... look on the bright side," I said cheerfully. "Maybe Mercer will get caught in the cross-fire and we won't have to worry about him anymore."

Dimples groaned. "Just stay home tonight. Don't go any-where." As an afterthought he added, "By any chance, did you tell the FBI about Mercer?"

"Uh... no. I didn't think about that. I guess I was hoping he'd be in custody by now." That was probably not the nic-est thing to say, and I immediately regretted it. He groaned again, letting me know I'd hit him below the belt, and I felt bad. "I shouldn't have said that. It's not your fault"

"Just tell me who the FBI agent is so I can call him and let him know about Mercer."

I gave him the name and he hung up, promising to call me if he heard anything new. It was a phrase that was starting to sound familiar.

Now I had to tell Chris that Mercer was still out there. How would he take it? There had to be something I could do. Then it hit me! What an idiot I'd been. The solution to the problem was in front of me all along. If Ricky had known who Mercer was, I was sure Ramos knew him, and probably Uncle Joey as well.

All I needed to do was tell Uncle Joey to let Mercer know I was off limits, and if he ever came near me, he was as good as dead. Mercer would understand those kinds of threats. If that didn't work, I could always offer him money not to kill me. I had five million dollars for Pete's sake. That idea probably wouldn't work, since there were so many things wrong with it, but it was something to think about.

So really, Chris was on the mark when he wanted to talk to Ramos, only in a different way than he was thinking. I shouldn't hesitate to use the resources I had to keep my family safe. I tried not to think about how this might keep me indebted to Uncle Joey, but seriously, he owed me. Big time.

"You look like the cat who ate the canary," Chris said, startling me. "Who was on the phone?"

"Dimples," I answered. "They didn't arrest Mercer because he's nowhere to be found. But I think I just solved that problem."

"Tell me," Chris said.

I explained what I was thinking, and Chris listened with calm detachment. I tried to probe his thoughts, but he had sealed them up tight. I wasn't sure how I felt about that, but I knew right now he needed the space. When I was done, he nodded his acceptance of the plan.

"I think that's our best option," he agreed. "I don't want to get back on Manetto's payroll, but your plan just might work. In the meantime, I'm going to sleep with this under my pillow." He held up his gun with a flourish, and stuffed it away.

"Really?" I wondered how well Chris could sleep with a gun under his pillow. He didn't toss and turn like a lot of people, so maybe it would be all right. But what if he accidentally pushed the trigger somehow. I didn't think I could sleep next to a loaded gun.

"How about if you put it on the night stand instead?" He pursed his lips in annoyance. "I just don't want to get my head blown off," I said in defense.

"All right," he relented, and put it on the night table.

"Thanks," I said, relieved. "And make sure if you hear anything, like footsteps or something, you turn the light on before you shoot. I don't want to get shot because I had to go to the bathroom."

He huffed, but didn't answer.

"Oh, and one more thing," I continued. "If you hear someone out in the hall, make sure it's not one of our kids getting up to use the bathroom either."

"Are you done?" he asked.

"Nope. I'm sure I can think of something else."

"Okay, I get it. I'll put the gun in the drawer." He slipped it inside. "How's that?"

"Better," I said, and got into bed. I fluffed up my pillow until he got under the covers and turned off his light. "Are you going to sleep now?" I asked.

He sighed. "I don't think so."

"Good," I smiled, turning toward him. "Because..." I kissed his lips, and his neck, and nibbled on his ear. "I don't think... I can sleep... yet."

His low growl was music to my ears, and much later, I was able to drift off to sleep with the panic and fear of the day tucked harmlessly away.

Chapter 9

The next day dawned cloudy with a chance of rain. During the course of the morning, I checked the street several times to see if the FBI surveillance car was still there. It was. It looked like as long as I stayed home, I was pretty safe from everyone that might be after me.

I still wanted to talk to Ramos, and as soon as everyone was gone, I checked the recent calls on my phone until I found his number and called him.

"Yes?" His low voice was barely above a whisper.

"Ramos... it's Shelby," I said, equally quiet. "I wonder if you have some time to talk today? I need your help."

"Would you like to meet about noon?"

"Well," I hedged. "I would, but I'm kind of stuck here."

"What do you mean?" he asked

"After yesterday, the FBI put a surveillance team to watch my house in case any of those guys came back."

"I see," he said. "Then you should be okay for a while. What is it you wanted to tell me?"

"Just that those guys are not the only ones after me. There's this guy, Mercer, who wants to kill me too. I was hoping that maybe with Uncle Joey's influence, he would be willing to back off. Do you know the guy I'm talking about?"

Ramos was silent for a moment. "Yes. I've heard of him. Why does he want to kill you?

"Let's just say I was involved with his first arrest, but they let him go because of lack of evidence. After that, I helped the police find the evidence to charge him for murder, but when they went back to arrest him he was gone."

"How do you know he intends to kill you?" Ramos asked.

"After he got out the first time, he found me in front of Chris' office and threatened me. Ricky was there. You could ask him."

"I will," Ramos said. He was silent for a while, and I crossed my fingers, willing him to help me.

"I think I know what to do," he said. "But I'll need your help."

"Sure," I agreed, my pulse fluttering. "Anything."

"Hmm..." he grunted. "You may be sorry you said that. This could be dangerous."

"Not any more dangerous than it is already," I answered. "Considering I've got three different groups of people after me."

"You've got a point there," he said. "Let me figure out the details and I'll get back to you. In the meantime, stay put."

"Okay." He disconnected and I pocketed my phone. Staying put was the easy part. It gave me lots of time to worry about what he wanted me to do to get out of this mess. Maybe I shouldn't have agreed so easily. In fact, I should have insisted he take care of it without me, since this was all Uncle Joey's fault in the first place.

Except for Mercer. I did that all on my own. Okay, so maybe I could forgive Uncle Joey as long as he got rid of Mercer for me. That would make us even as far as I was concerned. It was a good trade-off. Hopefully, he would think so too.

Today was my day to go to the gym, but that probably wasn't a good idea, so I did a few push-ups and crunches. After running up and down the stairs a few times, I called it good and hit the shower. I applied a little make-up and, with nowhere to go, pulled on my standard jeans and a t-shirt.

For breakfast, I poured some cereal into my bowl and glanced out my window to check on the surveillance car. It was gone, and my stomach clenched. I scanned up and down the street, but couldn't find it anywhere. Before the panic set in, I tried to reason it out. Maybe they just needed a potty break. And food was important. They could have left to grab something to eat.

Both of those explanations made sense, but I still couldn't shake the dread in the pit of my stomach. Without taking a bite, I dumped my cereal down the disposal, too upset to eat.

I probably should call someone, but whom? The FBI? The CIA? Ramos? Chris? Dimples? I knew all the doors in my house were locked, but suddenly, it felt more like a trap than a safe haven. Like a target was painted on my roof pointing out to everyone that "hey, here I am, come get me." All Mercer, or anyone else, would have to do was break a window or kick in the door, and bam... they were in.

I practically flew into the bedroom and grabbed my stun flashlight. Thankfully, it was recharged and ready to go. I hesitated over the drawer that held the gun. Should I take it? Was I ready to use it? I didn't know if I could actually shoot someone, but if it was them or me, I probably could.

I got it out, checked the safety, and found an extra purse to put it in. The kidnappers still had my favorite one in their van. I ran back to the window and glanced out, realizing that all of this preparation was probably just me being paranoid, and they'd be sitting there like usual.

Nope, they were still gone. But it had only been five minutes since I'd discovered it. I could give them some more time, and while I was waiting, I'd call Agent Bristow. His card was around here somewhere. The kitchen counter was where everything seemed to end up, so I started there. Moving junk mail, bills, and a magazine, I gave a little victory yelp when I finally found it. I grabbed the phone and put the call through.

"Bristow," he answered.

I let out my breath, relieved to reach him. "Agent Bristow, this is Shelby Nichols. The FBI guys are gone. Do you know anything about that? Were they only staying until this morning? I would have called them, but they didn't give me their card like you did," I rushed to explain.

"Um... they're probably just gone for a break or something."

"Oh. So I shouldn't be worried?"

"No. I'm sure they'll be back." When I didn't say anything, he continued. "But why don't you call me if they're not back in an hour."

"Okay," I said, disappointed.

"You haven't heard from the Mexicans again have you?" he asked.

"Nope."

"You should be fine," he said, dismissively. "I don't think they'll involve you anymore, and I have a feeling Manetto will take care of them for us."

I thanked him and disconnected. He didn't seem too concerned, but then he didn't know about Mercer either. Trying to decide who to call next, my phone rang, startling me. I checked the caller ID and it said Thrasher Development. Was Uncle Joey back? Why didn't Ramos tell me?

I'd better answer it. "Hello?"

"Shelby, it's Jackie. I'm supposed to call and tell you not to worry about Mercer anymore. It's been taken care of."

Surprise shot through me. "Really? When I talked to Ramos this morning, he said he'd get to work on it, but I didn't think it would be so fast. What happened?" She hesitated and I wondered what was going on. Too bad I couldn't read minds over the phone.

"Mr. Manetto got involved. He's back, and he took care of it."

"That's great," I said, not really feeling so great about it, knowing he was probably going to want something from me. "When did he get back?"

"He'd like to talk to you soon," she continued, ignoring my question. "But don't worry, as long as you still have the money, everything should be fine. You still have it don't you?"

"Well, I didn't give it to the Mexicans, if that's what you're thinking," I said, a tiny bit offended.

"Then there's nothing to worry about."

The way she said it gave me the creeps. Like I should start worrying. "Good," I managed to say.

"When can you come in?" she asked. "Ramos did tell you Mr. Manetto wanted the money back, didn't he?"

"Yes, but now's not really the best time," I hedged. I really needed to talk to Ramos about this. "I have the FBI watching the house because of the problem yesterday with the Mexicans. I think I'd better wait a few days until they're not watching my every move. The FBI would probably wonder why I was talking to a crime boss."

"Oh," she said. "All right. I'll let Mr. Manetto know, and see what we can set up for later."

She disconnected before I could say another word. What was up with her? Uncle Joey usually called me himself when he wanted something. Was she serious about Mercer? Was he really out of the picture? How had Uncle Joey taken care of him? Something didn't add up, and I wasn't about to let down my guard.

I checked out the window again, and there they were. The FBI was back. I guess Bristow was right, and they were only gone for a break. I sank onto the couch, relieved and yet still anxious.

The only person who could help me feel better was Ramos, so I dialed his number. It went straight to voice mail, dashing my hopes. I left him a quick message to call me and hung up. I hated when that happened. Now I had to wait and worry, which wasn't good for my digestive system, especially on an empty stomach. A piece of toast was about all I could handle, but it should help the queasiness go away.

I thought about calling Chris, but I didn't want him to worry. As long as the FBI was watching, I should just try and chill. I could tell him all about it when he got home. I spent the next few hours doing laundry with the phone never far from my side. Three o'clock came and went, with no calls from anyone. Was Ramos all right?

At five o'clock, I was grateful it was my turn to pick up Savannah from dance class. It meant I could finally leave the house. Just opening the door gave me that euphoric feeling of freedom. I backed the car out of my driveway and gave a little wave to the FBI agents. They didn't wave back, but started their car and followed me.

I was halfway to class when my phone rang. My heart skipped a beat to see it was Ramos. Quickly pulling over to the curb, I answered the phone. "Hello?"

"Hey," Ramos said. "I've got things worked out. I'm on my way to pick you up."

"Um... I just left to pick up Savannah from dance class. But it won't take me more than about twenty minutes to get back."

"You left the house?" He sounded worried.

"Don't worry, the FBI agents are following me, so I should be all right."

A loud pounding sounded on my window, and I jumped. One of the FBI agents stood by my door, giving me a clear view of his white shirt and tie. "Just a minute," I said to Ramos. I rolled down my window to explain where I was going, and the agent leaned down.

The words stuck in my throat. It was the guy who'd kidnapped me! Before I could react, he poked a gun in my face and told me to move over. I scrambled to the other side, thinking I could get out of the car before he got in. I pulled on the handle, but his accomplice was there, and pushed it shut.

He leaned down to stare at me. His eyes squinted to tiny slits, and his jaw thrust out with anger. I was so screwed. The cold barrel of a gun poked into my ribs and I gasped. "Okay, you got me." I slid the phone to the area by my feet, hoping Ramos was still listening, and raised my hands in surrender. "What happened to the FBI guys?" I asked, a little loud.

The second man jumped into the back seat, signaling for the car to take off. "Where are we going?" I practically shouted.

"Silencio!" the driver hissed. He pulled into traffic and turned several times, getting on the main street that would take us west. Several miles later, he pulled behind a building that had a big 'for lease' sign on it. We parked next to the white van.

I had to let Ramos know where I was. "My daughter's dance class isn't far from... ouch!" The driver shoved the gun back in my ribs. He glared at me and I closed my mouth.

"Get out," he said. The other guy opened my door and I slowly reached down for my purse. "What are you doing?" he said.

"I need my purse. It's got all my bank account numbers in it. Don't you want the money? Isn't that what this is about?"

"All right," he said. "But don't make any sudden moves."

I grabbed my purse, and pushed the phone under the seat with my foot. I got out of the car, and stood, the man in the back seat right behind me. The driver led the way to the door and unlocked it. He ushered me inside, and the other man jerked my purse out of my hands.

"Hey!" I made a grab for my purse, but the driver put the gun in my face.

"This way," he said, ushering me down a hallway and into a large room. It was dark inside, but light from a desk lamp sitting on a table cut through the dimness. Other than that, the place was empty. He marched me to the desk and opened the laptop that was set up there. After powering it on, he typed in his password. Turning toward me with a satisfied smile, he pulled out the chair in an invitation for me to sit.

"Now," he began. "We will begin the money transfer from your account to mine."

"Okay," I said meekly. "I need the account numbers. They're in my purse." If I could get to my gun, I might have a chance to get out of here.

The guy with my purse opened it up and his eyes widened. From the string of Spanish words in his mind, I knew he'd found my gun. "What is this?" he asked, pulling the gun from the bag. He put it in his pocket, and rummaged through my purse some more. I held my breath, hoping he wouldn't take the stun flashlight too. He pulled something shiny out, and my heart sank.

He examined it, and I realized he was the one I'd used it on. He realized it at the same time, and a glint of something dark flashed in his eyes. Oh great! Now I was going be tortured before they killed me.

He handed me my purse, which was basically empty, and brushed the flashlight against the back of my neck. Shivers ran down my spine and I cringed. He smiled with a hint of anticipation, and my stomach clenched. My mouth went dry, and my head tingled like I was going to faint or something.

I started to slump, and the other guy grabbed my arm, holding me up. He spoke rapidly in Spanish, and jerked me back into a sitting position. Kneeling down in front of me, he roughly patted my cheeks. Next he handed me a bottle of water. "Drink this," he commanded. I eagerly took it, and gulped down a few swallows.

"That's enough." He grabbed the bottle from my hands and gestured toward the computer. "I have it all set up. Just put your bank account numbers in this area, and the transfer will be complete."

He had his account numbers already in the 'transfer to' field, but unfortunately, I had lied. I didn't know what my account number was and it wasn't in my purse. Besides that, the money wasn't just in one account. It was in several.

I rummaged through my purse and tried to think of what to do next. Should I try putting in some fake numbers? No, that didn't seem too smart. Then it hit me. "You know what? This is the wrong purse. The account numbers are in my other purse. The one I left in your van yesterday."

Some swearing in Spanish came from his mind. "I don't think so," he said. "Or we would have found it when we did a thorough search."

"Oh," I said. "Okay, the truth is, I don't know the account numbers." The gunman tensed, raising his gun to my head. "But I can get them from my bank account. I just need to login on the Internet to my bank."

His teeth clenched and he spoke loudly in Spanish. Getting control, he took a deep breath and lowered the gun. "Fine. Open another window and do it."

I took my time finding the bank on the Internet. Once there, I logged in, hoping I had the right password. I was so rattled I wasn't sure what one I'd used before. It said 'incorrect password' and kicked me out. The gunman beside me groaned. "I'm trying to remember the right password," I said. "Just give me a minute."

He huffed out a breath. "Sure. But if you don't get it right, we start hurting you. Maybe that will help jog your memory."

I felt the blood drain from my head, and my hands started to shake. "Okay. I get it. I'm doing the best I can." What was the stupid password? I tried another one, and it still didn't work.

"You have one more chance," the gunman said. "You'd better make it count."

I typed in another one, but hesitated. What if this one was wrong too? I knew it had both letters and numbers. That's when it came to me, and I deleted it and put in the one that had to be right. This time it would work. Still, I hesitated to push the enter button. Had I given Ramos enough time to come after me?

A small creaking sound, like a door opening, came from behind us. The gunmen turned, raising their weapons. One of them hurried to the door and disappeared out of sight, while the other put his hand on my shoulder. "Keep working," he said. It didn't look like he was going to leave my side.

Hope broke through my fear. Was Ramos here to rescue me? Another scuffling sound came, followed by silence. What was going on? The gunman swore under his breath, and put the gun next to my head. "I will kill her!" he yelled. His arm wavered, and he shouted something in Spanish.

A whizzing sound cut him off, and he fell back against the table, blood oozing from a bullet wound between the eyes. As he slipped to the floor, the gun dropped harmlessly from his hand and I screamed, jerking back in my seat.

I swallowed the bile that rose in my throat and took deep breaths. Ramos had saved me just in time. My eyes watered with relief, and I blinked the tears away. Footsteps approached, and I glanced up.

Horror twisted my stomach, sending shards of fear through my veins. Instead of Ramos coming toward me, it was Mercer! Shock froze my breath and I couldn't seem to move. How could this be?

"Hello Shelby," he said conversationally. "You look surprised to see me." He smiled and lowered his gun. Holding it sideways, he began unscrewing the silencer with glove-clad fingers. It came off, and he put it in a space on his belt. Next, he slipped the gun into a holster. "It seems you have friends in high places."

With the gun put away, I found my voice. "You're not going to kill me?" It came out kind of squeaky, and he chuckled.

"Not today."

"Really?" I couldn't seem to get my brain to think straight.

"That's right," he answered. He stepped closer to me, pulling a cloth from his pocket, and I cringed away. His lips curled in response to my fear. "You might want to turn that off." He nodded toward the computer.

I focused on the screen, willing to do whatever he said. Since I'd never logged in, it was easy to exit the site and turn off the computer.

"Good," Mercer said. "Besides the computer, what else did you touch?" His dark eyes gleamed in the light, but his expression remained aloof and professional.

"Um... just the desk in front of the computer and the chair."

He nodded, and briskly wiped down the computer, moving to the desk and chair. I stood to get out of his way.

"Anything else?" he asked.

I glanced around and tried to avoid looking at the dead man sprawled on the ground. My gaze was drawn to him anyway and I shivered, knowing that it could have been me lying there with dead, sightless eyes.

"No," I said, pulling my gaze away with a determined swallow. "Except for my purse." I picked it up from the floor and remembered my gun and stun flashlight. "The other guy..." I glanced at Mercer. "He took my gun and my flashlight out of my purse. I think he put them in his jacket."

"Your gun?" Mercer's brows rose into his forehead. "Well, we'd better get it back. You may need it sometime."

I felt the blood drain from my face, and he smiled, thinking taunting me was more fun than it ought to be. Strangely, that thought helped settle me down. He was already walking out the door, and I hurried to catch up with him.

The other guy was sprawled near the outer door, his head tilted at an unnatural angle. Mercer knelt beside him and quickly found my gun and flashlight. I was hoping he wouldn't notice the flashlight was a stun gun too, in case I ever needed to use it on him, but no such luck.

"Hmm... is this the one that carries one million volts of attack-stopping power?"

"Yes," I sniffed. Did everyone know?

"Does it work pretty well?"

"Yeah, pretty good. I used it on him yesterday, and it dropped him flat." I nodded toward the dead guy and suppressed a shudder.

"Nice," Mercer said, and handed it to me. "Well, that just about does it." He glanced at me sharply. "It would be best if we pretended that you'd never been here."

"Um... okay," I said, understanding the threat.

He checked his watch. "You are a little late to pick up your daughter, but if you leave right now you should still get there in time."

"Oh, right!" I hurried over to my car. "Wait. My keys."

"Are in the ignition," he finished my sentence.

I glanced at him. "Who sent you?"

His smile came slowly. "You'd better get going." He wasn't going to answer me, so I searched his thoughts. He was thinking that I looked a little shell-shocked, and he hoped I could drive home without killing anyone.

Flustered, I got in my car and poured all my concentration into driving. I pulled up to Savannah's dance class, and she ran out with a smile on her face, happy she'd done so well on a new dance she'd learned. Running on automatic, I asked her about her day and let her voice pour over me in a soothing cascade of normalcy.

I got to my street, and a spurt of anger shot up my spine to find the FBI surveillance car parked across from my house. Where had they been earlier? How had the Mexicans taken their place? I turned into my driveway and pulled into the garage, wondering if they'd even known I was gone.

Anger surged over me. I told Savannah to go inside and marched over to their car. I didn't recognize either of the men inside, but that didn't mean anything, since I'd never seen them in the first place. I waited while the driver rolled down his window.

"Can I help you?" he asked.

"Yes," I said defiantly. "Where were you this afternoon? Because you weren't here, so don't lie to me."

The man squinted, put off by my anger. He glanced at the other agent before turning to me. "We got called away... but we're back now. Is there a problem?" He was thinking that I had no idea how lucky I was for the protection they were giving me. No one ever said they would be watching my house around the clock, but they'd been there most of the day, even when there were a lot of cases more important than mine to spend time on. I should be grateful they were there at all.

That last thought about did me in. I was ready to take the gun out of my purse and shoot the tire or something. Instead, I took a deep breath and let out a big sigh. "You know... you might as well leave," I began. "Go and take care of those more important cases. I don't need you anymore."

His thoughts clouded with confusion. How had I known he was thinking that? I must be a great reader if I could pick that up. It was an asset the FBI regarded highly.

I shook my head and turned to leave. I did not want to have this conversation.

"Wait," he called. "What happened?"

I wasn't about to tell him. Not after Mercer's veiled threat. Besides, I didn't know if Ramos was involved in any of this, and I certainly didn't want to mention Uncle Joey. "Nothing," I said. "I guess I was just mad you weren't here when I left to pick up my daughter." It galled me to do it, but I decided I needed to make an attempt at being civil, otherwise, they'd know something wasn't right. "Sorry I got mad. You can stay if you want."

He wasn't sure he believed me, but sometimes when people were scared, they said stupid things, so he let it go.

Grateful he'd accepted my explanation, I hurried back to my house. After closing the garage, I entered my kitchen and sagged against the counter. I probably shouldn't have said anything. Once they found out those guys were dead, would they question me? Of course, how did I know they'd even find them? Maybe Mercer was going to get rid of the bodies and no one would ever know.

It was all starting to get to me. I ordered pizza for dinner and disappeared into the bathroom. Without consciously deciding it, I put in the plug and turned on the bathtub faucets full blast. Next, I dumped a ton of my favorite bubble bath into the filling tub. While it filled, I stripped and stepped into the hot water, drawing the scented air into my lungs with a deep breath.

I settled back, sinking into soft steaming water. I held it together until something Mercer said came back to haunt me. My heart pounded with the realization that he knew it was my turn to pick up Savannah. He knew where she was.

From there, it went downhill. I couldn't keep the memory of the blood, bullet hole, and sightless eyes of the dead gunmen out of my mind. Knowing they were going to kill me only made it worse. The burning question remained. Who had hired Mercer? And where was Ramos?

With that, I realized my phone was still in my car under the seat. I should probably get it, but for now, it was all I could do not to cry.

Half an hour later, my fingers and toes were turning into prunes and the water was getting cold. I figured I could hide in the bathtub for a while longer, or pull myself together and take charge of my life. I had two things going for me. First, I wasn't dead. And second, I had a husband and children who loved and needed me.

It made me remember when I was a young wife and mother. I'd wondered how I could keep going when I felt overwhelmed by crying babies and little sleep. It was a twenty-four/seven job that gave me little time for myself. I had to focus on different things, like making it through the day without losing it when one of my kids had a major meltdown in the grocery store, or some other public place.

I learned to take things in stride, and to face unpleasantness that pushed me to the limit with fortitude and patience. It also made me realize that there was a lot I could deal with. I didn't need to fall apart. I could find the strength to do what needed to be done.

Now was one of those times. I needed to act with that strength. I got out of the tub and put on a fresh set of clothes. The t-shirt I'd worn had tiny blood splatters on it, so I bunched it up and took it outside to the garbage can. I noticed the surveillance car was gone and shrugged, not allowing myself to care. On the way through the garage, I opened.the car door and found my phone. It was still working, but Ramos must have hung up since I had several missed calls from him.

I hit redial and the call went straight to his voicemail, so I quickly explained that I was safe and not to worry. I didn't know what was going on between him, Jackie, and Uncle Joey, but I wanted to save that for when I could talk to him.

The pizza arrived and I took it into the family room where Josh was playing a video game. I called to Savannah and persuaded them to watch a show with me while we ate. Josh wondered what was wrong with me, since this was out of the ordinary, but decided not to complain.

I got out the first season of Castle, one of my favorite detective shows, and admired how Kate Beckett hardly flinched when she saw a murder victim. If she could handle it, even with all that blood, so could I. In less than an hour, the case was wrapped up and the bad guy caught. It gave me hope. The fact that it was only a TV show hardly bothered me at all.

At least that's what I told myself. Chris got home just as the show ended, surprised and confused to find us watching TV. He took in my haunted eyes and his brows drew together in a frown. His concern hit a nerve and my eyes filled up with tears. Chagrined, I hastily got up from the couch and offered him some pizza.

"Looks good," he said. "How about we go in the kitchen." He could tell I was upset and wondered what had happened.

As soon as I set the pizza down, I rushed into his arms. I knew it wasn't fair to let him worry, but I needed a moment to feel his protective arms around me.

"What happened?" he asked. "Where's the surveillance car?"

"Let's go out on the deck," I suggested. "I don't want the kids to hear."

"Sure," he agreed, and opened the patio door, pulling me behind him. We squeezed onto the faded couch, and I began my story, holding nothing back. By the time I was done, my hands were shaking, and my stomach was in knots.

Chris paled and pushed his feelings of helplessness aside with a surge of raw anger. "What happened to the FBI? They were supposed to be guarding you."

"They were here when I got back." I explained my little chat with them. "They must have taken me at my word and left."

"Or else they found the dead guys," Chris added.

"That's a possibility," I agreed.

"The question remains. Who sent Mercer? Since he knew about that place, had he been following them? Or was he following you? Is that what Jackie meant when she told you not to worry about him? Because Manetto had hired him to take care of the Mexicans?" Chris pursed his lips, a sure sign that he was agitated, but trying to work things through. "What happened to Ramos? You said he called and that's when you pulled over. Tell me what he said again."

"He just said that he had a plan and was coming over to get me. He seemed pretty upset that I'd left the house. That's when the Mexicans shoved the gun in my face. I'm pretty sure Ramos heard what was going on. I thought he was the one who had come to save me."

"You called and left a message, but he hasn't called you back, right?"

"Uh-huh," I said. "Something's going on with Jackie, Ramos and Uncle Joey. I just don't know what it is. Hopefully, Ramos will call me back, and we'll know."

Chris nodded, but he was thinking that we shouldn't count on Ramos for anything. He was loyal to Manetto first, and it was time I understood that.

"Do you think we have to worry about Mercer anymore?" I asked.

"I don't think we have to worry that he'll kill you... unless someone pays him to do it." His words made me shiver. In response, he put his arm around me.

"So what do we do now?" I asked.

"I think the next step is to arrange a meeting with Manetto. This has gone on long enough. We need to get this settled and give him back his money."

"I think you're right," I agreed, relieved to do something. "I'll call Uncle Joey tomorrow and set it up."

"Good," Chris said. "And this time, I'm coming with you."

My heart swelled, and I smiled up at him. He gazed into my eyes, thinking that I'd nearly been killed again. It shook him up, and he wondered how I was holding up so well after witnessing such violence. Seeing a guy get shot in the head had to be horrific, let alone...

"I'm trying not to think about that," I said. "It would help if you didn't either."

"Oh, sorry," he said, instantly contrite. "I just can't imagine how awful that was for you."

I sighed. "I'll probably have nightmares. But I'm trying to put it out of my mind."

"Yeah, I get that," he said. "I'll try not to think about it either."

At that, my eyes filled up with tears. I was a total moron. Here he was, trying to understand how I felt, and I was chewing him out. How could I be so mean? I wasn't supposed to be listening anyway. Where were those stupid shields?

"Shelby? It's okay," Chris said. "I'm not mad that you read my mind."

"You should be," I said. "I'm mad at myself. How could I be so insensitive? You're being supportive and understanding, and here I am chewing you out for it."

"It's not a big deal," he said. "I promise." He turned so he was facing me and gazed into my eyes. "What matters to me is that you're alive. That we're here together. I love you, and nothing's going to change that. Not your mind-reading. Not this mess. Nothing."

My tears quieted. "Are you sure?" I asked.

"Of course," he said. "I love you."

"I love you too."

"Now... if you stopped cooking... I might have to think about it, but other than that..."

"What?" I pushed against him and he caught me in his arms and soundly kissed me. My stomach unclenched and I relaxed in his arms. It was going to be all right. Somehow we'd get through this mess.

Chapter 10

The next morning, I called Uncle Joey's cell phone. A loud tone sounded with a recording that said the number had been disconnected. I sighed, remembering what Ramos had told me about Uncle Joey's lost phone, but that was the only number I had. Now what?

I was worried since I still hadn't heard from Ramos, and decided to try him again. I wasn't expecting him to answer, so when he did, it surprised me. "Ramos? This is Shelby," I said. "Are you all right?"

"I'll live," he answered. His voice was hardly more than a whisper.

"What happened?"

"Took a bullet," he said. "I thought Salazar had you... guess I was wrong."

"Where are you?" My heart pounded with worry. "Are you in the hospital?"

"No... home."

"In the apartment at Thrasher?"

"No... other home. I'll be fine. Heard you got away. That's good. Don't worry about Salazar." He paused. "These pills make me sleepy. I'll call you back... when I'm awake." The line clicked, ending the call.

Guilt swamped my senses, and I sagged into a chair overlooking the street. Poor Ramos. No wonder he never called me back. I felt sick. How bad was he hurt? Was he home alone? It sounded like no one was there to take care of him. Maybe I should find out where he lived and take him some soup or something.

A familiar car pulled up to my house, and two men got out. I recognized the FBI agents from yesterday, and my stomach clenched. Had they found the dead Mexicans? Were they here to question me? What did they know? I started to panic before remembering that I could read their minds. That gave me a huge advantage. There was nothing to worry about.

The doorbell rang, and I flinched. So much for my pep talk. Did I really have to open the door? I took a deep breath for courage and marched to the door. Might as well get it over with.

"Mrs. Nichols," the agent said. "Do you have a minute? We won't take long, but we wanted to tell you what was going on."

"Of course," I said. "Come in."

"Thanks." He introduced me to the other agent and took a seat on my couch. "We just wanted you to know that we found your kidnappers, so you don't need to worry about them anymore." He was thinking that if I didn't act surprised enough, it might indicate that I already knew they were dead. Then he'd know if I was involved, or had anything to do with their deaths.

"Oh, that's great news," I said and waited for him to tell me more. When he didn't, I asked, "So... are they in jail?"

"No," he admitted. "They're both dead."

"Oh," I grimaced. "What happened? Did they resist arrest or something?"

"No. Someone killed them," he answered and paused.

This whole dancing around the issue was getting on my nerves. "You know, for coming here to tell me what's going on, you're doing a pretty lousy job." Did I just say that out loud?

The other agent spoke up. "You're right. Sorry. It's just that we were wondering if you knew anything about it." Asking me that made him realize how silly it sounded. The only reason they even wondered was because I was gone about the same time the shootings happened. That didn't mean I was involved. How could I be? Insinuating that I was that kind of person didn't make any sense.

"About who killed them?" I said, incredulously.

He was ready to apologize when the other agent spoke up.

"I know it sounds a bit farfetched, but we still had to ask." He was remembering how angry I was when I talked to him yesterday. Like he hadn't been there to protect me from the bad guys. That set him off that something wasn't right. Then, when they'd found the bodies and figured the time of death, it clicked in place, and he wondered if I knew who killed them. Of course, it was a long shot. His boss figured it was all part of the drug dealers taking care of 'loose ends' and didn't really care who shot them, but he felt it his duty to ask.

I was shaking my head. "I don't have a clue."

The other agent was embarrassed and quickly stood. "Thanks for your time." He stuck out his hand to shake mine.

I stood, shaking his hand. "Sure. So does this mean we're done? You won't be watching my house anymore?" Did

Dimples tell them about Mercer? I remembered that he was going to mention it to them. Should I say something?

"No reason to. They won't be bothering you anymore."

"Okay. Thanks."

The other agent thought I was being sarcastic with my thanks. Especially when they hadn't really done anything.

"I'm glad you were here," I looked at him. "Who knows, they might have come back otherwise. So thanks again." I quickly opened the door. He was thinking that I was really good at picking up emotions. I would make a fantastic 'reader'. They were always looking for people with that ability. That reminded him of Detective Harris, and it all fell into place.

"Detective Harris said you were helping him with a case," he said. "I remember now. What do you do for him?"

Oh great. This guy was way too smart for his britches. And why had he forgotten about Mercer – the reason Dimples talked to him in the first place? I gave an embarrassed smile and shrugged. "I'm a paid consultant. I sometimes get premonitions about things. When he's stumped with a case, he'll give me a call and see if I can help. Sometimes it works, sometimes it doesn't."

"Hmm... well, we'll have to keep that in mind." He was thinking it probably wasn't premonitions at all. I was just good at picking up non-verbal cues and reading facial expressions. I could probably tell pretty quick if someone was lying. "Do you have a business card?" he asked, thinking if I helped the police, maybe he could hire me as well.

"Not yet," I said, caught off guard.

"Here's mine." He handed it to me. "If you are ever interested in a job with the FBI, give me a call."

"Oh... okay. Thanks." I took his card and waved them out the door with a friendly smile. Whew. That wasn't too bad, but it was sure a relief to have them gone.

Hungry, I wandered into the kitchen. As I scrambled an egg, I wondered what it would be like to work for the FBI. I could probably help them out a lot. Maybe even save the world. Kidnappings, bombings, murderers, I could take them down. I chuckled. Now I was getting carried away. Besides, I wasn't sure I wanted to know about all that stuff. Helping Dimples was hard enough, and look at the mess I was in now. Still, it wouldn't hurt to get some business cards made.

I needed to concentrate on my next move to give Uncle Joey back his money. But now that the Mexicans, along with Salazar and probably Mercer, were out of the picture, I wasn't as anxious to talk to him. What if he guessed my powers were back? It made sense that he was the one who'd hired Mercer to kill the Mexicans. He wouldn't want them to get the money, and that was a good way to take care of it.

What bothered me was that Ramos didn't seem to know what was going on. He was Uncle Joey's right hand man. He knew everything. I tried to think of our conversation earlier. He'd said that he heard I got away. Who told him? Uncle Joey? Jackie? Mercer?

I needed to talk to Ramos before I did anything else. Maybe I could call Jackie about talking to Uncle Joey next week, and find out where Ramos lived so I could take him some food. Of course, then she'd wonder why I wanted to wait until next week and, since the FBI weren't watching me anymore, I wouldn't have an excuse.

I decided to call Chris. He could help me figure this out. Besides, he wanted to be there when I talked to Uncle Joey. I placed the call and was surprised when he answered.

"You actually answered your phone," I said. "What's the deal?"

He huffed. "You make it sound like I never have time for you." I didn't know what to say, since that was pretty much right. "Okay, so maybe I've changed my priorities. After the last few days, I thought I'd better take all your calls. Just in case you needed me to save you or something."

I chuckled. "That's nice to know. Can we meet for lunch? We need to talk."

"Yes, that should work. I've got a light schedule today, so how about noon?"

"Sounds great, I'll come to your office." We disconnected, and I checked the time. If I hurried, I could get in a quick run before my shower. It hit me that for the first time in a while, I didn't have to worry about looking over my shoulder. It felt amazing.

I pulled into Chris' parking garage five minutes late and hurried to the elevators. I was proud that I hardly even cringed in his parking garage anymore. Maybe it was because I was used to being shot at. There was something wrong with that thought, but I didn't want it to mar my good mood, so I shoved it to the back of my mind.

Chris was on the phone, so I gave him a warm smile and quick wave when I entered. He glanced at me appreciatively, noticing how nice I looked in my short denim skirt and new cowboy boots. I knew I was a distraction when he had to ask the person on the other end to repeat what he'd just said. I couldn't help the grin that spread over my face.

A few minutes later, Chris hung up and came around the desk to my side. "Babe," he purred. "You look great."

"Thanks," I said. "Ready to go?"

"Yeah." He was thinking that after seeing me he wasn't hungry for food anymore.

I playfully swatted his arm and pulled him out the door. "You may not be hungry for food, but I certainly am." He frowned, but his heart wasn't in it. "Hey," I said in defense. "You hardly have to be a mind reader to know what you were thinking."

"Where do you want to go," he said, choosing to change the subject.

"Some place where we can talk."

"I know just the place." He tucked my hand through his arm and pulled me down the hallway. As we left his office, his secretary was thinking what a cute couple we made. I sent her a big grin and she sighed, wondering if she would ever find love like ours. It made me even more determined to solve my dilemma and get Uncle Joey out of our lives.

We walked to a nearby café and found a corner booth where we wouldn't be disturbed. "So what's going on?" Chris asked.

I told him about my visit from the FBI and how they were hoping I'd know what happened to the Mexicans. "They gave me their card, in case I want to join up. Can you believe it?" I said playfully.

Chris stilled. "Why did they do that?" He was hoping I didn't give myself away again.

"I didn't give myself away. The guy thought I had good instincts. He called it 'reading' people, picking up on their facial expressions and being able to tell if they were lying." At Chris' frown, I continued. "Of course, he didn't say all that to me, but that was the gist of it."

"Tell me you're not considering it," he said, his brows drawn together in worry.

"Not right now. I only told you because... well... I guess I was flattered. I was thinking about having some business cards made up. You know, since I'm getting paid as a consultant for the police, it might look good to have a few on hand."

"Yeah, I guess," he said, unenthusiastically. "What would you put on them?"

"I was thinking something like... Shelby Nichols Consulting Agency... with my cell phone number on it. That way I wouldn't need an office or anything. Since I'd be calling it a consulting agency, I wouldn't be expected to do other things, like private eye stuff. I don't think I'd like that so much. What do you think?"

"Sure." He nodded reluctantly and heaved a sigh. He was thinking that our lives had changed drastically since I could read minds, and worried what would happen next. He never imagined living like this... he glanced at me sharply. Damn, had I just heard all that?

I ignored his thoughts and continued my story. "Anyway, I tried to call Uncle Joey, but the number I have was disconnected, so I didn't get through. I thought about calling Jackie, but decided to try Ramos first."

"Did you get him?" Chris asked.

"Yes," I said. "He didn't say much, but it sounded like he thought it was Salazar who got me yesterday, so he went after him." I went on to explain that he'd been shot, but told me I didn't have to worry about Salazar anymore. "I guess that's why he didn't call me back last night. He was pretty out of it, but he said he'd call me back after the pain pills wore off."

"Did he know about Mercer?"

"I don't know," I answered. "He said he heard I got away from the Mexicans, but that doesn't tell us much."

"So, who hired Mercer?" Chris asked.

"Take your pick. But I don't think it was Ramos. That leaves Uncle Joey. It must have been him. What should we do now?"

"I guess our next step is to contact Manetto and give him back his money." I nodded, but without much enthusiasm. Chris noticed my reticence. "What is it?" he asked.

"I'm afraid he'll guess my powers are back," I admitted.

"I'll be there with you," he assured me. "And I'll do whatever it takes to keep him out of our lives."

"Okay," I said. "Then I'd better call Jackie and set something up." Chris nodded his agreement. "Should I talk to Ramos first?" I asked.

"I don't think it matters. If he's been shot, he's out of the picture anyway. Manetto's the only one who can make this right. He's the one we need to talk to."

"All right," I said.

"Why don't you put in the call right now, while I'm here. Let's get this over with." He took my hands and squeezed them, sending the encouragement I needed to go through with it.

I squeezed back, then released his hands to rummage through my purse for my phone. He noticed my stun flashlight and grinned. "Good call," he said. "Is the gun in there too?"

"No. It's at home," I answered. "But I think we should take it to Uncle Joey's when we meet with him."

"I'll take it," he said. "You'll have your flashlight. We'll be all set."

He made it sound so easy. If only it were true. I found my phone and called Thrasher Development. Jackie answered right away. She didn't seem surprised to hear from me, and was ready to set up a meeting. "Let's see... can you come in to Thrasher tonight? Say... eight o'clock?"

"Tonight? Why so late?"

"Mr. Manetto has a lot to do today, so he can't fit you in until then, but he'll want to take care of this as soon as possible."

"Can't we wait until tomorrow morning?" I asked, put off by her eagerness.

"Mr. Manetto wouldn't like that. It's a lot of money. I'm sure you understand."

"All right," I agreed. "But I'm bringing my husband with me."

There was a pause on the other end. "That should be fine," she said. "Don't be late." She disconnected, leaving me listening to the dial tone. For some reason it sounded ominous.

"That was strange." I told Chris what she said.

"I don't like it," he agreed. "But then, it sounds typical based on who Manetto is."

"Do we have to go?" I asked.

"We've got to take care of this sooner or later," he shrugged. "Why not sooner? Then it will be over, and we can put it behind us."

"All right," I agreed.

"Hey, it will work out," he said. "If you hear anything you don't like, we can leave. We have the money, so we'll have the upper hand."

I nodded, but for some reason that didn't reassure me like I hoped. "Do you think we should put all the money back into one account so we can transfer it more easily?"

"Oh, I didn't think of that," he said. "That's probably a good idea. Do you want to go to the bank right now and take care of it? I think it will require both our signatures."

"Yes. Plus, we can see how much money we earned in interest, and it will make me feel better." Chris glanced at me sharply. "Not that I want to keep the money. It's just... you know... five million dollars. Don't think I haven't thought about what we could do with that much money."

"I know... I've thought about it too," he agreed. His thoughts were centered on paying off the house and getting out of debt. He didn't think we needed a nicer house or cars. Having that much money and not looking like it would suit him just fine. I frowned. His ideas were not at all like mine. It kind of made me ashamed.

My phone rang, sparing me more guilt. "It's the police," I told Chris. "I'd better answer."

"Go ahead," he said. "I'll pay the bill."

I answered, hoping it wasn't bad news. "Hello?"

"Hey Shelby, it's Harris. I heard the news about the drug dealers who kidnapped you. Did the FBI tell you?" Dimples asked.

"Yes, they came by this morning. I'm relieved I don't have to worry about them anymore. Have you got any news on Mercer?" I thought I'd better ask since it would look funny if I didn't.

"No, but we're not giving up. We think he might still be in the city, which doesn't make sense on a practical level, unless he has some unfinished business..." he trailed off, probably because of how that might sound to me.

"Like me?" I asked.

"Oh, I'm sure it's not you. I mean, I don't think he would come after you. From what I've been able to pick up, he's the kind who gets paid a lot of money, so I don't think he'd kill someone for free."

"If you're trying to make me feel better, it's not working." Seriously? What was he thinking?

"Oh. Yeah, that didn't come out right." He hesitated. "On a brighter note, I just got a call from Jessica Palmer. She has some information about the museum robbery and wants to meet with us right away. Are you free?"

"Um... yeah. I can do that. I'm already downtown having lunch with my husband, so I could come over now."

"That would be great! And don't worry, you'll be compensated."

What could I say to that? "Sure, I'll be there in a few minutes." He thanked me and hung up.

Chris heard what I said. "What's going on?" he asked

"The museum curator wants to talk to us. Do you think we could go to the bank after? I doubt it will take long, but it sounded urgent, and I'd hate to miss out on what she has to say."

"Okay, that should work." We left the café and hurried to Chris' office. He gave me a quick kiss. "Just give me a call when you're done."

"I will," I promised. "See you soon."

I took the elevator to the parking garage and started the car, realizing that in all the commotion, I had completely forgotten about the stolen art. As I drove, I wracked my brain to remember the guilty guy's name. Then it came to me, Greg Bowman. Relieved, I let out a sigh; grateful I wouldn't sound like an amateur since I'd forgotten.

Once again, I went into the police station. This time no one paid me any particular attention and, from their thoughts, I could tell they were getting used to seeing me come in. I took it as a good sign. Dimples waved me over, and I followed him out the back to a waiting car.

"Thanks for doing this," he said. "Ms. Palmer sounded a little panicked when she called, but wouldn't tell me anything over the phone."

"What do you think is wrong?" I asked.

"I'm not sure," he answered.

"Did you do any checking with Interpol about Greg Bowman?"

"I haven't had time yet." He felt guilty about not checking, especially since he'd probably let me down, but he just had too much on his plate right now.

"It's okay," I said. "I sort of forgot about the art theft myself. Maybe if Greg is there I can figure out where the art is, and we can be done with the case."

"Yeah," he agreed, smiling, but inside, he didn't think it would be that easy. Nothing was that easy. Then he mentally shook himself and decided to think positive. My premonitions had always been right, and he might as well take a chance. He smiled again, and this time, the smile was genuine.

We pulled into the museum parking lot and hurried into the building. Entering the offices, we noticed the receptionist was gone. A chill of unease ran down my spine. Dimples narrowed his eyes, but he was thinking it was still close to lunchtime, so he wasn't too concerned. I followed him down the hall to Jessica's office. The door was closed, and he knocked, calling her name. She didn't answer, so he turned the handle and pushed the door open. Empty.

"Did she tell you to meet her in her office?" I asked.

"Yes," he paused. "Something's not right." Dimples glanced around the room. "See this? The pencil holder's been knocked over." He was thinking that Jessica might have found out about Greg, which explained the agitation of her phone call. If Greg suspected she knew, or had walked in on her while she was talking to him, she might be in danger. That would explain why she wasn't here. If Greg had her now, he might kill her if he was desperate enough.

"Maybe he's got her, and he's going to kill her," I said, repeating his thoughts.

"I was thinking the same thing," he said. "Wait here. I'm going to see if they're still in the building." He started down the hall, and I followed. I didn't want to wait. What if Dimples needed me? If Greg was there, and thought of killing someone, I would know before he did it.

Dimples stopped, realizing I was right behind him. "What are you doing? I told you to wait."

I shrugged. "I think I'll come with you. You might need me."

"No. Go back to the office. This could be dangerous, and I don't want you hurt." He was also worried that I would get in the way and mess everything up.

"I won't get in the way. I promise."

Dimples froze. Did I just say exactly what he was thinking? How... it must be the premonitions thing. He shook his head. "I don't have time for this. Please go back."

"I have a feeling that you need me. I'll be fine. Let's go before Jessica gets killed."

He huffed out a breath. "Fine." He was angry with me, and hoped he wasn't making a big mistake. He continued down the hall and focused all his attention on finding Jessica.

I opened my senses wide, hoping to pick up any stray thoughts that might belong to Jessica or Greg. We went through the offices, and turned down a hallway that led to some double doors with 'storage' marked above them. Dimples cautiously pushed the door open, finding a staircase leading downward into a warehouse-like area.

Walking down the staircase was like walking into a cave. Dim light from an area to the right gave us enough light to see where we were going. At the bottom of the stairs, we found rows of shelves spaced vertically in front of us, and to the right was an open area with larger items. Here, the lights were turned on, and faint sounds of someone moaning came from that direction.

Dimples drew his gun and inched forward toward the sound. Rounding the corner, we found Jessica. She was at the far end of the room, propped up against a crate. Her hands and feet were bound with rope and her mouth tied with a gag. Blood oozed down her side and pooled on the floor. Had she been shot?

Dimples glanced around, wondering where Greg was. I listened for him, but could find no trace of his thoughts. That didn't mean he wasn't here, and my stomach clenched. Maybe I should have waited in the office and called for backup.

With the chance that Jessica was bleeding to death, Dimples had no choice but to help her. Keeping his gun out, he slowly crossed the floor in her direction. He was wishing I were a real detective with a gun so I could back him up, but there was no help for it now.

I inched forward as well, keeping out of the light with my back against the row of shelves. As Dimples closed in on Jessica, I caught the thought of *stay steady and squeeze*. My pulse leapt, and I yelled. "Look out!"

Dimples dropped and rolled just as a shot rang out, missing him by inches. I didn't know where Greg was, but from the cursing in his mind, I knew he was close. Dimples was thinking the shot had come from somewhere behind me, and I ducked down, ready to crawl to a more protected area. Lucky for me, there was a large wooden crate on the bottom shelf a few feet away, and I took shelter behind that.

Another shot fired, this one tracking Dimples as he ran back toward the stairs. He was trying to draw the shooter after him, away from Jessica and me. I wasn't sure that was such a good idea, especially when I heard footsteps running down the other side of the row of shelves. They stopped directly behind the crate, on the other side of the aisle from me, and I cringed. Greg was thinking that I had to be close, and maybe he could take me hostage.

Dimples realized his mistake when Greg didn't follow. He also thought he couldn't shoot at Greg because I could

get caught in the crossfire. So instead, he decided to nego-
tiate.

"Give it up, Greg," he called. "We have the museum surrounded. There's nowhere to go. Don't make things worse.
Surrender peacefully, and let me get Jessica the help she
needs before she bleeds to death. You don't want her murder on your hands."

A string of profanity came from Greg's mind. How did
we know it was him? Where was I hiding? I was his ticket
out if he could only find me. I had to be close. Thinking he
might see where I was if he looked under the shelf, he
dropped down to his knees.

Knowing he'd see me, I frantically pushed against the
crate, hoping to topple it onto him. It barely budged, and I
pushed harder, putting my back into it. It started to give,
but too slowly to catch Greg. In a move I didn't anticipate,
he pulled the crate toward him and onto the ground. I
jumped up to run, but he reached through the shelf, and
caught one of my legs with his hand.

I shrieked, and slipped down onto my hands and knees.
My purse fell to the ground right in front of me. As Greg
scrambled through the shelf after me, I grabbed my stun
flashlight. Before he could get through the hole, I planted
the flashlight against his neck and pushed the button.

One million tooth-jarring volts of power slammed into
him, and he flopped like a fish before his eyes rolled back
and he passed out. Breathless, I scooted back, relieved he
was no longer a threat. Dimples rushed toward me at a dead
run.

Skidding to a stop beside me, he glanced between us.
"What did you do to him?" Then he noticed my flashlight.
"Is that a stun gun?" Wow, was he ever impressed. "Way to
go, Shelby." He raised his hand to give me a high five, but I
was shaking so bad, it took a while to get my hand up. We

connected, and Dimples began his examination of Greg, taking his gun and checking his pulse.

"Is he dead?" I asked. Sometimes people died from being stunned, and he looked awful. His face was white with dark circles under his eyes, and drool was running from his mouth. Kind of like a zombie. I wondered if the Mexican had looked like that too. Of course, I hadn't stuck around long enough to see.

"Nope. Just out cold. Your stunner must carry a lot of power." He pulled Greg the rest of the way through the shelf and cuffed him. Next, he hurried over to Jessica, and called for the paramedics and an ambulance.

I took a deep breath and concentrated on getting my legs under me. They were a little shaky, so I grabbed onto the shelf for support. Getting to my feet made me feel a little better, but it was another moment before I could walk. I was surprised at how much getting my ankle grabbed like that shook me up. After all I'd been through lately, I should be used to stuff like that by now. Maybe it was starting to get to me.

By the time I shuffled over to Dimples, he had the gag and ropes off Jessica. He laid her flat and propped her feet up. It looked like she had been shot in the shoulder, and Dimples was thinking that she should be all right, but even the shock of a wound like hers could still kill her.

All that blood was making me woozy and I leaned against the wall for support. I didn't want to think about what a close call I'd had, so I focused on the sound of sirens and wondered what had happened to the receptionist. Had she been out to lunch all this time?

That's when I heard her. She knew something was wrong down here, and was thinking what a fool she was to believe that Greg had dumped Jessica for her. Then it all came together in her mind, hitting her like a ton of bricks. Greg was the one who had stolen the paintings, and she had helped him. Coming further into the room, she caught sight of Greg in handcuffs, and Jessica hurt and bleeding. With a little scream, she ran forward, thinking Jessica was dead.

"She's not dead," I told her.

She glanced at me and started sobbing. "I didn't know. He had me run some errands for him so he could talk to Jessica down here. I left him the keys... a few times... I didn't know what he was up to."

"It's all right," I said. "Jessica's going to be fine, and Greg will go to jail. Especially if you cooperate with the police and tell them everything you know."

She was berating herself and thinking how stupid she was. I pulled in my senses to block out her thoughts, and did what I could to calm her down. The cops and paramedics rushed down the stairs, and I sagged with relief, eager to let them take care of the receptionist and Jessica.

By then, Greg was stirring, and when the police got him up, he managed a halting gait with their help. He had a dazed look on his face, and his hair was poking up, kind of like he'd been shocked. Big time. I couldn't help the satisfied smile that curved my lips.

I glanced at Dimples and noticed the same smile on his face. He caught me looking at him and smiled even bigger. It made his dimples swirl in and out, and my attention was caught by that crazy dance they did.

Dimples took charge, explaining what had happened to the detectives and cops that were helping out. My legs were still a little shaky, so I found a chair to sit on while I waited. It was beautifully carved out of old wood, and I hoped it wasn't the kind that you were meant to look at but not touch.

The police motioned to me, and Dimples told them that I would give a statement after we got back to the police station. Once he had everything settled, he was ready to leave and came over to my side.

"You did good," he said. He was proud of my resourcefulness, and glad that I hadn't fallen apart under the stress. "That stun gun was a great idea." Then he thought about how I hadn't stayed upstairs like he'd asked, and how close I'd gotten to being killed.

I didn't like him thinking about that part, so I defended myself. "It's a good thing I came down here with you. I think he was waiting to kill you. Jessica must have told him you were coming, and he didn't have time to finish her off and leave before we showed up."

"Yeah, but I never should have come down here without backup," he answered. "I put you in danger."

"Probably, but Jessica's life was at stake. You didn't want her to die because you waited upstairs. Coming down here so fast probably saved her."

He thought about it and secretly agreed with me, but now he'd have to think twice about how much he involved me in the future. If anything happened to me, it would be his fault, and he didn't think he could live with that.

"You ready to go?" he asked. None of his thoughts showed on his face.

I was touched that he didn't want me to get hurt, and thought he was probably right. I didn't need to worry that helping him would kill me. I was involved with plenty of other things that would do that already. "Yes," I answered with enthusiasm.

"Let's go then," he said, and took my arm to help me up the stairs.

It was nice to lean on him a little, since my legs hadn't decided to work properly yet. I took solace in the fact that I had done a good thing here, and it made me feel less shaky. Soon, I had enough strength to walk out of there without

Dimples' assistance, but I kept my arm in his anyway. Why spoil a good thing?

Chapter 11

We got to the police station, and promptly went to work on my statement. Dimples helped me fill it out, but it was a long, drawn-out process. It gave me a deeper appreciation for everything the detectives had to do.

With a jolt, I realized I was supposed to meet Chris at the bank. I checked the time and gasped. How had it gotten so late? I quickly called him. "Is it too late to go to the bank?" I asked.

"No, they don't close until six. We can still make it. What took you so long?"

"It's a long story. I'll tell you all about it later." I checked the form and realized I wasn't quite done. "I can be there at five-thirty. Will that work?"

"Sure," he replied. "See you then." We disconnected, and I hurried to finish up. At five-thirty, I handed my statement to Dimples.

"Looks good," he said. "I'll walk you out to your car."

"Thanks." I picked up his thoughts, that he owed me a lot and felt bad that I still had to worry about Mercer. I wondered how he would feel if he knew Mercer had saved my life. He probably wouldn't believe it. It was still hard for me to believe.

"Don't forget to recharge your stun gun," he said, smiling.

"Ha. That's one thing I won't forget to do," I answered.

"Good. See you later."

I drove away, completely worn out. After today, I wasn't sure I had it in me to meet with Uncle Joey. Maybe I could call and set it up for tomorrow. That would be much better.

I spotted Chris' car in the bank's parking lot and hoped he hadn't been waiting too long. He was talking to Blaine, the bank manager, as I walked in. He caught my gaze and smiled, sending my heart into little flip-flops. It made me a bit nervous to tell him what I'd been doing this afternoon. Maybe I could give him a watered-down version that didn't have any shooting in it. More likely, he'd find out the truth, and then I'd be in trouble.

It only took a few minutes to make the transfer back into my old account. If it was that easy, giving it back to Uncle Joey should be a piece of cake. There was no need to be nervous. It would all work out.

Chris and I checked to see how much interest we'd earned from the five million. My visions of lots of money were dashed to find a measly two thousand dollars. With nearly three weeks of having five million dollars in my bank account, that's all we'd made?

Chris wasn't too surprised, since he knew interest rates were pretty low. But it was still disappointing. My fantasy of being nicely compensated on the interest was destroyed. It left me depressed, thinking that what I'd been through had definitely not been worth it. Maybe I'd have to rethink my strategy about giving all the money back.

We finished up with the bank manager and, after politely shaking hands, walked out to the parking lot.

"Are you okay?" Chris asked. He was thinking that I was unusually quiet and lost in my own little world. "How did it go with Dimples?"

"Great." His question caught me off-guard, and I had to switch gears back to the heist. I decided to put a positive spin on the case and leave a few details out. "With the curator's help we caught the thief."

"Was it the person you thought it was?" he asked.

"Yes," I smiled. "That's why it took me so long. I had to stay at the station and give a statement. But at least I don't have to deal with that case anymore, so that's positive."

Chris nodded, knowing that when I talked about something being positive, it usually meant there was a whole lot of negative to go along with it. He raised his brows. "So what exactly happened?"

I sighed, knowing that he wouldn't relent until I told him all the details. Still, I had to try. "Quite a bit actually. Do you want to hear the long version or the short version?"

"Okay," he said, his suspicions correct. "You wouldn't tell me that unless there's something you don't want me to know. Spill it. What happened?"

"Maybe we should wait until we get home." I really didn't want to tell him yet. "I mean; it is a long story."

Chris huffed, knowing he was getting the run-around. "Fine. I'll see you at home."

I got in my car with guilt flaring down to my toes. I knew he would worry all the way home, but seriously, I was right there and I was okay. So what did it matter? But that wasn't right. It mattered to him. Who was I trying to kid? Did that mean I couldn't work with Dimples anymore? Maybe when I explained to Chris that Dimples had realized he'd handled it wrong, and had decided not to put me in danger like that again, it wouldn't bother Chris so much. That's what I'd tell him at the beginning; then he wouldn't get upset when he heard the whole story.

Feeling better, I followed Chris home with a lighter heart. It was always good to have a plan. That was my new motto. From now on, I'd think things through and figure out a plan. So what was the plan for meeting with Uncle Joey tonight? Take Chris, take the gun, and take my stun flashlight. If I could get him to give me twenty thousand dollars for my trouble, that would be even better.

I arrived home to find two hungry teenagers. It was the one thing I could always count on. "I'd better fix dinner right away," I said to Chris. Telling him my story would have to wait until after this crisis.

He narrowed his eyes, but was resigned to waiting. I whipped up some spaghetti and meatballs. By the time dinner was over, it was nearly seven-thirty and hardly any time at all before we had to leave for our meeting with Uncle Joey. With a gasp, I realized I hadn't recharged my stun flashlight and quickly plugged it in.

That was all the encouragement Chris needed. "You used your stun gun," he said. It was not a question. He leaned against the kitchen counter with his arms folded and his eyebrows slightly raised, a clear invitation to talk.

"Yeah," I said. "It was pretty crazy." I spilled my guts and told him everything, including how Greg grabbed my ankle and I stunned him in the neck. "That thing really carries a wallop."

Chris shook his head. "That's it," he said emphatically. "No more working with the police."

"I was afraid you'd say that," I answered. "If you want to know, Dimples felt really bad about it. He was thinking that he would never let anything like that happen again. So, I could probably still work with him."

"It doesn't matter what he thought," Chris said. "Can he guarantee that you'd never be in harm's way? No, he can't. And you... you're not trained for this kind of work. Maybe if you were a police officer or something, it would be different... but you're not. You can't do this anymore."

"Okay," I said, deciding to agree for now. I put my arms around him. "I didn't mean for this to happen. It scared the crap out of me too. These last few days have been..." I couldn't think of a word that could adequately describe the horror I'd felt.

"Worse than awful?" Chris filled in. "Worse than your worst nightmare?"

"Well, maybe not... but pretty close. At least, I don't think it can get any worse. Once we give the money back, things will get better." I leaned my head against his chest. "I think I need a vacation."

He chuckled. "I agree, just the two of us. We could take a cruise or something."

I smiled up at him. "Sounds good to me."

"Okay, I'm glad that's settled." He was thinking he was relieved that I had agreed not to work for Dimples anymore. But knowing me, it was probably only a matter of time before I changed my mind.

"Oh no," I said, wanting to stop him thinking about my duplicity. "What time is it?"

He checked his watch. "Nearly eight. Are we supposed to be there at eight-thirty?"

"No! Eight o'clock." My heart skipped a beat, and panic clenched my stomach. "I'm not sure I'm ready for this."

He grimaced. "I'll get the gun. You get your stunner. We'll talk about a plan on the way."

"Maybe I should call and cancel. I really don't feel good about this."

He paused. "It's just nerves. You'll feel better when it's over. We need to get this taken care of. I'm sick of what it's done to us."

"Yeah, but... Ramos never called me back. Maybe I should call him first."

Chris sighed and his shoulders sagged. "All right. But it will make us late."

"I know, just give me a minute." I couldn't stop the foreboding that seeped up my spine. If this was the right thing to do, it only made sense that Ramos would know about it. He knew everything Uncle Joey did.

He answered on the fifth ring. "Hi Ramos, it's Shelby. Are you feeling any better?"

"Yeah," his voice was low and rusty. "Sorry I didn't call you back."

"That's okay. Do you need anything?" Chris shook his head, wishing I would get right to the point. Ramos could take care of himself.

"No, I'm good. But thanks. What's up?"

"I called Jackie to set up a meeting with Uncle Joey so I could give the money back to him. She set it up for eight tonight. I was hoping you could tell me if that was a good idea or not."

"What?" Ramos sputtered. "She said to come tonight?"

"Yeah," I answered.

"That doesn't make any sense. He won't even be here tonight. Mr. Manetto is flying in tomorrow."

My breath caught. "Then why did she say that?"

"I don't know." He was silent for a moment, then added, "Just sit tight tonight. I'll see if I can figure out what's going on."

"Okay, thanks. Let me know what you find out."

"Yeah," he said and disconnected.

"What did he say?" Chris asked, anxiously.

"He said Uncle Joey is flying in tomorrow. He's not even here, and Jackie set up this meeting anyway."

"Whoa. It's a good thing you called," Chris said.

"I know. He said to sit tight and he'd see if he could figure out what's happening. Hopefully, he'll call me back and let me know."

Chris narrowed his eyes. "This is Jackie's doing. What's up with her? Do you think she wants the money?"

"That's the only thing I can think of. But why would she take Uncle Joey's money? I mean... she works for him; he'd know it was her."

"Good question." Chris couldn't figure it out. Who in their right mind would take Manetto's money? He was bound to come after them. It didn't make any sense. "Maybe she has some bills she needs to pay."

"Hmm..." I said. "Maybe she'll call when we don't show up and we can ask."

Chris shook his head. "Who knows? I guess the plan now is to wait and see."

"True," I agreed. "But we're not doing anything until we hear from Ramos."

"Sounds like a good plan to me," Chris agreed.

We spent the rest of the night waiting for a phone call that never came. Around eleven-thirty, we finally went to bed. I was hopeful that Ramos had taken care of the problem. Still, it was a long time before I could fall asleep.

Chris left early the next morning for work. It was his day in court for the divorce case, and he couldn't miss it. I promised I would call him if I heard anything. After the kids left for school, I thought about going to the gym, but the last few days had taken their toll, and all I wanted to do was sit around in my pajamas. Maybe I'd watch an old movie or two, and eat a lot of popcorn.

I worried that I hadn't heard back from Ramos, but I didn't want to be a pest and keep calling him. There was also the matter of Uncle Joey. When was he due to arrive? It was only a matter of time before I had to face him. I wished there was something I had on him that I could bargain with.

There was the money, and the fact that I wanted some of it for compensation was probably not too smart. But giving it all back for nothing was harder than I thought. After all the trouble it had caused, I shouldn't have a problem giving it back. So, did wanting to keep some make me a bad person? I figured I could play it by ear. As long as he didn't find out about my mind-reading ability it could work out.

I was just popping some popcorn when the phone rang. I didn't recognize the number, but thought I should answer it anyway. "Hello?"

"Shelby."

My heart raced. It was the only person that could strike fear into my heart by just saying my name. "Uh... Uncle Joey?"

"Yes, it's me." When I didn't say anything, he continued. "I think you know why I'm calling. You have something of mine that I need back."

The way he said it raised my hackles. "Hey, you're the one who put it in my account. I didn't take it from you." There was silence on the other end so I kept going. "And you know what? I've nearly been killed a few times because of it. I'm not very happy about that."

He sighed. "Yes, that is regrettable. I'm back now though, so I can take it off your hands." Before I could say anything, he continued. "My driver should be there in about ten minutes." He disconnected.

"Wait... damn!" It didn't sound like bargaining was going to be an option. Then I realized I was still in my pajamas without a hint of make-up, and only ten minutes to get ready.

"Damn!" I rushed into my bedroom and threw on some black slacks and a black top. It hit me that I was wearing all black. Just the way he liked it. How had that happened?

With no time to change, I put on some eye shadow and mascara, wondering why I cared. But I did. Looking good was important when I faced Uncle Joey. Why was that? It was like he had some kind of strange power over me, making me do his bidding. What could it be? Fear. Plain and simple. I was terrified.

There was one more thing I had to do before leaving, and that was call Chris. I checked the clock and groaned, knowing he was in court and probably wouldn't answer. The call went straight to voice mail, confirming my fears.

Uncle Joey's driver pulled up and began walking to my door. After the beep for voice mail, I quickly explained to Chris what had happened and slipped the phone into my purse. I was just about to answer the doorbell when I remembered my stun flashlight and ran back to my room to get it.

The doorbell rang again, but I ignored it and pulled the flashlight out of the charger. As I slipped it into my purse, the knocking started. Totally rattled, I took a deep breath, funneling my nervous energy into indignation. Taking my time, I walked to the door and yanked it open.

"I'm coming, you don't have to..." I flinched back with shock. Mercer stood there with a gun in his hand. I nearly wet my pants, and my heart pounded so hard I thought it was going to burst. "What..."

He grabbed my arm, pulling me effortlessly out of my house. "Come along, we have an appointment to keep."

"But you…"

"Don't worry Shelby. I'm not here to kill you." He smirked, thinking that the look on my face was priceless. Something he would cherish for years to come. It made everything he'd gone through worth it.

Bile rose in my throat. "I think I'm going to be sick."

"Oh no, you don't," he said, jerking my arm so I faced him. "I told you I'm not going to kill you. I'm just doing a job for Mr. Manetto. He doesn't want you dead. All right? You don't have to worry."

I was still having trouble breathing, but his words finally began to penetrate my shocked sensibilities. "You're not?"

"Nope," he said. "Now pull yourself together. Mr. Manetto doesn't like it when people fall apart."

"How do you know?" I asked before I thought.

He smiled. "It's part of what makes me good at what I do." He opened the back passenger door to the limousine and ushered me inside. "Make yourself at home. There's a drink in the cooler if it will help settle your nerves."

I sat back in plush opulence, unable to enjoy the luxury that surrounded me. On impulse, I jerked open the cooler, finding mini-bottles of all kinds. With a huff, I slammed the lid, not giving in to the temptation. This was not the time to indulge. I needed my wits about me. Besides, drinking would probably interfere with my mind-reading abilities, and I needed all the help I could get.

Feeling a little better, I sat back and took stock. I had my stun-flashlight. I had my mind-reading. I had my phone. I had Uncle Joey's five million dollars. Chris knew where I was… unless we weren't going to Thrasher Development. Panic kicked in, but I pushed it down. He still knew I was with Uncle Joey. Things weren't so bad. I was pretty sure I could get through this without getting killed.

Ramos was on my side, right? So where was he? How come Mercer was driving? Did Uncle Joey even know that Mercer the Assassin was his driver? Had Mercer killed Uncle Joey's driver and taken his place? No... Mercer had to be working for Uncle Joey. He had killed the Mexicans for him and saved me. Whatever the reason, Uncle Joey was behind it all, and soon, I would find out what was going on. Hopefully that knowledge wouldn't make me a liability.

I could always bargain for my life again by disclosing my mind-reading was back, but that was the last thing I wanted to do. There had to be a way out of this mess. If only I could figure out what it was.

Relief turned my insides to jelly when Mercer maneuvered the limo into the parking garage of Thrasher Development. At least that was one thing I didn't have to worry about.

He pulled up to the elevator doors and stopped, then hopped out and opened my door. I thought about stunning him right then and there, but decided it was too early to use it, especially when I might need it later. He stood at attention like a real limo driver, and offered his hand when I emerged. I ignored it and stepped out.

"Go on up," Mercer said. "Mr. Manetto is waiting for you." He closed the door behind me, got back into the limo, put it in gear, and drove off to park the car. That was weird.

Not wanting to be there when he came back, I hurried to the elevators and pushed the call button. As I entered, I pushed the twenty-sixth floor and popped open my phone to leave another message for Chris. My heart sank to find there was no reception in the elevator shaft. Almost there, I took a deep breath to calm my nerves, and my mind went totally blank. This was insane. What was I going to do? I envisioned myself emerging from the elevator screaming like a crazy person. Everyone would probably run for their lives. For some reason, that tickled my funny bone.

When the elevator doors whooshed open, I couldn't hold back a chuckle. I stepped out and my laughter got bigger, in fact, the more I tried not to laugh, the worse I laughed. The doors to Thrasher Development stood open and I stepped toward them with pursed lips to hold in the laughter. This was serious. Get a grip.

Jackie stood inside the doors at her desk. One look at her was enough to curb my insane laughter. She was not a happy camper. I probed her thoughts and she was thinking that it was a good thing I was there. Now maybe she could straighten out this mess. She could have done it last night if I would have just shown up. Oh well, today would work just as well. Maybe even better.

What did that mean? What the heck was she planning?

"Mr. Manetto is waiting for you in his office," she said icily. I just nodded and turned down the hall. My spine tingled as she followed close behind. What was she up to? I raised my hand to knock, but she quickly opened the door.

"Shelby's here," she announced and ushered me inside.

Uncle Joey sat behind his desk, but it was the person leaning against it that caught my attention. Tall and thin, with shoulder-length, curly, dark hair, she had to be somewhere in her fifties, but it was hard to determine because she was in such great shape. She straightened when I came in, sizing me up, and wondering why Joey had given all that money to me when it was rightfully hers. What was that supposed to mean?

"Thanks for joining us Shelby. This is Carlotta... and this is Miguel." He motioned to the young man sitting at the table, glued to his computer.

"Nice to meet you," Carlotta said in a low, stiff voice.

Miguel tore his gaze from the computer and stood, a bright smile on his face. He made his way around the table and shook my hand warmly. "It is so good to meet you, Senora. My father has told me many great things about you." He released my hand and glanced at Uncle Joey to see if he'd done it right. Uncle Joey gave him a slight nod of approval and Miguel beamed.

In that moment I realized several things. Miguel idolized Uncle Joey and would do anything to please him. Uncle Joey had not only saved Miguel from a horrible death, but also killed all the men who had kidnapped him. That act alone earned his unfaltering loyalty. Plus deep down, he knew what had happened to him was his mother's fault. He loved his mother, but it was nice to have a father too... if he really was his father.

Carlotta had just learned I had the money, and this grated on her. That money rightfully belonged to her after everything she'd gone through, and she was determined to get it back. Guilt that Miguel would be dead if not for Uncle Joey's help wouldn't keep her from taking it from him. It was her money, and she would persuade Uncle Joey of that fact. Then she would leave him. He wouldn't dare harm her. Not as long as he believed she was the mother of his son.

Jackie hated Carlotta. Jackie was the woman who loved Uncle Joey. It was she who had taken care of him all these years. If Uncle Joey was blind to this floozy's real intentions, Jackie wasn't about to leave without some compensation. She'd take the money for herself, and let him stew over that. It served him right.

I pulled away from these thoughts with a physical step back. Whew. Was Uncle Joey ever in trouble. I could understand Carlotta's strategy to get the money, but how did Jackie plan on getting it?

A knock sounded on the door and Jackie immediately pulled it open. Mercer came in toting a gun, and my question was answered. Jackie had hired Mercer. "Which one should I kill first?" he asked her.

Chapter 12

I glanced at Uncle Joey. He caught my gaze and was thinking that I shouldn't worry because he had everything under control. I nodded before I caught myself, but it was too late. His eyes lit with victory. Damn!

Without pause, he focused on Jackie. "What's this all about?"

"I want the money in Shelby's account," Jackie said. "Or Carlotta dies." Jackie had told Mercer it was me she was going to threaten since I had the money, but things had changed now that Carlotta was here. If Uncle Joey wanted Carlotta, he'd have to pay for it in money or blood, and she didn't much care which.

Carlotta gasped and leaned back against Uncle Joey's desk, pulling Miguel to her side. For a moment I thought she was going to put Miguel in front of her, but thankfully, she didn't.

"All right," Uncle Joey said. "You can have the money. But first tell me why."

"After everything I've done for you? You have to ask me that?" Jackie was furious. "Can't you see that all she wants from you is your money? If you pick her over me, then the least you can do is give me the money."

Uncle Joey frowned. "This isn't about picking one or the other of you," he said.

"Well, you can't have us both," Jackie shouted.

"Of course not," Uncle Joey said, his voice placating. "There's only one of you that I want."

The tension in the room increased, and everyone focused on Uncle Joey. "I can think of only one way to settle this," he continued. "We'll start with Mercer. I don't know how much Jackie is paying you to kill Carlotta, but I'll double it if you won't."

Mercer glanced at Jackie, then back to Uncle Joey. "Fifty grand. So that will be a hundred and fifty to you."

Uncle Joey narrowed his eyes. "I said double it. What part of that didn't you understand?"

"Oh I understand all right, but I'm the one with the gun, and I say a hundred and fifty, or someone dies. I don't much care which one." He glanced at me and smirked, swiveling his gun to point at me, then Carlotta and last at Miguel.

Uncle Joey tamped down his anger, which kind of surprised me. "All right," he said. "I'll pay your price."

"But..." Jackie turned to Mercer, fuming. "You can't do this. I hired you first."

"Sorry," Mercer said. "But it's nothing personal." He handed her his card before pointing the gun in her direction. "Give that to Mr. Manetto." With a sigh of frustration, she did as he told her. "That's my account," he continued. "I'll wait while you transfer the money."

I couldn't believe how calmly Uncle Joey was taking this. He sat in front of his computer and completed the transaction. "It's done," he said.

Mercer took out his phone and checked his account. "Nice doing business with you." He smiled and was out of the door in a flash.

Before anyone could say a word, Uncle Joey took charge. "Now that he's gone, we can solve this little dilemma." Jackie and Carlotta both began to protest. "Not a word! Both of you sit down." Now he was getting flustered, and I tried to hold back a smile.

"Since you both want the money, I've decided to split it up," he announced. That silenced them. "Two point five million is enough to keep you happy, but I think Shelby should get a share as well, since she's had to deal with this mess."

This surprised me, but before I could say anything, Carlotta jumped to her feet. "But Joseph! That money belongs to Miguel and me. I know you didn't say it was ours, but I thought after everything we'd been through it was only fair and right that we get it. If it wasn't for me, we wouldn't have been able to get the money in the first place. I'm the one who knew the passwords to their bank accounts."

"Thank you Carlotta." Uncle Joey was wondering what he ever saw in Carlotta. Had it always been about the money? If it wasn't for Miguel... how could he keep his son and live with this woman? "Please sit down. I want to hear what Jackie has to say for herself."

Jackie shook her head, keeping her gaze in her lap. After a moment of silence, she finally glanced up. "Divide it how you like. I quit." With tears in her eyes, she jumped up and ran from the room.

Uncle Joey pursed his lips, but his heart was breaking. He realized that he loved Jackie and didn't want her to go. But he couldn't keep them both, and there was Miguel to consider.

Carlotta was relieved to have her gone, but could tell that Uncle Joey was upset. She made a soothing noise and attempted to help him feel better. "Darling, I'm sorry she was upset. I guess money really does bring out the worst in people. It's hard to believe she was willing to kill for it." She shuddered, hoping to sound sympathetic and repulsed at the same time.

Uncle Joey wasn't fooled. In fact, things were becoming clearer to him by the moment. "Well, that leaves Shelby." He glanced at me. "How much do you think she should get?" He directed this question to Carlotta. I wisely kept my mouth shut.

"Oh, I don't know. She's already had the money for about a month. She could just keep the interest. I think that would be fair." Carlotta was hoping I would agree and that Uncle Joey's reputation would scare me into complying with her wishes. How had Ramos ever thought she looked down on organized crime? She was already a master at it.

I focused on Miguel and realized he was worried. He was thinking his mother was going to blow it, and this man whom he had come to admire was going to send them away. He was sick of worrying about his mom's schemes, especially since the last one had nearly killed him. But he didn't know what to do. Maybe his father would let him stay, no matter what his mother wanted.

It was the kid's worry that decided me. "Fine," I said with reluctance. "I'll make the transfer." That's what I was there for, and what Uncle Joey did about Carlotta and Jackie wasn't my problem.

Uncle Joey sighed, but gave me a tight smile. "Very well," he agreed. "Carlotta and Miguel, you may go home. I will meet you there shortly."

"But the driver..." Miguel said.

"Oh right," Uncle Joey said. "I'll have Jackie..." He flushed, realizing that was no longer possible. "Just wait in the conference room for me." His growling tone let them know of his frustration, and they fled the office.

As soon as the door shut, he glanced at me. "I'm not used to this bickering between women." His eyes glowed with speculation, knowing I must have lied to him when I denied I could read minds a month ago. "Now that I know you have your powers back, you can help me with this problem."

"Wait a minute," I broke in. "Who said my powers were back?"

His brows rose in surprise, then his eyes narrowed. "Nice try Shelby, but you can't fool me. I had a feeling you were lying before I left for Mexico, and now I know you are. The way you purse your lips and fidget in your seat gives you away. Face it, you're just not a very good liar."

I opened my mouth to deny it, but what could I say? He was too good at this and I was out of my league.

"I need your help with this situation and, in return, I'm sure we can come up with something to compensate you for your ability."

He sounded so reasonable and compromising that I didn't know if I'd ever have a better chance to bargain for what I wanted. I could still deny it, but knowing him, he could just threaten my family again, and I would lose any bargaining power I had.

He could tell I was waffling, so he continued with his plea. "You know what Jackie and Carlotta were thinking. You can help me figure out what to do. I didn't realize Jackie felt so strongly... and Carlotta is not what I thought. I don't know how to take care of this. I could really use your help."

It had surprised him that Jackie would hire an assassin, although it showed a lot of spunk, and now she was gone. "Jackie's gone," he continued, "and Carlotta... I'm beginning to think I never knew her. It seems all she wants is money. I'm usually not so blind. Then there's my son."

He glanced at me and smiled, his eyes lighting with joy. "Can you believe it? I have a son? It's something I've wanted for a long time, and I guess lately with everything that happened with Kate, it really hit me, that I had no one. Now I have a chance again. But with Carlotta, it's not so easy. How can I keep him without keeping her?"

He actually touched his hair and rubbed the back of his neck. I'd never seen Uncle Joey so unsettled and emotional. He was always in control and coldly detached, with his clothing immaculate, his shoes polished, and not one hair on his head out of place.

"There is a way." I gave in, jumping on my chance to keep him out of my life. "But you have to promise me full immunity... or whatever it is you call it."

His movements stilled, and he considered my proposal. If he agreed, he'd lose his right to my powers, but maybe there was a way around it. He twitched and glanced up. Had I just heard that? My smile was all the answer he needed.

"I might be willing to consult with you once in a while," I said. "But only by my choice and not yours." He was listening, so I continued. "Certain conditions would have to apply, mainly that it wouldn't put my life in danger. I'm getting tired of getting shot at." He nodded his agreement.

"Plus you would accept it if I turned a job down," I said. "I would only work for you if I wanted, and not because of any type of coercion on your part." He pursed his lips, but motioned to continue. "And last, of course, you would pay me."

I couldn't believe what I was doing. It felt like I was bargaining with the devil himself. But what choice did I have? He knew about my power. I had to make some concessions or he wouldn't even consider it.

He was thinking that I drove a hard bargain, but at least he'd have access to my ability. In his dealings, he'd always known everyone had a price. He'd just have to make his offers enticing enough that I'd always agree to what he wanted. It was something he was good at.

Oh please! If he thought he could always buy me out, he was in for a rude awakening. Of course, part of what he was thinking was true. I did want some of the five million, but wouldn't most people? Dammit! I decided not to ask for it. I wouldn't be bribed. It was the only way this might work out.

"Agreed," he said. "Now tell me how to take care of this situation."

I let out a breath of relief, and tried to keep my cool.

"All right," I began, jumping in before he could change his mind. "First of all, I think I know a way to get rid of Carlotta and keep Miguel. As you've already guessed, Carlotta is only in it for the money. She's planning on taking it and leaving you. She figures that since she is the mother of your son, you won't harm her."

I let him digest this news before I continued. He was taking it pretty well, which made me realize he had already accepted what motivated Carlotta. Now was the hard part. Should I tell him that Miguel probably wasn't his son? Maybe it was better to save that for the end.

"The best way to get what you want is to give Carlotta the five million with the understanding that you get to keep Miguel. She can visit or talk with him at any time. He just lives with you now. If she doesn't agree, then she doesn't get the money. Tell her you're prepared to pay for his schooling and college education. Remind her that once he is eighteen, he can live where he chooses."

"But what if he wants to live with her?" Uncle Joey asked.

"He won't," I said with a smile. "He idolizes you. You saved him from something he views as his mother's fault. As long as he knows his mother is taken care of, he'll be happy not to worry about her anymore. I don't think Carlotta realizes how deep Miguel's loyalty to you has become, and it would be best if you didn't share that with her."

Uncle Joey relaxed in his chair. This was going much better than he thought. Only he couldn't give Carlotta the full five million since it had cost him close to two million to get her and Miguel out of that mess. But once he pointed that out to her, he was sure she would agree to his reasoning. Three million was still a lot of money.

"So how do I get Jackie back?" he asked. That would be the hard part.

I thought about it for a moment. He was right about it being hard. "She loves you. I don't understand it, but she does. Somehow, you've got to get Jackie to realize that you're kicking Carlotta out because you want to be with her. Can you do that?"

"I'm not used to groveling," he said. "I don't even like people who grovel. So how am I supposed to get her back without groveling? That's something I just won't do."

"She wouldn't expect that from you," I assured him. "In fact, she'd probably want something a little more dramatic. Like kidnapping her and locking her in your room until you can convince her that she is the love of your life." Uncle Joey raised his brows, thinking I had read too many romance novels. "Hmm, you might be right about that. So... you figure it out. I'm sure you can come up with something. Just make sure Carlotta is out of the picture first. That's very important."

He huffed, thinking I had a low opinion of him if I didn't think he already knew that.

I smiled and shrugged. "Well, that about covers it. You might want to make Miguel's parentage official by legally adopting him or something. Just in case... you know... Carlotta decides he's not really yours."

"I can just get a blood test," he said.

"Umm... not a good idea." I shook my head. "How much do you want him as your son?"

"He is my son," he said in a low voice. "He looks just like me... well... a lot like me at that age." He thought it over and realized I had a point.

"Miguel wants to believe you are his father, but he's not sure. Carlotta is using that card right now, but she's not sure either. If you go ahead with a blood test, well... you see what I mean. If it doesn't come back positive, you'll lose him."

Uncle Joey thought it over. He didn't need a blood test to accept Miguel as his son. But if he ever did, he could make sure it came out right. He glanced at me sharply, had I just heard that? Hmm... this was harder than he remembered. He had a lot of secrets he didn't want me to know.

"Just a thought," I said. "But for the sake of your son, you might want to consider going straight. Get on the right side of the law and all that. It would be sad if he ended up in jail or killed by one of your enemies."

He smiled at my audacity. "You're good for me, Shelby. I appreciate your suggestion. I'll consider it."

Was he making fun of me? I couldn't tell. "Why don't we make that transfer?" I said brightly, changing the subject. "Then I can get out of your hair." The further from him, the better. It just wasn't good to get involved in his life.

"Yes," he agreed. "Let's do that." He was thinking that I had a lot of potential, but with our arrangement, there was a chance that I could find out a lot of his secrets. He was pretty sure he could trust me, but it wasn't something he was used to. Most of the people who knew too much about his personal life didn't live very long.

"Hey, you know my secret, so let's just call us even and move on."

He smiled widely. "You do have a head for this," he exclaimed. "Maybe I should adopt you too." He laughed, loving the look of horror on my face.

"Ha, ha," I said, hoping he'd think I knew it was a joke. He didn't.

We spent the next few minutes doing the money transfer. I sighed with a tinge of regret when the full five million left my account. Then I felt selfish and shook it off. I didn't need his money. As I stood to leave, a thought occurred to me. "Did you know Mercer had replaced your driver?"

"Of course," he answered.

"So you knew Jackie's plan all along?"

"Yes, Shelby. There's little I don't know." He opened the door. "Oh, and you'd better give Chris a call. He's probably frantic by now. I'm sure he'd be happy to pick you up." I narrowed my eyes at his presumption, and he smiled. "If I were you," he said softly. "I wouldn't tell him about our little arrangement. He would probably do something stupid if he knew that I knew your secret, and that you're working for me again... even if it's only occasionally."

He shut his office door before I could reply. Damn. It hit me that most of the times I ever swore were because of Uncle Joey. It figured. At least I didn't have to worry about the money anymore. Even better, I had withstood the temptation to bargain with him about keeping some. The interest was still mine and that was better than nothing. That was positive, and probably a good place to start when I talked to Chris.

But was Uncle Joey right? Should I tell Chris? He would probably be upset, but would he be upset enough to do something stupid? I remembered his thoughts from a few days ago when he wanted to put a few bullets in Uncle Joey, but I knew he would never do something like that for real. Still, maybe I shouldn't tell him the whole story.

Carlotta and Miguel were in the conference room, and looked up at me as I walked by. I paused outside the door. "Uncle Joey would like to see you now," I said sweetly. I knew he didn't, but I was mad at him, so this was my way of getting even.

Carlotta glared at me, wondering if Joseph was really my uncle. If that was the case, it made sense that he sent the money to me, but why I was willing to part with it didn't. She'd have to keep her eye on me.

Miguel glanced at me with sudden interest, and I realized he thought we were related. That would make me his cousin. Then he thought it was too bad I was so old.

"Thanks," Miguel said. "See ya."

I twisted my lips into a semblance of a smile. I wasn't that old. Carlotta looked down her nose at me, and I hoped that was the last I'd see of her. I got to Jackie's empty desk and paused. She was gone along with Mercer. I didn't think I had to worry about Mercer anymore, but decided to call Chris before leaving the office anyway. He answered after the first ring.

"Are you okay?" he asked.

"Yes. I'm still at Thrasher Development, but I'm done. I just have one problem."

"If it's just one, then it must not be too bad, unless he found out your secret. So what is it?"

I wasn't ready to tell him about that, so I went with the immediate problem. "I don't have a way home. Do you think you could come get me?"

"Oh... that's the problem? Your life wasn't threatened or anything like that?"

"Not exactly," I hedged. "But I'd rather tell you about it when you get here."

"Okay," he paused. "You do know I'm in court don't you?"

"So... does that mean you can't come?" I asked.

"Basically. At least not until we have a recess. I shouldn't even be talking to you right now."

"Okay," I said. "I'll figure something out."

"The courthouse is only a few blocks from Thrasher," he said. "Maybe you could come over here and when there's a break, I can take you home."

"Sure," I agreed. "I'll walk over. Should I go to your office or the courthouse?"

"The courthouse," he answered. "I'm in the same courtroom as before, room 401."

"Okay. The courthouse it is. See you in a bit." I disconnected and sighed. I did not want to go to that courthouse. Just the thought of going over there made my stomach clench. But going was better than staying here. I glanced down the hall toward the opposite side of Uncle Joey's offices. There was an apartment down there that Ramos often stayed in. How was he doing? If Uncle Joey was here maybe Ramos was too. Should I go knock on his door and see if he needed anything?

I wandered in that direction and then thought better of it. That's when I noticed the door was ajar. Was someone in there that shouldn't be? I knocked on the door and it opened wider, allowing me to sneak a peek inside. I couldn't see anyone and, feeling like a trespasser, decided to leave it alone.

Reaching to pull the door closed, I heard footsteps inside. Jackie stepped into view and saw me standing there. Surprise and something like embarrassment flushed over her features and she glanced down the hallway behind me before ushering me inside.

"Are they still here?" she asked.

"You mean Carlotta and Uncle Joey?"

"Yes," she said. I nodded and her shoulders sagged. "When I left, this was as far as I got," she explained. "Ramos isn't here and I just couldn't leave yet. I can't stand it that Carlotta has taken advantage of Joe. He never falls for that kind of thing. It must be the kid. He's always wanted a kid, and now she's digging her claws into him. She's going to bleed him dry."

"Come on Jackie," I chided. "You know Uncle Joey's not like that. He's a lot smarter than you think."

"I hope so." She shook her head. "You probably think I'm crazy. I guess maybe I am, but I love him. All these years, I never knew how much until she came into the picture. I hired Mercer to threaten you so you'd give me the money. I suppose he saved you from the Mexicans so it worked out all right. When you didn't show up last night, I decided it would work just as well to take the money in front of Joseph, rather than behind his back, but I didn't expect him to outbid me." She laughed bitterly. "I thought if I had the money, he'd have a reason to come after me. But now I have nothing."

"That's not true," I said. "He may have loved Carlotta once, but I think he's over her. There's only one person he loves now, and that's you."

She gasped and glanced at me. "How can you be so sure?"

"Easy. He puts up with her because of the boy, but he's already got plans to get her out of the picture. Just hang in there." I patted her shoulder. "I should go."

"Don't tell him I'm here," she said.

"I won't." I walked toward the door. "Hey, how's Ramos? Is he doing any better?"

"Yeah, lots. He was here earlier, but Joe sent him on an errand."

"Good. Well, see you." I slipped out the door and hurried out of the office to the elevator. It took me down to the main level, and soon, I was out the revolving door to the street. My heart felt lighter; it was good that I'd talked to Jackie. I didn't like the fact that she'd hired Mercer, but like she said, he'd saved my life, so I couldn't be too upset about that.

It was crazy that she thought she had to threaten me to get me to do what she wanted, but it was probably because of Uncle Joey's influence. If she had asked me for the money and explained why she wanted it, I probably would have given it to her. That was the insane part.

It was a good day for a walk: not too hot and the sun was shining. About halfway to the courthouse I realized someone behind was keeping pace with me. It was the middle of the day, so I wasn't too worried, but they seemed awfully close, almost like they were about to step on my heels. I glanced back and caught a glimpse of a man in jeans and a baseball cap. He was looking down, so I couldn't see his face.

Irritated, I decided to move off the sidewalk so he could go around me. I let down my shields so I could hear what he was thinking, but his focus to move quickly overshadowed other thoughts. I stepped off the path and he hurried by, knocking against my shoulder. What a jerk.

I waited until he was further down the street before continuing my walk, and soon lost sight of him in the crowd. Something about him seemed familiar, but I couldn't place it. Just then, another person pushed by. This one had ugly legs and huge hair. Could that be the same guy dressed like a woman from the courthouse? I'd forgotten all about him. He passed by so fast that I couldn't catch his thoughts, and other than thinking it was strange, I brushed it aside. I had bigger things to worry about. Like what to tell Chris.

Shame washed over me. How could I even think of not telling him? Of course I'd tell him everything. How could I not? He was my husband. Keeping a secret like this would be bad for both of us. I needed to talk about this and get his advice, plus he needed to be able to trust me.

I paused in front of the courthouse. Maybe I could just wait out here. That way I wouldn't have to worry about what I'd hear inside. I glanced around the building and noticed a garden area off to the side. There were some pretty bushes behind a bench. And with the trees and shrubbery in that area, it was somewhat secluded.

Relieved I didn't have to enter the building, I sat down and pulled out my phone to let Chris know where I was. As I found his number, someone sat down on the bench, sliding into me, and grabbing the phone from my fingers. "Hey..."

His arm came around me and something hard pressed into my ribs, causing my heart to race with fear. "I could kill you right now," Mercer said. A baseball cap covered his face, but I recognized his voice. "But I'd rather not." My breath caught. He was the one who'd nearly run me down a few minutes ago.

"What's going on?" I said, bewildered. "Uncle Joey paid you off. You don't have to kill me anymore."

"Yes I do. I was always going to kill you." He was close enough to whisper in my ear. I realized that anyone passing by would only think we were sharing an intimate moment and nothing was wrong.

"I wanted to wait a little longer," he continued, "but I have to leave town. Your Uncle Joey doesn't like it when people double-cross him. And since I took more of his money than we agreed on, I'm afraid I can't stick around. Unfortunately, that means I had to hurry this along."

"You don't want to do this," I said breathlessly, my voice shaking with fear. "If you do, you're a dead man. Uncle Joey will never let you live. Your life will be over. You'll never get another job, let alone live to spend the money you've already got."

He stilled, considering what I said. I'd always called Manetto my uncle and, if it were true, that could be bad. But if he was my uncle, what was I doing working for the police? It didn't make sense, and from what he'd gathered from Manetto, he didn't see the connection. Mercer wanted to kill me so bad it hurt. I had humiliated him. He couldn't allow that to go unpunished. But I was right. Manetto had a lot of influence. He just had to decide if killing me was worth the risk.

I knew when he made his decision. I crunched my eyes together and hoped it wouldn't hurt too much. A whine, followed by a wet splatter across my face, startled me. Mercer's arm around me slackened, and his head fell onto my shoulder.

I cringed but found I couldn't move. Was that blood? A shadow fell over me, and I glanced up to find Ramos at my side. He took my phone from Mercer's hand and pulled me to my feet, sliding his arm around my waist. "Just walk away," he said. "Put your arm around me and keep walking."

I focused on his voice and did as he said, amazed I could move at all. Mostly, Ramos was dragging me, but once I figured that out, I started moving my feet a little.

"That's right," he said. "You're doing great." He took a cloth from his pocket and wiped at my cheek and nose. It came away red. "That's better," he said, and tucked the cloth back in his pocket. My legs wobbled, and I started to shake.

"Keep it together, Shelby. We're almost to the car. You can do this."

He turned us off the main walkway and down a sidewalk that entered the parking garage. There were a lot of steps going down, and my knees started to buckle. Ramos held me to his side and took most of my weight. We made it to the bottom, and he stopped to catch his breath. That was when I remembered he'd been shot. It probably still pained him wherever it was, and he'd had to basically carry me down the steps. It made me feel even worse. I leaned over and took big breaths, concentrating on fighting down the bile rising in my throat. I won, but just barely.

Ramos recovered before I did. "This way." Once again he put his arm around me for support, but this time my legs were working and he didn't have to take so much of my weight. We reached his black sports car, and he helped me inside. I still felt a little lightheaded, so I put my head between my knees. By the time he got in and put on his seat belt, I felt well enough to sit up.

I slipped on my seatbelt while Ramos backed out of the parking spot. He drove up the ramp and deftly pulled into traffic. The sound of sirens raised the hair on my arms and sent a shiver down my spine. Ramos eased the car over to the side of the road. In a moment, two police cars coming from the opposite direction raced by. As soon as they were gone, Ramos pulled back onto the street.

"You're safe now," Ramos said, noticing how tightly my hands were clenched. He was thinking it was a close call, and he was glad he'd been trailing Mercer.

"So, you were watching Mercer?' I asked, finally managing to speak. "Did you know he was going to try and kill me?"

"I had an idea he might," he answered. "After you told me he killed the Mexicans, I figured someone within our organization had hired him. It didn't take long to find out it was Jackie. Mr. Manetto didn't think Mercer would try anything until after he was paid, and I agreed. I knew he would make his move today, and when I overheard you telling Chris you'd meet him at the courthouse I hurried over."

"You heard me?"

"Yeah, I was in the apartment. I went out the back way."

"Oh, now it makes sense." That's why the door was ajar and maybe why Jackie looked guilty. They'd been eavesdropping on my conversation.

"I never thought Mercer would try to kill you in plain sight though," Ramos continued.

"Yeah, that was a shocker. I never thought it would happen that way either." I glanced at him. "How did you know he was going to pull the trigger?"

"The set of his shoulders." He glanced at me, thinking it was really that I had crunched my eyes together. "It's easy to spot if you know what to look for. Luckily, he was so focused on you that he didn't notice me." He was thinking it was a close call. If he'd been any later, I'd be dead too. He was relieved he'd made it in time. That was cutting it too close for his taste.

"Yeah," I agreed. "You got him just in the nick of time. He was going to kill me. I'm still in shock that I'm alive. I don't ever want anything like that to happen ever again. I think I've aged ten years. My hair will probably go gray overnight. I can't believe what happened. You killed him. And we just walked away. How gutsy is that?"

I couldn't stop talking. It was like the plug got pulled, and my mouth wouldn't stop running. "And it worked! We got away. They'll never know it was us, or what happened. And since he's a killer, everyone will be glad he's dead. I'll bet they won't even look hard for who killed him. It wouldn't do them much good anyway since there's no evidence or anything to tie him to you." Ramos was thinking I was losing it, and something I'd said earlier had him baffled. It was almost like I'd read his mind.

"Oh my... goodness," I said, realizing he was right. "I'm so sorry. I'm babbling like a crazy person." I swallowed and took a deep breath, letting it out slowly to get a hold of myself. Tears gathered in my eyes, but I fought them back. Talking had kept them away, but now... now it was hard not to cry.

Ramos could tell I was about to cry, and it made him nervous. He hated it when a woman cried. Especially when it didn't make any sense. Mercer was dead. I was alive. What was there to cry about? He glanced at me and was just about to tell me it was okay if I kept talking, but the look I was giving him made him confused. It was almost like I'd heard his thoughts, and I didn't approve.

I snapped my mouth shut and glanced out the window. "It looks like you're taking me home," I said, hoping to distract him. "I should probably call Chris and tell him that you gave me a ride." I reached into my purse for my cell, and realized it wasn't there.

"I've got it."

"That's right," I said, remembering he'd taken it from Mercer's lifeless fingers.

"What's right?" He asked, glancing at me.

His lips hadn't moved and his mouth was shut tight, and it hit me that he hadn't been speaking out loud. My pulse raced, but there was still a chance I could cover it. "You took it from Mercer. That was fast thinking on your part. Can I have it back now?"

"Sure." He handed it over. He was wondering if it had worked. Had I just read his mind? If I had, it all made sense. Everything about me fell into place. Why Mr. Manetto had kept me around. Why I'd been at all his meetings. Why I was still on the payroll, and why he'd sent the five million dollars to me. What he couldn't figure out was how I could do it. But he guessed that really didn't matter in the long run.

A tiny smile curved his lips. I was tempted to say something sarcastic, but that would give me away for sure. He may think he had it figured out, but I was not going to talk about it. Ever.

I pushed send to call Chris, and when he answered, it was hard not to cry again. "Hi honey," I said.

"Shelby! Are you all right?"

"Yeah I'm fine. Sorry I didn't call... something came up and I didn't have to come to the courthouse for a ride after all. In fact, I'm on my way home right now."

"You'll never believe it," he said. "They found Mercer. Dead. Someone shot him in the head."

I swallowed and licked my lips. "Really? What happened?"

"No one knows. They found him sitting on a bench outside the courthouse."

"And he'd been shot?" I asked, hoping I sounded normal for someone who'd just heard that the man threatening to kill her was dead. Probably not.

"Yes." Chris was quiet, and it made me worry that he was putting things together.

"Wow," I said. "That's crazy. I wonder who killed him."

"Hmm... me too," he said. Uh-oh, this was not good. "How are you getting home?" he asked.

"Um... Ramos said he could take me. I was really happy about that too, since I didn't want to walk all the way to the courthouse. So it worked out great." I was repeating myself, and it made me sound suspicious. Probably something Chris would easily pick up on.

"So you never came to the courthouse?" he asked.

"Nope," I said.

"Hmm... I wonder what Mercer was doing there."

"Yeah, me too."

"So... is Ramos with you right now?" Chris asked.

"Uh-huh. We'll have to talk about it when you get home, okay?"

"Um... what you're really saying is you can't talk about it now, right?" he asked.

"That sounds about right," I answered. "I'll see you soon then. Love you!" I ended the call. I winced just a little, but figured Chris would understand when I explained the whole story.

Ramos was thinking that if I really could read minds, it would suck to be Chris. I sniffed in response, but managed to keep my mouth shut. He glanced at me and chuckled.

"What's so funny?" I asked.

"Nothing," he said. If I wasn't going to say anything, he wouldn't either.

We pulled up in front of my house, and relief came over me like a soft blanket. I was alive and I was home. I turned to face Ramos. "Thanks," I said. I knew it was inadequate, but it was all he wanted to hear.

"No problem," he said. "Are you going to tell him?"

He meant Chris. "I don't know... but probably."

He nodded, thinking that was a chance he'd have to take. But since he'd just saved my life, he didn't think Chris would mind enough to do anything about it.

I opened the car door and got out. Before shutting it, I leaned in. "He'll be fine with it," I said, and shut the door. I hurried up the sidewalk and unlocked my door. Safe inside, I glanced out the window. He was still sitting there. I gave a quick wave, and with a nod, he drove off.

Chapter 13

Ramos thought he knew about me, but it didn't make me panic like I thought it would. Probably because I didn't think he'd tell anyone. Especially since the only person I had to worry about already knew.

I did what I always did after nearly getting killed. I began filling up the bathtub with hot water and "stress relief soothing eucalyptus and mint" bath salts. I glanced in the mirror and found spatters of blood on my hair, face and neck. Grabbing a paper towel, I washed it off, then noticed the blood all over my shirt. Now I knew why Uncle Joey preferred black. The blood didn't show up as easily. Yuck. I pulled off the shirt and threw it in the garbage. Even if I got the blood out, I could never wear it again. At this rate I would have to get a whole new wardrobe.

Once I finally got into the tub, the tears began to flow. It seemed like I'd just done this. When was it ever going to stop? I really needed a vacation. It would be wonderful to get away from all this. I took a deep breath. The aroma from my bath soothed me and calmed my mind.

It was over. Mercer was dead. He was no longer a threat to me, and everyone else who wanted to kill me or take the money was dead and gone as well. I was finally safe. I let out a sigh and settled back, finally relaxing into the scented water. Uncle Joey knew, but I could work with that. Now all I had to decide was how to tell Chris.

A half hour later, I decided it was time to get out of the tub. I wracked my brain to remember what day it was, and if I needed to do anything. Like picking up Savannah from dance, or taking Josh to a soccer game.

My mind drew a blank. So much had happened in the last few days, I couldn't even remember what was going on in my real life. I remembered I'd already picked up Savannah from dance because that was the day the Mexicans had tried to kill me. Was that just two days ago?

That meant today was Friday. I smiled, pleased with myself that I'd figured it out. Even better, it also meant I could order pizza for dinner. I got dressed and placed the order, asking for it to be delivered at six, which wasn't for another three hours. I found my bag of popcorn still in the microwave and threw it in the garbage. I needed warm popcorn and put in a fresh bag to pop. Time to watch a show.

Josh came home and promptly guzzled the milk straight from the carton. He was slurping the last of it and came in to find me in front of the TV. What was going on? He remembered the same thing happening the other day. Was something wrong with me? Stuff like this just didn't happen.

I said hello, and Savannah walked in, taking in my slouch and noticing the episode of Castle I was watching. "Mom!" she said forcefully, appalled and confused. "What are you doing?" This was weird. How could I act like a kid? That wasn't cool. I was supposed to be the example. I was the adult. Then her thoughts turned into worry. Was I having a midlife crisis? Did that mean I was going to divorce her dad and get a tattoo?

I turned off the TV and managed to keep a straight face. "Hi guys. How was school?"

Savannah relaxed. That was more like it. After hearing about school, even the parts they didn't exactly tell me, things were back to normal. I pushed the near-death incident to the back of my mind, determined not to dwell on what might have happened. Ramos was right about that part. Mercer was dead, I wasn't... so what was there to cry about?

Chris came home early. I wasn't expecting him to walk in, so when he did, my eyes got misty. I hugged him tight, holding him a little longer than usual. Tears welled up at how close to death I'd been. Again. A few tears leaked out, but I managed to stop from gushing, and the moment passed.

"Are you okay?" he asked.

"Yes," I said wiping my eyes. "I'm good now."

"So what happened?" He was dreading my news, hoping I wasn't involved in any way, shape, or form with Mercer's death.

Knowing what he thought made it even harder. Should I tell him everything? Would it be worse for him to know Mercer had almost killed me? I'd been thinking about what to tell him all afternoon. Now that he was here, I still didn't know.

"Did you know I just realized something today?" I asked instead.

"What's that?" he said.

"That I mostly only swear when I'm around Uncle Joey."

Chris chuckled. "I'm not surprised." Then he got serious. "So tell me what happened."

We went outside on the deck, and I began by explaining that Uncle Joey had called me, saying his driver would be there to pick me up. "It turned out Mercer was the driver. I had no idea what was going on or who he was working for, but it scared me to death."

He could hardly believe it. "So why did Mercer pick you up? Who was he working for?"

"I think by then he was working for Uncle Joey, although Jackie thought he was working for her." I explained how Jackie brought Mercer in to threaten Carlotta's life if Uncle Joey didn't give her the five million, and how Uncle Joey paid Mercer one hundred and fifty grand not to kill Carlotta.

"So Mercer took the money and ran?"

"Basically."

"So how did he end up dead at the courthouse?" he asked.

I sighed. "That's another story. Let me finish this part first."

The phone rang before I could say another word. I checked the caller ID. It was the police. "I think it's Dimples. I'd better take this." Chris hid his irritation with a quick nod, and left to change his clothes.

"Hi Shelby," he began. "Just thought I'd better let you know that Mercer is no longer a threat. We found him shot in the head on the courthouse grounds."

"Yes, I heard. Chris was there and called me. Do you have any idea who did it?"

"None," he said with alacrity. "But we're thinking it was a professional, like someone took a hit out on a hit-man." I could hear the smile in his voice. He cleared his throat. "Do you happen to know anything about this?"

"Me?" I squeaked. "No, not a clue." Of course he had to ask, but was it because of my premonitions? Or because of my ties with Uncle Joey? I should have been prepared for the question, but I wasn't.

"Well, okay," he said. "We don't have much to go on. No one saw anything suspicious, and there are no leads, but I thought I'd pass it by you. If you hear anything or get any premonitions... you'll let me know. Right?"

"Sure," I said. "Anything I can do to help." I bit my lip, knowing I was lying through my teeth. And Uncle Joey thought I was bad at it?

"Thanks again for your help yesterday. How are you holding up? After what happened I was a little worried."

"I'm good," I said. If he knew everything I'd been through, he wouldn't be asking. Yesterday was nothing compared to what had happened today. "Is Jessica Palmer going to be all right?"

"Yes, which reminds me... the mayor has requested that you and Chris come to the Official Museum Opening Gala two weeks from tonight. He has something he wants to present you, but I promised him I wouldn't tell you what it was. Can you come?"

"Um... I think so."

"That's great. Since you're the guest of honor it will mean a lot to have you and Chris there. I'll send along the invitation. Just be sure to mark it on your calendar." He thanked me again, and we disconnected.

Chris had come back while I was still on the phone and opened his mouth to ask what Dimples wanted. Before he could say a word, the doorbell rang. It was our pizza.

"That's dinner," I said brightly, rushing toward the door.

"Didn't we just have pizza the other night?" Chris was remembering that night. It was right after the Mexicans had nearly killed me. If I'd ordered pizza again so soon, did that mean it was the same scenario and Mercer had almost killed me? He shuddered. Did he really want to know?

I called the kids to come and eat, grateful for this little reprieve. Chris was too. He was hungry and figured the pizza would help fortify him for what was to come. Everyone snarfed down the pizza, and in no time, dinner was over.

Both Savannah and Josh had plans with their friends. Savannah was watching a movie at her friend's house, and Josh was playing soccer. I made them both promise to be home by eleven, or call and let me know what they were doing. They grumbled, but when I wouldn't back down, finally accepted it. Especially with Chris backing me up.

They left, and Chris tugged me into his arms. "Good job with them," he said.

I smiled and kissed him. "Hey... and we're home alone. What could be better?"

"I'd like to show you," he said. "But I guess I'll have to wait until you finish your story. I think I'm ready to hear it... as long as it's not too long." He was really thinking that part of him dreaded knowing what happened. Mostly because he wasn't sure he'd like it. "So Mercer picked you up as Manetto's driver, but it was Jackie who hired Mercer in the first place?" he asked.

"Yes," I said, pulling him onto the couch where we could get comfortable. "She wanted to get the money before Uncle Joey did. She thought if she had it, Uncle Joey would have a reason to find her and leave Carlotta. I don't think she was counting on Uncle Joey's son Miguel."

Chris raised his brows. "His son was there?"

"Yes." I told him about Miguel and Carlotta and how neither one of them was sure he was really Uncle Joey's son.

"Wait a minute," he interrupted. "So is he Manetto's son or not? Weren't you able to pick that up?"

"No, I mean yes... I'm telling you what I picked up, not what they said. When I told Uncle Joey Miguel might not be his son, he said he didn't care. He was willing to claim him without knowing for sure."

"Wait," Chris frowned. "You told him that?"

Oops. Chris caught the guilty look on my face and closed his eyes. He was swearing. A lot. "I can hear that," I said.

He took a deep breath and caught my gaze. His brows were drawn together and he was thinking this was the worst thing that could happen. Somehow I had let Manetto know my power was back. This was why he should have been there. He could have helped protect me from myself. How could I be so stupid?

"I can still hear you," I repeated. "And it's not what you think."

"You mean he doesn't know?" His voice brightened with hope.

I shook my head. "He knows," I said defeated. "But he tricked me." That sounded pretty lame, but what Chris was thinking was worse. Did he really think I was that stupid? That the only way I could have gotten out of it was if he'd been there to "protect" me? Anger simmered, and I fought against indignation.

Chris realized I was mad, but he didn't want to think it was anything he'd done. He was mad too... and disappointed. What was I thinking? How could I let Manetto know? Now our lives were ruined. Manetto would never let me go. How could we ever live normal lives again? Manetto would always be there. This was a disaster, and it was all my fault!

"Chris," I whined. "Stop it! Do you think for one minute that I wanted this? It happened. Maybe it's my fault, maybe it isn't, but your blaming me isn't helping!"

His gaze jerked to mine, and he realized I'd heard every one of his uncharitable thoughts about me. I blinked back tears and he felt even worse. But he was still mad, and he couldn't let it go.

"It's not as bad as you think," I reasoned. "If you'd just calm down and give me a minute to explain, you'll see that."

I wiped the tears away and caught that now he was upset that I was reading his thoughts. Where were my shields? What happened to that plan? He'd say something to remind me, but he knew that wouldn't help, even though it made him angrier than ever. Plus I'd probably just picked all that up and heard it anyway. So what difference did it make? He was screwed no matter what. Maybe he should just leave until he was under control. Take a drive or something. He didn't want to hurt me...

"Chris," I growled. "Just say it... say what you're thinking."

"Fine," he said. "I don't want to hurt you. I'm sorry you heard my thoughts, but you're not supposed to be listening, and when I'm upset, I can't control everything I think."

"I know." I put my arms around him. "It's all right." He slowly raised his arms until he was hugging me back, and I sighed. "I know this is hard, and I'm sorry. I wish it was different."

"It's okay," he said. "Could you just put up your shields for now? I need to know you're not going to hear my thoughts, because I'm still pretty mad. I would never say anything to hurt you, but not thinking them, even just a little, is too much to ask right now."

He was right. I thought mean things about people when I was upset, but I would never say them out loud. "Sure," I agreed. "You're right. Just give me a minute."

I concentrated on turning off the switch that let me hear him, and got an instant headache. But at least I knew it was working. It was almost like the pain blocked the thoughts. So as long as it hurt, I was good to go.

"Okay," I said. "I can't hear you anymore. Think whatever you like." I said that with a smile so he'd know I wasn't mad, but I don't think he appreciated it, from the set of his jaw.

Oh well. We sat in silence for a minute, each gathering our composure.

"So how did Manetto find out?" he asked, his voice even and steady.

"Hmm... I think it was when Mercer came in asking Jackie who he should kill first. Mercer smirked and pointed the gun at me. It made me nervous. From his thoughts, I knew he wanted to kill me. I glanced at Uncle Joey and when our eyes met, he was thinking that he had everything under control. I nodded, and that's how he knew."

"Just from a nod?" Chris asked, incredulous.

"Well... not exactly. There was a lot more to it than that," I said forcefully.

Chris blew out his breath. "So what happened?"

"After Mercer took the money and left, Uncle Joey told Jackie and Carlotta he would divide the money between them, but Carlotta didn't want to do that. She felt like it was hers and Miguel's. Anyway, Jackie said she didn't want it anymore and ran out. Uncle Joey didn't know what to do, since that was when he realized he loved Jackie and not Carlotta. But he also wanted to keep Miguel. So you can see the dilemma he was in."

I waited until Chris nodded before continuing. "He sent Carlotta and Miguel out so he could talk to me, hoping I could help him out. I denied that my powers were back, but he wasn't having any of it. He claims I'm a bad liar. So that's when I made a bargain with him."

"What kind of bargain?" Chris asked, his eyes narrowing.

My shields dropped a bit, so I pushed real hard and the headache came back. That was close, but I could still tell that Chris was not happy. "I told him I would help him, but only on my terms. I told him it couldn't involve anyone shooting at me. I could accept or decline any time I wanted, and if I accepted, he had to pay me."

"What did he say?"

"He agreed," I said.

"Well, I'm not surprised," Chris said. "He's a master at finding out someone's price. I mean, consider yours. Wouldn't you say the price of your children was worth helping him?"

"Oh no," I said. "He was thinking about money. He knows I would never agree to help him on any other terms, and I'm too valuable to alienate. I know too much."

"Hmm... that might be true," Chris conceded. "So what happened after that?"

"I told him to give the five million to Carlotta in exchange for letting Miguel stay with him. She was planning on leaving him anyway, so this way he had leverage. With Miguel being seventeen and only one year away from independence, it wasn't that much of a stretch. Plus, he adores Uncle Joey. I signed over the money and left. Oh... and he doesn't think I should tell you any of this."

"Yeah," Chris fumed. "I'll bet he doesn't. So what happened at the courthouse?" He was dreading... oops, I caught the shields and the pain came back, blocking his thoughts.

"Uncle Joey thought Mercer might try something, so he sent Ramos to watch out for me. I walked to the courthouse like I told you I would, but I didn't want to go in. I saw the bench there and sat down, pulling out my phone to call you. That's when Mercer sat next to me and shoved a gun between my ribs. He said he'd always planned to kill me."

I licked my lips, dreading this part. "Just before he pulled the trigger, Ramos came up from behind and shot him." I paused to gain my composure. "He pulled me to my feet and we just walked away."

"Damn... that was pretty gutsy," Chris said. "But I'm sure glad Ramos did it." He closed his eyes and took a deep breath. "So... he brought you home after that?"

"Yes." I decided not to tell him that Ramos thought he knew my secret. It wouldn't serve any purpose other than make him angrier than he already was. "I told him I would probably tell you, but it didn't seem to bother him."

"No, I suppose not," Chris said. "After all, he saved your life."

Chris just sat there. He didn't take me in his arms or anything. This wasn't the way I expected him to act. It made me a little nervous. "So we don't have to worry about Mercer anymore. That's positive," I said, hoping to bring him out of it.

He smiled and glanced at me. I let out my breath, relieved. We fell into each other's arms. His kiss was almost savage with pent-up frustration. I couldn't hold onto my shields, and his worry and anger hit me hard. So did his love. They were both so much alike it amazed me. After the torrent of our emotions was spent, we held each other close. "How long before the kids get home," he asked, a gleam in his eyes.

I checked the clock and smiled wickedly. "Not for another hour or so."

Much later, I remembered Dimples' phone call. "Do we have any plans two weeks from tonight?" I asked.

Chris thought for a moment. "I don't think so. Why?"

"When Dimples called, he told me the mayor wanted us to come to the opening gala for the museum. He said I was the guest of honor and the mayor had something to present me. What do you think it could be?"

"I don't know," he answered. "Maybe there was a reward for the paintings, and he wants to present you with a check."

I laughed. "Wouldn't that be something? We'll have to be sure and go. Who knows? Maybe we'll get some fast money after all."

Our invitation came two days later. It was a black tie affair and, not including my old prom dress, which I had kept all these years, I had nothing to wear. Luckily, the mall was open. I searched until I found the perfect dress. It was a long cherry-red, one-shoulder, chiffon gown with a side slit. Next, I found some gorgeous black platform pumps. I couldn't wait to show them to Chris. Of course they weren't cheap, so I went to the ATM to check on the account from Uncle Joey. Who knew, maybe there'd be another five million dollars in there.

The balance came up showing an extra eight thousand dollars. Not too bad for the advice I'd given him, minus the two or three times I'd nearly been killed. Add to that all the stress, and I figured it mostly evened out. I could live with that. I could also live with using some of it to buy the dress and shoes. I smiled all the way back to the store.

Another week passed with no contact from Uncle Joey, and I began to relax. Dimples called me a couple of times. The first was to see if I got my invitation and was still planning on attending the gala. The second was to make sure I got the check for my consulting fee. It had arrived the day before, and gave me a feeling of satisfaction that I'd done something good... plus making a little money didn't hurt either.

Maybe I could go somewhere with my own consulting agency. On a whim, I spent some time picking out business cards and ended up ordering some. My business card said, "Shelby Nichols Consulting Agency" with an S on one side and an N on the other. With a smaller C and A in the middle above the words, it made the acronym of SCAN, which I thought was pretty cool since that's what I do when I read minds.

On the Internet, I bought my domain name, shelbynicholsconsulting.com, and set up a website for a pretty good price. I put my cell phone number and my website on my business cards and was good to go. The best part was that my first check from the police paid for everything, with some left over.

The day my business cards arrived, I knew it was time to talk to Chris about my idea. I'd been putting it off until things died down, but now I hoped enough time had passed that I could talk to him about it. Of course, I hid the business cards, realizing I'd done it all backwards, but he didn't have to know that.

I had to wait for the right moment, so just before bed one night I broached the subject. I decided to start with the check I got for helping consult with the police. "Look what came in the mail." I held it up. "It's a check for three hundred dollars! Can you believe it?"

"Let's see that," Chris held out his hand, his brows drawn into a frown. It was hard, but I used all my will power to block his thoughts, knowing it was essential to our relationship. "What's it for?"

"My work with the police. Dimples told me to keep track of my hours and they'd pay me. So here's my first paycheck."

"That's nice," he said, handing it back.

I couldn't tell what he was thinking, and I wanted to drop my shields so bad it hurt. "So, what do you think? It's great, right?"

He glanced into my hopeful face and sighed. "Sure."

Frustrated that he wasn't telling me what he thought, I decided to take advantage of the situation. "Yeah, I'm thinking it might not be a bad idea to set up a business account at the bank. I could call it the Shelby Nichols Consulting Agency, and keep it separate from our other accounts. Do you think I'd have to get a small business license or something?"

He mulled it over. "You really want to do this? After everything you've been through?" Put me through was what he was thinking. Oops. But in a way, he was right.

"I do," I said. "It's a way to put my power to good use. And... I can make sure I only take cases that won't involve getting killed. Besides, it's not like it's a detective agency or anything. Consulting doesn't mean investigating... mostly just talking to people, and helping them figure out what to do based on what I pick up."

He still wasn't convinced, so I plunged ahead. "I talked to Dimples about helping him in the future, and he said that what happened in the museum was a mistake, and that he wouldn't involve me in anything dangerous like that again. It would mostly just be giving him my premonitions and he'd follow up on them. So it wouldn't be dangerous at all."

Chris raised his brows, so I kept going before he could object. "Plus, if Uncle Joey knows I have my own agency and that I'm helping the police, he might not be too interested in involving me very often. I think it might be a deterrent for him, and if I'm helping him with his business, why not help the good guys too? Then I wouldn't feel so guilty about helping him once in a while."

"It's also something that could get you into a lot of trouble," Chris added. "Don't you see the conflict of interest this would involve? The police and Manetto together could prove difficult, at least as far as Manetto is concerned. Manetto wouldn't like it."

"Exactly," I said. "So maybe he'll just leave me alone. That would be good, right?"

"Well, yes, but... I'm not sure that's wise. Manetto might find a way to use that to his advantage."

"Not if I don't let him," I said. "Hey... I'm stuck with helping Uncle Joey once in a while... that's just the way it is, but if I can make a difference helping the police, I could live with it."

Chris lowered his head in defeat. "I might be willing to agree if you took some self-defense classes or something."

"That's a great idea!" I said. "If I can learn to anticipate someone's moves... which shouldn't be too hard considering my mind-reading skills... I could know what they're going to do before they do it. That would give me the edge for sure."

Chris shook his head. How the hell could he stop me now? He could tell I'd already made up my mind about this. In fact, I'd probably gone ahead and ordered business cards and who knows what else?

I ducked my head to hide my guilt, and he glanced at me sharply. I clenched my eyes together, knowing I'd been caught. "Shelby..." Chris growled.

"Do you want to see them?" I asked. "They're pretty cool."

Chris ran his hands through his hair. "Why not?" He sighed with defeat.

On that note, I hurried to the closet where I kept them in a box and took one out. "See? It's pretty cool, right?"

He took it from me and a reluctant smile twisted his lips. "SCAN?" he said. He was thinking it was kind of silly.

"It's not... I mean... well... I think it's great," I said, doing some back-pedaling. "Since that's kind of what I do." I decided I liked it better when I talked to people who didn't know I could read their minds. It seemed I was always getting into trouble with Chris.

"Okay," he said reluctantly. "I can see you've already made up your mind about this. So, I'll just have to live with it. But let's make it legitimate and legal. We'll need to get a small business license and figure out startup costs and tax information."

"It might be nice to have an office somewhere too. If I get a lot of clients," I added.

He took a deep breath. "Let's take it one step at a time for now."

"Sure," I said, smiling brightly. My chest fluttered with excitement. This was going to work! My own business! How cool was that?

I got a pad of paper and pen and we wrote a list of everything I'd need. Chris knew a lot about the business part since he was a lawyer, and having him involved gave me a lot of ideas. "We could work together," I said. "I could help with some of your cases like I did with Hodges. The other lawyers in your firm might want my help too."

"Maybe," he said. "But you're forgetting that we don't want it to get out that you can read people's minds. That would be bad."

"Oh," I said. "You're right. I could help you though, and if you needed my help with someone else's case we could be discreet."

"Umm... we'll see," he said. He glanced at me sharply as a new thought occurred to him. "If you do this, you're going to have to be careful. Real careful, as in 'not letting anyone know how you find the answers' careful."

"Yeah, I know what you mean, but I can do it. Dimples accepts that I have premonitions, others would too."

"I hope you're right."

"I'll be careful," I promised. "No one will ever know." We both knew that wasn't true. "Besides Uncle Joey," I amended. "By the way," I said. "He put eight thousand dollars in my account."

Chris raised his brows, then drew them together. "Blood money," he said.

I didn't like the sound of that. "It's not that bad," I said. "He's just paying me for all I went through because of the five million. And don't forget I helped him solve his little problem with Carlotta and Jackie."

He nodded his agreement, but he still didn't like it. "Have you heard from him?" he asked, suddenly concerned that I wouldn't tell him if I had.

"No," I said. "Not a peep."

"Good," he said, and his gaze met mine. "Promise me you'll tell me if he calls and what he wants. I want to be included in your dealings with him."

"Sure," I agreed. "I'd like that." I wanted Chris' help, but I didn't think Uncle Joey would want Chris involved. So I left it at that, never actually verbalizing how or what his involvement would entail.

That's when the realization hit me that I didn't want Chris to ever be in the same room as Uncle Joey. I couldn't imagine that going well. It even made me sweat a little. The other thing I didn't want to admit was that even though Uncle Joey's five million dollars had nearly gotten me killed, it had nothing to do with Mercer. That was because of an unhappy coincidence. So since Uncle Joey had basically saved my life, did that mean I had to spend the rest of my life paying him back?

Chapter 14

The day of the Museum Gala arrived. I picked up the black tuxedo I'd rented for Chris and brought it home. It reminded me of our wedding day, and a little thrill of excitement ran up my back. After a long hot shower, I did my make-up and hair with special attention. I couldn't wait to put on my beautiful red dress and see the look in Chris' eyes.

The invitation said the evening included food and drinks along with a band and dancing. The governor and mayor would be in attendance, and it made me a little nervous. At least the invitation didn't say I was the guest of honor. The mayor probably just wanted to thank me for helping the police crack the case, and Dimples made it sound more important than it was to make sure I'd come.

Chris got home early enough for a quick shower, and soon he was dressed and looking like he belonged on the set of a movie with him as the dashing hero. I waited until the last minute to put on my dress. It hugged my body in all the right places, and was long enough to do justice to my tall black pumps.

I added the diamond earrings the bank had given me, happy that they didn't make me give the earrings back when I transferred the five million out. After applying my perfectly matching red lipstick and a spray of my favorite perfume, all I needed was my purse. The small black clutch purse was just the right size to hold my lipstick and some gum. I threw in a few business cards, then caught sight of my stun flashlight sitting on the dresser and decided to add it since it would fit. I shrugged, who knew? With the way my life was going, it might come in handy.

Chris was reading the paper in the living room when I came out. His eyes widened. "Wow," he said, dropping the paper and standing. "You look amazing."

"Thanks." I smiled. "So do you."

He came to my side. "Shall we?" he asked, his slow smile devouring me. I floated to the car and looked with anticipation to a wonderful evening. Chris was thinking how great I looked in red, then his thoughts turned to how much a dress like that must have cost, and he hoped I hadn't spent too much. Were those shoes new too? They looked expensive. What about the earrings? Were they real diamonds?

I had promised myself that tonight I wouldn't read his thoughts, or say anything if I did. I wanted to make this evening as normal as possible, without either of us getting angry, or having hurt feelings. I glanced at Chris and my resolve crumbled, he was still fretting about the money. Why couldn't he just put it aside for this once?

"Honey," I said. "Just so you know, I bought the dress with the money from Uncle Joey, so you don't need to worry about it... just in case you are," I quickly added. "And the earrings are from the bank, remember?"

"Oh, yeah," he said, disgruntled that I had read his mind. He was hoping that tonight he wouldn't have to worry about that.

Irritation buzzed through me. Why was he offended that I'd told him something to ease his worries? He should be grateful, not mad. I closed my eyes and decided to let it go. It wasn't worth being mad about, and I wanted to have a good time.

Maybe the best way to do that was raise my shields for real. I hated doing it, but if I wanted tonight to be normal, it was my only choice. "Chris, I'm going to try hard to keep my shields up all night. I don't want you to worry about it, okay? I really want to have a good time."

"Okay," he said. "I do too. Thanks." I closed my mind and got a small headache, but I could tell it helped since Chris relaxed into his seat, and we were able to visit like normal people.

After the short drive, we pulled into the parking lot and around to the valet parking. I waited for Chris to open my door and escort me up the red carpet to the doors. I couldn't stop smiling at how cool it was to be at the gala with Chris.

I recognized a few people because I'd seen them on the news and in magazines. They were the rich who had a lot of money to throw around, with a few politicians thrown in for good measure. There were even news reporters with cameras surveying the crowd. Chris and I didn't really fit in, but I wasn't going to let that stop me from enjoying the evening.

Inside, we were ushered onto the main floor that served as the gathering place. Sculptures, paintings, and a twinkling chandelier made it the perfect setting. Off to the side, another area was set up with round tables and chairs, and a huge buffet table behind them. At the front of the hall a makeshift stage held a draped podium and several chairs. I recognized the governor and the mayor with their wives standing nearby. Not far from them, I spotted Dimples, who noticed Chris and me at the same time.

"Shelby, Chris... it's so good to have you here," Dimples said, joining us.

"Thanks. Good to see you too," I said. "Wow, this is quite the gathering."

"Yes. We have a number of patrons who donate a lot to the arts. There is someone else here who would like to talk to you." He craned his neck to scan the crowd. "I don't see her, but Jessica Palmer wanted to thank you."

"Oh, that's nice she could come. How's she doing?"

"Very well, especially since we recovered the paintings," he answered.

"What about the receptionist? Did she come too?" I asked, remembering how badly she felt for helping Greg Bowman without realizing it.

"Yes. She's here somewhere." Dimples checked his watch. "It's almost time to start. Are you ready?"

"Just exactly what do I need to be ready for?" I asked, suddenly nervous.

"You'll see." He smiled mysteriously, and left to join the people at the podium.

"Did you pick up anything from his thoughts?" Chris asked softly.

"I wish. I put up my shields, remember? But right now, I'd sure like to know what's going on."

"You can take them down, Shelby. It's okay with me."

"With this crowd, I'm not sure I want to," I smiled at him. "Maybe I'll lower them just a little if I think I need to. Is that okay with you?"

"Of course," he replied. "I think it might be fun to know what all these people are really thinking. You'd have to let me in on it, though."

I shook my head. "You'd be surprised."

"So what are they thinking?" Chris indicated a group of people standing to the side of us. There were two couples with another man. I let down my shields and only caught bits and pieces through the crowd.

"Mostly the women are concentrating on not squinting their eyes, and hoping they don't look as old as their friends. The men are a little harder to read... but one of them is hungry and just wants to eat and get out of here."

Chris chuckled. "Sounds pretty normal to me."

A waiter approached, passing out drinks on a large tray. Something about him seemed familiar, but I couldn't place it. Did I know him? Curious, I scanned his thoughts. He glanced at me, then quickly looked down, hoping I hadn't figured out who he was. It would ruin his plans.

Before I could listen further, the mayor stepped to the microphone and asked for everyone's attention. When I looked for the waiter again, all I could see was his retreating back. Who was that guy? I knew him from somewhere, but where? Had I seen him at the police station? That seemed the most likely place, but something was different.

"Shelby," Chris said, startling me. "They're calling for you. You need to get up there. To the podium."

"Oh," I said, rattled. "Okay." I made my way to the podium and, with my shields down, I could hear all kinds of thoughts about me. Most were nice enough, if a little curious, wondering what I had done to deserve this attention since they'd never heard of me before. I passed one guy who was thinking 'nice butt' and it took all my will power not to look at him. I could feel a blush creeping up my neck. Maybe letting down my shields wasn't such a good idea.

"Thanks for joining us Shelby." The mayor shook my hand, then turned back to the microphone. "As most of you know, some of our most treasured paintings were stolen during the move to this fine building. Detective Harris enlisted the help of this young lady to recover them, and it was due to her skills that we found the thief and recovered the stolen art.

"That is why we would like to honor Shelby Nichols tonight with this." He held up a bronze plaque with my name on it that said 'with gratitude for your service.' "This plaque will be permanently attached to the wing which holds the paintings she helped recover. Also we have this."

He set the plaque down, and held up an ID badge with my picture and name on it. "Which makes her an honorary member of our city's finest detective force, with the hope that she will continue to help us in the future."

He handed it to me and shook my hand. "Thank you again," he said. I nodded and smiled, while everyone clapped politely. He picked up the plaque and turned toward a photographer for a few pictures, thinking the publicity would be good for his image. It also didn't hurt that I was a real babe.

It was hard not to start laughing right then, but I somehow managed to keep it together. This certainly wasn't the money I'd hoped for, but the plaque was cool. Only... didn't they usually put those in the museum for people who were dead? Like 'in loving memory,' or something? He motioned me to take a seat on his left, and invited the governor to come forward for a few words.

I zoned out the governor's speech, and studied the badge. How was this an honor? The only use the badge held was to make me look more official. On that note, maybe I could add this to my résumé, or put 'honorary member of the detective force' under my name on my business cards. Yeah, right.

The photo looked like a mug shot, and I wondered where it had come from. Then I realized it was my driver's license photo. No wonder it was so bad. I held back another laugh and glanced into the audience to find Chris. He was going to love this.

He caught my gaze and smiled, thinking I was probably disappointed my 'honor' didn't include some sort of monetary compensation. Then he was thinking that the slit in my dress was exposing a lot of leg and I looked totally hot. I grinned and crossed my legs, letting the material fall even further.

His gaze jerked to mine and his eyes narrowed. He was thinking that was far enough, and I'd better cover up if I knew what was good for me. I sat back, and noticed he wasn't the only one enjoying the view. I quickly covered up, but couldn't keep the self-satisfied smile off my face.

From here, I had a great view of the people, and glanced around the room. A couple entered in the very back and I recognized the full silver head of hair and commanding presence of Uncle Joey. I tensed, wondering who he was with, and relaxed when Jackie stepped beside him. They were together, so it was a good guess that he got everything straightened out, and Carlotta was out of the picture.

The governor finally finished his speech, and everyone stood and clapped, mostly because he was done and they could get on with the party. I slipped the badge into my purse before I lost it. Chris made his way to the stage and helped me down the steps. He took my hand and placed it possessively in the crook of his arm. I grinned. I could get used to this.

"Uncle Joey's here," I said under my breath. "But at least he's with Jackie."

Chris tensed, not sure he was ready to face Manetto. At least without punching him in the face. "He must have enough clout, even with his reputation, to move in these circles."

"Makes sense," I added, not sure I was ready for Chris to talk with him either. I had to figure out something to alleviate the tension. "But you know what?" I continued, looking fiercely at Chris. "I don't care if he's here. I want to have a good time, so let's just forget about him. All right?"

Chris caught my attitude and smiled. "Sure," he said, willing to let his animosity fade for me. "Besides, we can't leave without eating some of that good food over there."

"That's right," I agreed. I glanced in that direction and noticed the mysterious waiter again. "Hey," I said to Chris. "See that waiter?" I motioned with my chin, not wanting to be obvious.

"The bald guy?" he asked.

"Yes. He looks familiar to me. Do you know him?"

"Nope," he said.

"When I saw him earlier he was thinking that it wouldn't be good if I recognized him. It would ruin his plans. We need to keep an eye on him until I figure out what's going on. I wish I knew where I'd seen him before."

It was the baldness that threw me. I pictured him with hair, and it came to me in a flash. He was the guy who normally dressed like a woman with a wig and heels. He was at the courthouse when Mercer killed the bank robber. He was also there the same day Mercer tried to kill me. What was he doing here? And more important, why didn't he want me to recognize him?

I turned to tell Chris, but Jessica Palmer found us first. "Shelby," Jessica said. "I'm so glad you're here. I wanted to thank you personally for helping me that day."

"No problem. How are you doing? You look great." She wore a beautiful long black dress, and her hair was coiled on top of her head. I introduced her to Chris, and we exchanged pleasantries until we got to the buffet table and she excused herself.

"She seemed nice enough," Chris said.

"Yes," I agreed. "It's hard to believe someone could pull the wool over her eyes, but I guess it happens." I was preoccupied with finding where the waiter went. I needed to know what he was up to.

We got our plates of food and found an empty table. I set down my plate, grateful not to have spilled anything while holding my purse. After sitting down, I was ready to take a sip of my drink when a shadow fell over me.

"Shelby," Uncle Joey said. "May we join you?"

At the sound of his voice I sloshed my drink, and hurriedly put it down. "Um... sure." Jackie sat next to me with him on her other side.

"I don't think we've been formally introduced to your husband," Uncle Joey said.

I quickly made the introductions, and Chris managed to nod his head but didn't get up to shake Uncle Joey's hand. I held my breath, hoping this didn't turn into a scene, but Uncle Joey was used to this sort of thing and only smiled thinly. Whew, that was close. Why would Uncle Joey want to sit with us? What was he up to?

"I just wanted to thank you for your advice, Shelby. Everything's worked out for the best." He shared a glance with Jackie that seemed to thaw the ice in his veins.

"Glad to hear it," I said. Maybe there was hope for him after all. "How's Miguel?"

"Doing well. He's a very bright young man, and I'm very proud of him." He was thinking that having a son gave him a different perspective and he was seriously considering getting out of the business, although it would take some time.

Uncle Joey caught my raised brows and smiled. He glanced around the room, calculating how good it would be to know what some of these people were thinking, especially some of his business associates. He glanced at me again. I shook my head and he chuckled.

Chris was ready to punch him in the face. He could tell we were communicating with each other, and he didn't like it. I put my hand on his arm and widened my eyes, telling him to stop. He glanced at me with resignation, and started eating his food.

Two more couples joined our table, taking the pressure off us to do all the talking. They knew Uncle Joey. In fact, one of them was Blaine Smith, the bank manager, and his wife. He wanted to keep on Uncle Joey's good side since he liked having all his money in his bank. He was also excited to have an extra five million dollars to work with.

He recognized Chris and me and said a quick hello, then glanced between Uncle Joey and us. I could practically hear his brain putting it together that we had just transferred five million dollars out of our account. And here we were, sitting by Joe Manetto. *Hmmm...very interesting.*

Oh great! Now the bank manager was guessing I was in cahoots with Uncle Joey. Hopefully he wouldn't say anything. I was ready to put my shields back up when the waiter approached and offered us drinks. I nudged Chris to tell him he was the one, but Chris only thought I was telling him to take a drink.

The waiter wondered how he could get me alone. He realized I was sitting by Manetto 'The Knife' and his eyes got big. Is that how I did it? Now he really needed to talk to me. He thought about spilling a drink on my dress so I'd leave to visit the ladies room, and I blanched. He was not going to ruin my new five-hundred-dollar dress!

I pushed back my chair. "Excuse me," I said. "I'll be right back." The men stood when I did, surprising me. Chris couldn't believe I was leaving him there alone with Manetto. Uncle Joey couldn't believe it either, but when nature calls, you have to answer. The waiter couldn't believe his good luck.

Oh please! I grabbed my clutch and walked toward what I hoped was the restroom. The waiter took his tray to an empty table and left it to follow me. I rounded the corner to the hallway and followed it down to another hall where the restrooms were located. I flattened myself against the wall and took out my stun flashlight.

The waiter hung back. He was nervous about following me into the ladies' room without his disguise, but decided he might not get another chance. He came around the corner and jerked with surprise to find me waiting for him. I jammed the stun flashlight against his neck and pushed him against the wall.

With my tall shoes on, I was a couple of inches taller than him, and I hoped that made me more intimidating. "I know who you are," I said with as much venom as I could. "What do you want?"

I had almost scared the crap out of him, literally. He couldn't believe I had a gun against his throat. "Okay, okay. Don't shoot me. I just want to know where the money is. If you tell me, I'll forget I even know you. I won't tell anyone about your involvement, I promise."

"My involvement with what?" I asked.

"I know you had something to do with Mercer's death. Maybe you even killed him, but I don't care about that. I just want to know where the money is."

Now he really lost me. When I'd listened to him at the police station he was thinking about money then too, but it was the money from the bank robbery. Did he think I had it? The part about killing Mercer worried me.

"What makes you think I know anything about the money?" I asked, deciding to go with it. "You don't know what you're talking about."

He figured I was bluffing. He knew Mercer killed Bishop to keep the money safe. So he followed Mercer and that led him to me. Why else would I kill Mercer, if not for the money?

Huh? This guy had it all wrong. "Who are you?"

"You said you knew who I was," he answered. "Wait a minute..." He hit my arm hard and the stun flashlight fell from my hand and rolled across the floor.

"Oww," I yelped.

"That's a flashlight," he said, surprised. He grabbed my arms, twisting me around and pulling them together behind my back. Then he pushed my face against the wall. "Now you're going to answer some questions from me."

I struggled, but he just pulled my arms tighter. "You've got this all wrong," I said. "I didn't kill Mercer. He was a hired assassin. Somebody hired him to kill Bishop. He didn't do it for the money... well not that money. I'm sure he got paid for it, but he didn't have anything to do with the bank robbery."

"Then why did you meet with him all those times? You were trying to find out where the money was, and after he told you, you killed him. So, this is your last chance before I break both your arms. Where's the money?"

"You're nuts," I yelped. "I don't have it!"

"Fine. You asked for... aack!" His body jerked, and in a series of spasms he let me go and sank to the floor.

"Are you all right?" Chris asked, the stun flashlight still crackling in his hand.

"You came!" I said, rubbing my wrists.

"What happened?" he asked.

I stepped over the body into Chris' arms. "He thinks I know where the stolen money from the bank robbery is. But worse, he thinks I had something to do with Mercer's death."

"That's preposterous," Uncle Joey said.

I jerked with surprise and turned, finding a crowd of people coming to stand behind us. Among them was Uncle Joey and Jackie, as well as Dimples and the bank manager, Blaine Smith.

"You were at my office until Ramos took you home," Uncle Joey declared.

"What's going on here?" Blaine asked. "Who's that?"

"I don't know," I said. "He came after me, but Chris got him with my stun flashlight. What are you doing here?" I asked.

"Well... after you left and your husband followed... and then Mr. Manetto and Detective Harris after that, I figured something was going on, and I wanted to see what it was," Blaine said, which pretty much summed it up for all of them. "Say... is he all right?"

Everyone glanced at the waiter. His eyes were shut, and drool was running from the corner of his mouth. "Yeah," I said. "He'll be fine in a few minutes."

"Hey... I think I know that guy," Blaine said. He stepped closer and knelt down to get a better look at his face. "Yeah. He's the private investigator we hired to find the money from that bank robbery a few months ago. He said he had some leads," Blaine glanced at me. "So what was he doing following you?" It looked a little suspicious to him.

"He's got some crazy idea that I know where the money is because the bank robber's killer, Mercer, was after me. But of course I don't." Although remembering the bank robber's thoughts, I had an idea. I'd forgotten the mental image the bank robber had in his mind when he was getting onto the elevator in the courthouse. There was a box with a lid, kind of like a casket, and the word 'underwear' in his mind. I'd dismissed it since it didn't make any sense, but what if it was a clue?

"Why was Mercer after you?" Blaine asked.

"Because she implicated him in the murder of the bank robber," Dimples said, making his presence known. Everyone moved aside to let him come forward to stand beside me. "And from the evidence we were able to gather, it looks like she was right. So who's this?" he asked.

"I can't remember his name," Blaine said.

Dimples checked his pocket and pulled out his wallet. "His name is Rob Felt."

"That's right. I remember now," Blaine said. "The job was on a contingency basis," he added. "He only gets paid if he finds the money. That's probably why he was a little rough with you Shelby. Are you all right?" he asked.

"Yes, I'm fine."

"So you're the one who fingered Mercer for the bank robber's murder?" Blaine asked, studying me with interest.

"She was working with the police," Dimples answered for me. "Sometimes she has premonitions about things, so we've hired her as a consultant on a few of our cases."

"That's interesting." Blaine narrowed his eyes shrewdly, thinking that was why I'd received all the attention tonight. "Do you think you could help us find the stolen money?"

Everyone's attention zeroed in on me, wondering what I'd say. "Maybe I could take a look at the case," I answered. My purse had fallen to the floor so I picked it up and took out one of my business cards. "Here's my card. Why don't you give me a call on Monday, and we can discuss it."

Blaine took the card and smiled, willing to take me up on it, especially since this guy Felt, was a total failure. "Sounds great. I'll do that." He'd never heard of a bona fide psychic before, but if the police thought I was good enough to have on their payroll, he had no problem working with me.

Uncle Joey studied me. He had no idea I was working with the police, and it took him by surprise. I was a lot more shrewd than I'd let on. In a way he was proud of me. It showed I had a head for business and was willing to take advantage of my assets. Which was fine as long as it didn't interfere with his business.

Chris was wondering if I'd gone crazy. How in the world did I think I could find the stolen money? Especially when there was no one to talk to about the case. If I couldn't read their minds, I had nothing to go on. I would fail for sure.

The waiter, Rob, groaned and opened his eyes, saving me from more of Chris' unhelpful thoughts. He sat up and wiped his mouth on his sleeve, stopping in mid-wipe as he noticed all of us standing around him. Confusion clouded his eyes. "What happened?" he asked.

"I'll take care of this," Dimples said. "Why don't the rest of you go back to the party?"

That was fine with me. "Thanks." I took Chris' hand.

"Wait," Rob said. "You can't let her go. She killed Mercer. She knows where the stolen money is!"

"Mr. Felt," Dimples said. "If you continue with this kind of behavior, I'm going to have to arrest you for disorderly conduct."

"But..." Rob closed his mouth, knowing defeat when he saw it. He knew I was with Mercer the day he was killed because he'd seen me sitting by him on that bench outside the courthouse. His attention had only wandered for a moment when the next thing he knew, I was gone and Mercer was slumped over. He'd passed by the bench for a closer look, and it had spooked him to see all the blood. He was certain I'd killed Mercer. So what was my game plan? Was I working for someone like Manetto, or was I on my own? Whatever it was, he was going to get to the bottom of it.

Oh great! He thought I killed Mercer, and he wasn't going to let it go? The fact that he'd seen me with Mercer that day was awful. Now I'd have to figure out how to keep that guy away from me. Then it hit me that he wasn't going to be happy when he found out that the bank wanted to hire me to find the stolen money. But since he'd gotten everything wrong, it was his own fault. What kind of a P.I. was he anyway?

We rejoined the party, and I found that someone had cleared the table. My food was gone, and other people were now sitting there. "Where's my plate?" I asked. "I didn't even get one bite."

"It's okay Shelby, you can get another one," Chris said. He wasn't happy with the way things had turned out. At least he'd gotten there in time to stun that guy. What was wrong with me? Why did I take off like that, without even telling him what was going on? From the way Felt talked, he sounded pretty sure I'd killed Mercer. Had he seen me that day? If he had, he must have missed seeing Ramos.

"Thanks for coming after me." I squeezed his hand. "I had no idea that guy was going to threaten me. Let's walk through the gallery, and I'll tell you all about it." I explained that I'd seen him the first time at the courthouse dressed as a woman, and all the other times in between. "Who would have thought he was working for the bank?"

"That's pretty crazy all right," Chris said. "I'm concerned that he thinks you killed Mercer though. Did he see you there?"

"He was following Mercer, so yeah, he did see me sitting by him on the bench, but he must have missed the part where Mercer got killed by Ramos. We were gone by the time he saw that Mercer was dead."

"I noticed Manetto gave you an alibi," Chris said.

"Yeah, me too," I agreed, feeling better. "So it looks like it's Felt's word against mine. Luckily I have the police on my side."

"True, but it might be a problem in the future," Chris said. He turned to me with his brows drawn together. "Why did you tell the bank manager you could help him find the money?"

"Oh, I didn't tell you, but when I saw the bank robber, he thought about where the stolen money was. I didn't think it made any sense at the time, but maybe we can figure it out together."

"Together?" he asked.

"Well sure," I said. "Unless you don't want to."

"Shelby... of course I want to. I hate thinking of you involved in some of this stuff alone. So yes, I want to know what's going on. In fact... that's the only way I feel okay about you doing this whole consulting business." He was thinking it was the only way he could keep me out of trouble too.

"I guess you have a point," I said. "But a lot of the trouble I get in is not my fault!"

"Yeah, right," he said. "Which is exactly why I'm going to be involved. In fact, I think we should have a system where the cases you take have to be approved by me first."

"What?" I gasped.

"And I should be on the payroll."

"Where's my stun flashlight?" I reached for his pocket, and he caught my hand, pulling me against him.

"I know just how you're going to pay me too," he said, his voice deep and low. He kissed my neck, just below my ear, sending shivers up my spine. He could feel my pulse quicken, and his thoughts were smug and certain.

The crackle of the stun flashlight brought him up short, and I smiled at his surprise that I'd taken it from his pocket. "Two can play this game, you know."

He pulled away, thinking I wouldn't dare. His eyes widened, knowing I'd heard his unspoken challenge, and uncertainty washed over him. With great ceremony, I opened my clutch, and placed the stun flashlight inside.

"Just so you know," I said. "I would never stun you... unless it was an accident or something."

He shook his head and smiled. "Come on." Taking my hand, he pulled me back toward the party. "Right now, all I want to do is dance with my beautiful wife. We can worry about all this other stuff later."

We entered the hall, and he took me in his arms. He was thinking he wanted everyone in the room to know I belonged to him, and he was proud of it. He'd noticed the looks I'd gotten from many of the men there, and it stirred something primeval and protective in him.

I laughed, loving how good it felt in his arms. People watching us were thinking what a handsome couple we made, and my happy feelings intensified. If Chris wanted to help me with my cases, that was fine with me. We had our moments, but we loved each other, and that was what mattered most.

Before long, the evening drew to a close. As the bank manager left, he told me he'd give me a call on Monday. I agreed, realizing I still needed to fill Chris in on the clues I had. If Chris didn't think we could find the money, it would help me decide if I should take the job.

We started toward the door, and Dimples pulled us aside. "Just thought I'd let you know that the badge was my idea," he said proudly. "I thought it would help you get through the red tape when you helped me on future cases."

"Yeah, thanks. That's pretty cool," I said.

"I have one in mind, if you're willing to come down to the station on Monday." Beside me Chris frowned, and noticing, Dimples added, "I promise it's not dangerous."

"Sure," I said and smiled. "See you then."

Jessica Palmer hurried to my side. "Before you go, you need to see this." The plaque with my name on it had already been attached to the wall, and we followed her to take a look. Relief washed over me to find that it wasn't too prominently displayed.

"That's really nice. Thanks," I said.

We left the hall and made our way outside to the valet parking attendants. There were several people waiting ahead of us, two of which happened to be Uncle Joey and Jackie. We greeted them politely and Uncle Joey complimented me on my awards.

"I didn't know you were working with the police department," he said.

"Yeah, I help them once in a while." What else could I say? His accusatory tone put me on the defense. Almost like he'd caught me doing something bad.

"I might have a job for you, if you're interested." he said.

"What is it?" I asked, feeling Chris stiffen beside me.

"I think I know where Kate and Hodges are," he said. "If you could run into them, it would be nice to know what they did with my money."

"Where do you think they are?" I asked.

"Seattle." He glanced at Chris. "I'd be willing to send you both if you'd like to go. Think of it as a mini-vacation. On me of course."

Hmm... that sounded tempting. "We'll talk it over and I'll let you know."

Uncle Joey nodded with a knowing smile. He'd seen my eyes light up and figured it was an offer I couldn't resist. Chris was more cautious, but the thoughts of a free vacation had him thinking it might be fun. He glanced at me and caught my smile, realizing I'd 'heard' him. Oops. I just shrugged and kept my mouth shut.

We finally made it to the front of the line just as Uncle Joey's limo pulled up. Ramos got out of the driver's seat and came around to open the door for them. He glanced up and smiled with appreciation at the sight of me in my red dress. He thought I looked pretty hot.

Chris noticed him, and Ramos shifted his attention. They stared at each other, like they were having a duel with their eyes or something. Then surprisingly, Chris gave Ramos a slight nod. Ramos acknowledged it with a chin jerk and got back in his car.

It was on the tip of my tongue to say something, but at the last second, I decided it was best to ignore that exchange. Something unspoken between the two of them that had everything to do with me? Yeah, I should probably act like I didn't even see it.

Our car arrived, and I took Chris' arm. He glanced at me, thinking that with all the job offers and my consulting business, he was pretty sure our lives were about to change. How was he going to keep up with me? Then he smiled. Somehow we'd manage, just like we always did. He didn't know what the future held, but with me by his side, it was sure to be a wild ride.

ABOUT THE AUTHOR

USA TODAY AND WALL STREET JOURNAL BESTSELLING AUTHOR

As the author of the Shelby Nichols Adventure Series, Colleen is often asked if Shelby Nichols is her alter-ego. "Definitely," she says. "Shelby is the epitome of everything I wish I dared to be." Known for her laugh since she was a kid, Colleen has always tried to find the humor in every situation and continues to enjoy writing about Shelby's adventures. "I love getting Shelby into trouble...I just don't always know how to get her out of it!" Besides writing, she loves a good book, biking, hiking, and playing board and card games with family and friends. She loves to connect with readers and admits that fans of the series keep her writing.

Connect with Colleen at www.colleenhelme.com

Made in the USA
Columbia, SC
15 September 2019